Elizabeth Costello

Eight Lessons

J. M. Coetzee

Secker & Warburg
LONDON

Published by Secker & Warburg 2003

2 4 6 8 10 9 7 5 3 1

This page should be read in conjunction with the
Acknowledgements on page 233

First published in Great Britain in 2003 by
Secker & Warburg
Random House, 20 Vauxhall Bridge Road,
London SW1V 2SA

Random House Australia (Pty) Limited
20 Alfred Street, Milsons Point, Sydney,
New South Wales 2061, Australia

Random House New Zealand Limited
18 Poland Road, Glenfield,
Auckland 10, New Zealand

Random House (Pty) Limited
Endulini, 5A Jubilee Road, Parktown 2193, South Africa

The Random House Group Limited Reg. No. 954009
www.randomhouse.co.uk

A CIP catalogue record for this book
is available from the British Library

ISBN 0 436 20616 1

Typeset by Palimpsest Book Production Limited
Polmont, Stirlingshire
Printed and bound in Great Britain by
Mackays of Chatham plc, Chatham, Kent

Contents

1
Realism

THERE IS FIRST of all the problem of the opening, namely, how to get us from where we are, which is, as yet, nowhere, to the far bank. It is a simple bridging problem, a problem of knocking together a bridge. People solve such problems every day. They solve them, and having solved them push on.

Let us assume that, however it may have been done, it is done. Let us take it that the bridge is built and crossed, that we can put it out of our mind. We have left behind the territory in which we were. We are in the far territory, where we want to be.

Elizabeth Costello is a writer, born in 1928, which makes her sixty-six years old, going on sixty-seven. She has written nine novels, two books of poems, a book on bird life, and a body of journalism. By birth she is Australian. She was born in Melbourne and still lives there, though she spent the years 1951 to 1963 abroad, in England and France. She has been married twice. She has two children, one by each marriage.

Elizabeth Costello made her name with her fourth novel, *The House on Eccles Street* (1969), whose main character is Marion Bloom, wife of Leopold Bloom, principal character of another novel, *Ulysses* (1922), by James Joyce. In the past decade there has grown up around her a small critical industry; there is even an Elizabeth Costello Society, based in Albuquerque, New

Mexico, which puts out a quarterly *Elizabeth Costello Newsletter*.

In the spring of 1995 Elizabeth Costello travelled, or travels (present tense henceforth), to Williamstown, Pennsylvania, to Altona College, to receive the Stowe Award. The award is made biennially to a major world writer, selected by a jury of critics and writers. It consists of a purse of $50,000, funded by a bequest from the Stowe estate, and a gold medal. It is one of the larger literary prizes in the United States.

On her visit to Pennsylvania Elizabeth Costello (Costello is her maiden name) is accompanied by her son John. John has a job teaching physics and astronomy at a college in Massachusetts, but for reasons of his own is on leave for the year. Elizabeth has become a little frail: without the help of her son she would not be undertaking this taxing trip across half the world.

We skip. They have reached Williamstown and have been conveyed to their hotel, a surprisingly large building for a small city, a tall hexagon, all dark marble outside and crystal and mirrors inside. In her room a dialogue takes place.

'Will you be comfortable?' asks the son.

'I am sure I will,' she replies. The room is on the twelfth floor, with a prospect over a golf course and, beyond that, over wooded hills.

'Then why not have a rest? They are fetching us at six thirty. I'll give you a call a few minutes beforehand.'

He is about to leave. She speaks.

'John, what exactly do they want from me?'

'Tonight? Nothing. It's just a dinner with members of the jury. We won't let it turn into a long evening. I'll remind them you are tired.'

'And tomorrow?'

'Tomorrow is a different story. You'll have to gird your loins for tomorrow, I am afraid.'

'I have forgotten why I agreed to come. It seems a great ordeal to put oneself through, for no good reason. I should have asked them to forget the ceremony and send the cheque in the mail.'

After the long flight, she is looking her age. She has never taken care of her appearance; she used to be able to get away with it; now it shows. Old and tired.

'It doesn't work that way, I am afraid, Mother. If you accept the money, you must go through with the show.'

She shakes her head. She is still wearing the old blue raincoat she wore from the airport. Her hair has a greasy, lifeless look. She has made no move to unpack. If he leaves her now, what will she do? Lie down in her raincoat and shoes?

He is here, with her, out of love. He cannot imagine her getting through this trial without him at her side. He stands by her because he is her son, her loving son. But he is also on the point of becoming — distasteful word — her trainer.

He thinks of her as a seal, an old, tired circus seal. One more time she must heave herself up on to the tub, one more time show that she can balance the ball on her nose. Up to him to coax her, put heart in her, get her through the performance.

'It is the only way they have,' he says as gently as he can. 'They admire you, they want to honour you. It is the best way they can think of doing that. Giving you money. Broadcasting your name. Using the one to do the other.'

Standing over the Empire-style writing table, shuffling through the pamphlets that tell her where to shop, where to dine, how to use the telephone, she casts him one of the quick, ironic looks that still have the power to surprise him, to remind him of who she is. 'The best way?' she murmurs.

At six thirty he knocks. She is ready, waiting, full of doubts but prepared to face the foe. She wears her blue costume and silk jacket, her lady novelist's uniform, and the white shoes with which there is nothing wrong yet which somehow make her look like Daisy Duck. She has washed her hair and brushed it back. It still looks greasy, but honourably greasy, like a navvy's or a mechanic's. Already on her face the passive look that, if you saw it in a young girl, you would call withdrawn. A face without personality, the kind that photographers have to work on to lend distinction. Like Keats, he thinks, the great advocate of blank receptiveness.

The blue costume, the greasy hair, are details, signs of a moderate realism. Supply the particulars, allow the significations to emerge of themselves. A procedure pioneered by Daniel Defoe. Robinson Crusoe, cast up on the beach, looks around for his shipmates. But there are none. 'I never saw them afterwards, or any sign of them,' says he, 'except three of their hats, one cap, and two shoes that were not fellows.' Two shoes, not fellows: by not being fellows, the shoes have ceased to be footwear and become proofs of death, torn by the foaming seas off the feet of drowning men and tossed ashore. No large words, no despair, just hats and caps and shoes.

For as far back as he can remember, his mother has secluded herself in the mornings to do her writing. No intrusions under any circumstances. He used to think of himself as a misfortunate child, lonely and unloved. When they felt particularly sorry for themselves, he and his sister used to slump outside the locked door and make tiny whining sounds. In time the whining would change to humming or singing, and they would feel better, forgetting their forsakenness.

Now the scene has changed. He has grown up. He is no longer outside the door but inside, observing her as she sits, back to the window, confronting, day after day, year after year, while her hair slowly goes from black to grey, the blank page. What doggedness,

4

he thinks! She deserves the medal, no doubt about that, this medal and many more. For valour beyond the call of duty.

The change came when he was thirty-three. Until then he had not read a word she had written. That was his reply to her, his revenge on her for locking him out. She denied him, therefore he denied her. Or perhaps he refused to read her in order to protect himself. Perhaps that was the deeper motive: to ward off the lightning stroke. Then one day, without a word to anyone, without even a word to himself, he took one of her books out of the library. After that he read everything, reading openly, in the train, at the lunch table. 'What are you reading?' 'One of my mother's books.'

He is in her books, or some of them. Other people too he recognizes; and there must be many more he does not recognize. About sex, about passion and jealousy and envy, she writes with an insight that shakes him. It is positively indecent.

She shakes him; that is what she presumably does to other readers too. That is presumably why, in the larger picture, she exists. What a strange reward for a lifetime of shaking people: to be conveyed to this town in Pennsylvania and given money! For she is by no means a comforting writer. She is even cruel, in a way that women can be but men seldom have the heart for. What sort of creature is she, really? Not a seal: not amiable enough for that. But not a shark either. A cat. One of those large cats that pause as they eviscerate their victim and, across the torn-open belly, give you a cold yellow stare.

There is a woman waiting for them downstairs, the same young woman who fetched them from the airport. Her name is Teresa. She is an instructor at Altona College, but in the business of the Stowe Award a factotum, a dogsbody, and in the wider business a minor character.

He sits in the front of the car beside Teresa, his mother sits at the rear. Teresa is excited, so excited that she positively chatters. She tells them about the neighbourhoods they are driving through, about Altona College and its history, about the restaurant they are headed for. In the middle of all the chatter she manages to get in two quick, mouselike pounces of her own. 'We had A. S. Byatt here last fall,' she says. 'What do you think of A. S. Byatt, Ms Costello?' And later: 'What do you think of Doris Lessing, Ms Costello?' She is writing a book on women writers and politics; she spends her summers in London doing what she calls research; he would not be surprised if she had a tape recorder hidden in the car.

His mother has a word for people like this. She calls them the goldfish. One thinks they are small and harmless, she says, because each wants no more than the tiniest nibble of flesh, the merest hemidemimilligram. She gets letters from them every week, care of her publisher. Once upon a time she used to reply: thank you for your interest, unfortunately I am too busy to respond as fully as your letter deserves. Then a friend told her what these letters of hers were fetching on the autograph market. After that she stopped answering.

Flecks of gold circling the dying whale, waiting their chance to dart in and take a quick mouthful.

They arrive at the restaurant. It is raining lightly. Teresa drops them at the door and goes off to park the car. For a moment they are alone on the pavement. 'We can still abscond,' he says. 'It is not too late. We can get a taxi, drop by the hotel to pick up our things, be at the airport by eight thirty, take the first flight out. We will have vanished from the scene by the time the Mounties arrive.'

He smiles. She smiles. They will go through with the programme, that barely needs to be said. But it is a pleasure to toy with at least

6

the idea of escape. Jokes, secrets, complicities; a glance here, a word there: that is their way of being together, of being apart. He will be her squire, she will be his knight. He will protect her as long as he is able. Then he will help her into her armour, lift her on to her steed, set her buckler on her arm, hand her her lance, and step back.

There is a scene in the restaurant, mainly dialogue, which we will skip. We resume back at the hotel, where Elizabeth Costello asks her son to run through the list of the people they have just met. He obeys, giving each a name and function, as in life. Their host, William Brautegam, is Dean of Arts at Altona. The convenor of the jury, Gordon Wheatley, is a Canadian, a professor at McGill, who has written on Canadian literature and on Wilson Harris. The one they call Toni, who spoke to her about Henry Handel Richardson, is from Altona College. She is a specialist on Australia and has taught there. Paula Sachs she knows. The bald man, Kerrigan, is a novelist, Irish by birth, now living in New York. The fifth juror, the one who was seated next to him, is named Moebius. She teaches in California and edits a journal. She has also published some stories.

'You and she had quite a tête-à-tête,' says his mother. 'Good-looking, isn't she?'

'I suppose so.'

She reflects. 'But, as a group, don't they strike you as rather . . .'

'Rather lightweight?'

She nods.

'Well, they are. The heavyweights don't involve themselves in this kind of show. The heavyweights are wrestling with the heavy-weight problems.'

'I am not heavyweight enough for them?'

'No, you're heavyweight all right. Your handicap is that you're not a problem. What you write hasn't yet been demonstrated to be a problem. Once you offer yourself as a problem, you might be shifted over into their court. But for the present you're not a problem, just an example.'

'An example of what?'

'An example of writing. An example of how someone of your station and your generation and your origins writes. An instance.'

'An instance? Am I allowed a word of protest? After all the effort I put into not writing like anyone else?'

'Mother, there's no point in picking on me to fight with. I am not responsible for the way the academy sees you. But you must surely concede that at a certain level we speak, and therefore write, like everyone else. Otherwise we would all be speaking and writing private languages. It is not absurd – is it? – to concern oneself with what people have in common rather than with what sets them apart.'

The next morning John finds himself in another literary debate. In the hotel gymnasium he bumps into Gordon Wheatley, chairman of the jury. Side by side on exercise bicycles they have a shouted conversation. His mother will be disappointed, he tells Wheatley – not entirely seriously – if she learns that the Stowe Award is hers only because 1995 has been decreed to be the year of Australasia.

'What does she want it to be?' shouts Wheatley back.

'That she is the best,' he replies. 'In your jury's honest opinion. Not the best Australian, not the best Australian woman, just the best.'

'Without infinity we would have no mathematics,' says Wheatley. 'But that doesn't mean that infinity exists. Infinity is just a construct, a human construct. Of course we are firm that Elizabeth Costello is the best. We just have to be clear in our minds what a statement like that means, in the context of our times.'

The analogy with infinity makes no sense to him, but he does not pursue the issue. He hopes that Wheatley does not write as badly as he thinks.

Realism has never been comfortable with ideas. It could not be otherwise: realism is premised on the idea that ideas have no autonomous existence, can exist only in things. So when it needs to debate ideas, as here, realism is driven to invent situations – walks in the countryside, conversations – in which characters give voice to contending ideas and thereby in a certain sense embody them. The notion of *embodying* turns out to be pivotal. In such debates ideas do not and indeed cannot float free: they are tied to the speakers by whom they are enounced, and generated from the matrix of individual interests out of which their speakers act in the world – for instance, the son's concern that his mother not be treated as a Mickey Mouse post-colonial writer, or Wheatley's concern not to seem an old-fashioned absolutist.

At eleven he taps at the door of her room. She has a long day before her: an interview, a session at the college radio station, then, in the evening, the presentation ceremony and the speech that goes with it.

Her strategy with interviewers is to take control of the exchange, presenting them with blocks of dialogue that have been rehearsed so often he wonders they have not solidified in her mind and become some kind of truth. A long paragraph on childhood in the suburbs of Melbourne (cockatoos screeching at the bottom of the garden) with a sub-paragraph on the danger to the imagination of middle-class security. A paragraph on the death of her father of enteric fever in Malaya, with her mother somewhere in the background playing Chopin waltzes on the piano, followed by a sequence of what sound like impromptu ruminations on the influence of music on her own prose. A paragraph about her adolescent reading (voracious, unselective), then a jump to Virginia Woolf, whom she first read as a student, and the impact Woolf had on her. A passage on her spell at art school, another on her year and a half at post-war Cambridge ('What I mainly remember is the struggle to keep warm'), another on her years in London ('I could have made a living as a translator, I suppose, but my best language was German, and German wasn't popular in those days, as you can imagine'). Her first novel, which she modestly disparages, though as a first novel it stood head and shoulders above the competition, then her years in France ('heady times'), with an oblique glance at her first marriage. Then her return to Australia with her young son. Him.

All in all, he judges, listening in, a workmanlike performance, if one can still use that word, eating up most of the hour, as intended, leaving only a few minutes to skirt the questions that begin 'What do you think . . . ?' What does she think about neoliberalism, the woman question, Aboriginal rights, the Australian novel today? He has lived around her for nearly four decades, on and off, and is still not sure what she thinks about the big questions. Not sure and, on the whole, thankful not to have to hear. For her thoughts would be, he suspects, as uninteresting as most people's. A writer, not a thinker. Writers and thinkers: chalk and cheese. No, not chalk and cheese: fish and fowl. But which is she, the fish or the fowl? Which is her medium: water or air?

This morning's interviewer, who has come up from Boston for the occasion, is young, and his mother is usually indulgent towards the young. But this one is thick-skinned and refuses to be fobbed off. 'What would you say your main message is?' she persists.

'My message? Am I obliged to carry a message?'

Not a strong counter; the interviewer presses her advantage. 'In *The House on Eccles Street* your lead character, Marion Bloom, refuses to have sex with her husband until he has worked out who he is. Is that what you are saying: that until men have worked out a new, post-patriarchal identity, women should hold themselves apart?'

His mother casts him a glance. *Help!* it is meant to say, in a droll way.

'Intriguing idea,' she murmurs. 'Of course in the case of Marion's husband there' would be a particular severity in demanding that he work out a new identity, since he is a man of − what shall I say? − of infirm identity, of many shapes.'

Eccles Street is a great novel; it will live, perhaps, as long as *Ulysses*; it will certainly be around long after its maker is in the grave. He was only a child when she wrote it. It unsettles and dizzies him to think that the same being that engendered *Eccles Street* engendered him. It is time to step in, save her from an inquisition that promises to become tedious. He rises. 'Mother, I am afraid we are going to have to call a halt,' he says. 'We're being fetched for the radio session.' To the interviewer: 'Thank you, but that will have to be all.'

The interviewer pouts with annoyance. Will she find a part for him in the story she files: the novelist of failing powers and her bossy son?

At the radio station the two of them are separated. He is shown into the control booth. The new interviewer, he is surprised to find, is the elegant Moebius woman he had sat beside at dinner. 'This is Susan Moebius, the programme is *Writers at Work*, and we are speaking today to Elizabeth Costello,' she commences, and proceeds with a crisp introduction. 'Your most recent novel,' she continues, 'called *Fire and Ice*, set in the Australia of the 1930s, is the story of a young man struggling to make his way as a painter against the opposition of family and society. Did you have anyone in particular in mind when you wrote it? Does it draw upon your own early life?'

'No, I was still a child in the 1930s. Of course we draw upon our own lives all the time – they are our main resource, in a sense our only resource. But no, *Fire and Ice* isn't autobiography. It is a work of fiction. I made it up.'

'It is a powerful book, I must tell our listeners. But do you find it easy, writing from the position of a man?'

It is a routine question, opening the door to one of her routine paragraphs. To his surprise, she does not take the opening.

'Easy? No. If it were easy it wouldn't be worth doing. It is the otherness that is the challenge. Making up someone other than yourself. Making up a world for him to move in. Making up an Australia.'

'Is that what you are doing in your books, would you say: making up Australia?'

'Yes, I suppose so. But that is not so easy nowadays. There is more resistance, a weight of Australias made up by many other people, that you have to push against. That is what we mean by tradition, the beginnings of a tradition.'

'I'd like to get on to *The House on Eccles Street*, which is the book you are best known for in this country, a path-breaking book, and the figure of Molly Bloom. Critics have concentrated on the way you have claimed or reclaimed Molly from Joyce, made her your own. I wonder if you would comment on your intentions in this book, particularly in challenging Joyce, one of the father-figures of modern literature, on his own territory.'

Another clear opening, and this time she takes it.

'Yes, she is an engaging person, isn't she, Molly Bloom – Joyce's Molly, I mean. She leaves her trace across the pages of *Ulysses* as a bitch on heat leaves her smell. Seductive you can't call it: it is cruder than that. Men pick up the scent and sniff and circle around and snarl at each other, even when Molly isn't on the scene.

'No, I don't see myself as challenging Joyce. But certain books are so prodigally inventive that there is plenty of material left over at the end, material that almost invites you to take it over and use it to build something of your own.'

'But, Elizabeth Costello, you have taken Molly out of the house – if I can continue with your metaphor – taken her out of the house on Eccles Street where her husband and her lover and in a certain sense her author have confined her, where they have turned her into a kind of queen bee, unable to fly, you have taken her and turned her loose on the streets of Dublin. Wouldn't you see that as a challenge to Joyce on your part, a response?'

'Queen bee, bitch . . . Let's revise the figure and call her a lioness, rather, stalking the streets, smelling the smells, seeing the sights. Looking for prey, even. Yes, I wanted to liberate her from that house, and particularly from that bedroom, with the bed with the creaking springs, and turn her loose – as you say – on Dublin.'

'If you see Molly – Joyce's Molly – as a prisoner in the house on Eccles Street, do you see women in general as prisoners of marriage and domesticity?'

'You can't mean women today. But yes, to an extent Molly is a prisoner of marriage, the kind of marriage that was on offer in Ireland in 1904. Her husband Leopold is a prisoner too. If she is shut into the conjugal home, he is shut out. So we have Odysseus trying to get in and Penelope trying to get out. That is the comedy, the comic myth, which Joyce and I in our different ways were paying our respects to.'

Because both women are wearing headphones, addressing the

microphone rather than each other, it is hard for him to see how they are getting on together. But he is impressed, as ever, by the persona his mother manages to project: of genial common sense, lack of malice, yet of sharp-wittedness too.

'I want to tell you,' the interviewer continues (a cool voice, he thinks: a cool woman, capable, not a lightweight at all), 'what an impact *The House on Eccles Street* made on me when I first read it in the 1970s. I was a student, I had studied Joyce's book, I had absorbed the famous Molly Bloom chapter and the critical orthodoxy that came with it, namely that here Joyce had released the authentic voice of the feminine, the sensual reality of woman, and so forth. And then I read your book and realised that Molly didn't have to be limited in the way Joyce had made her to be, that she could equally well be an intelligent woman with an interest in music and a circle of friends of her own and a daughter with whom she shared confidences – it was a revelation, as I say. And I began to wonder about other women whom we think of as having been given a voice by male writers, in the name of their liberation, yet in the end only to further and to serve a male philosophy. I am thinking of D. H. Lawrence's women in particular, but if you go further back they might include Tess of the D'Urbervilles and Anna Karenina, to name only two. It is a huge question, but I wonder if you have anything to say about it – not just about Marion Bloom and the others but about the project of reclaiming women's lives in general.'

'No, I don't think there is anything I would want to say, I think you've expressed it all very fully. Of course, fair's fair, men will have to set about reclaiming the Heathcliffs and Rochesters from romantic stereotyping too, to say nothing of poor old dusty Casaubon. It will be a grand spectacle. But, seriously, we can't go on parasitizing the classics for ever. I am not excluding myself from the charge. We've got to start doing some inventing of our own.'

This is not in the script at all. A new departure. Where will it lead? But alas, the Moebius woman (who is now glancing at the studio clock) does not pick up on it.

'In your more recent novels you have gone back to Australian settings. Could you say something about how you see Australia? What does it mean to you to be an Australian writer? Australia is a country that remains very far away, at least to Americans. Is that part of your consciousness as you write: that you are reporting from the far edges?'

'The far edges. That is an interesting expression. You won't find many Australians nowadays prepared to accept it. *Far from what?* they would say. Nevertheless, it has a certain meaning, even if it is a meaning foisted on us by history. We're not a country of extremes – I'd say we're rather pacific – but we are a country of extremities. We have lived our extremities because there hasn't been a great deal of resistance in any direction. If you begin to fall, there isn't much to stop you.'

They are back among the commonplaces, on familiar ground. He can stop listening.

We skip to the evening, to the main event, the presentation of the award. As son and companion of the speaker he finds himself in the first row of the audience, among the special guests. The woman to his left introduces herself. 'Our daughter is at Altona,' she says. 'She is writing her honours dissertation on your mother. She's a great fan. She has made us read everything.' She pats the wrist of the man beside her. They have the look of money, old money. Benefactors, no doubt. 'Your mother is much admired in this country. Particularly by young people. I hope you will tell her that.'

All across America, young women writing dissertations on his mother. Admirers, adherents, disciples. Would it please his mother to be told she has American disciples?

The presentation scene itself we skip. It is not a good idea to interrupt the narrative too often, since storytelling works by lulling the reader or listener into a dreamlike state in which the time and space of the real world fade away, superseded by the time and space of the fiction. Breaking into the dream draws attention to the constructedness of the story, and plays havoc with the realist illusion. However, unless certain scenes are skipped over we will be here all afternoon. The skips are not part of the text, they are part of the performance.

So the award is made, after which his mother is left alone at the rostrum to give her acceptance speech, entitled in the programme 'What is Realism?'. The time has arrived for her to show her paces.

Elizabeth Costello dons her reading glasses. 'Ladies and gentlemen,' she says, and begins to read.

'I published my first book in 1955, when I was living in London, at that time the great cultural metropolis for Antipodeans. I remember clearly the day the package arrived in the mail, an advance copy for the author. I was naturally thrilled to have it in my hands, printed and bound, the real thing, undeniable. But something was nagging at me. I got on to the telephone to my publishers. "Have the deposit copies gone out?" I asked. And I would not rest until I had their assurance that the deposit copies would be mailed the same afternoon, to Scotland and the Bodleian and so forth, but above all to the British Museum. That was my great ambition: to have my place on the shelves of the British Museum, rubbing shoulders with the other Cs, the great ones: Carlyle and Chaucer and Coleridge and Conrad. (The joke is that my closest literary neighbour turned out to be Marie Corelli.)

'One smiles now at such ingenuousness. Yet behind my anxious query there was something serious, and behind that seriousness in turn something pathetic that is less easy to acknowledge.

'Let me explain. Ignoring all the copies of the book you have written that are going to perish – that are going to be pulped because there is no buyer for them, that are going to be opened and read for a page or two and then yawned at and put aside for ever, that are going to be left behind at seaside hotels or in trains – ignoring all these lost ones, we must be able to feel there is at least one copy that will not only be read but be taken care of, given a home, given a place on the shelves that will be its own in perpetuity. What lay behind my concern about deposit copies was the wish that, even if I myself should be knocked over by a bus the next day, this first-born of mine would have a home where it could snooze, if fate so decreed, for the next hundred years, and no one would come poking with a stick to see if it was still alive.

'That was one side of my telephone call: if I, this mortal shell, am going to die, let me at least live on through my creations.'

Elizabeth Costello proceeds to reflect on the transience of fame. We skip ahead.

'But of course the British Museum or (now) the British Library is not going to last for ever. It too will crumble and decay, and the books on its shelves turn to powder. And anyhow, long before that day, as the acid gnaws away at the paper, as the demand for space grows, the ugly and unread and unwanted will be carted off to some facility or other and tossed into a furnace, and all trace of them will be liquidated from the master catalogue. After which it will be as if they had never existed.

'That is an alternative vision of the Library of Babel, more disturbing to me than the vision of Jorge Luis Borges. Not a library in which all conceivable books, past, present and future, coexist, but a library from which books that were really conceived, written and published are absent, absent even from the memory of the librarians.

'Such, then, was the other and more pathetic side to my telephone call. We can rely on the British Library or the Library of Congress no more than on reputation itself to save us from oblivion. Of that I must remind myself, and remind you too, on this proud night for me at Altona College.

'Let me now turn to my subject, "What is Realism?"

'There is a story by Franz Kafka – perhaps you know it – in which an ape, dressed up for the occasion, makes a speech to a learned society. It is a speech, but a test too, an examination, a viva voce. The ape has to show not only that he can speak his audience's language but that he has mastered their manners and conventions, is fit to enter their society.

'Why am I reminding you of Kafka's story? Am I going to pretend I am the ape, torn away from my natural surroundings, forced to perform in front of a gathering of critical strangers? I hope not. I am one of you, I am not of a different species.

'If you know the story, you will remember that it is cast in the form of a monologue, a monologue by the ape. Within this form there is no means for either speaker or audience to be inspected with an outsider's eye. For all we know, the speaker may not "really" be an ape, may be simply a human being like ourselves deluded into thinking himself an ape, or a human being presenting himself, with heavy irony, for rhetorical purposes, as an ape. Equally well, the audience may consist not, as we may imagine, of bewhiskered, red-faced gents who have put aside their bushjackets and topis for evening dress, but of fellow apes, trained, if not to the level of our speaker, who can mouth complicated sentences in German, then at least to sit still and listen; or, if not trained to that pitch, then chained to their seats and trained not to jabber and pick fleas and relieve themselves openly.

'We don't know. We don't know and will never know, with certainty, what is really going on in this story: whether it is about a man speaking to men or an ape speaking to apes or an ape speaking to men or a man speaking to apes (though the last is, I think, unlikely) or even just a parrot speaking to parrots.

'There used to be a time when we knew. We used to believe that when the text said, "On the table stood a glass of water," there was indeed a table, and a glass of water on it, and we had only to look in the word-mirror of the text to see them.

'But all that has ended. The word-mirror is broken, irreparably, it seems. About what is really going on in the lecture hall your guess is as good as mine: men and men, men and apes, apes and men, apes and apes. The lecture hall itself may be nothing but a zoo. The words on the page will no longer stand up and be counted, each proclaiming "I mean what I mean!" The dictionary that used to stand beside the Bible and the works of Shakespeare above the fireplace, where in pious Roman homes the household gods were kept, has become just one code book among many.

'This is the situation in which I appear before you. I am not, I hope, abusing the privilege of this platform to make idle, nihilistic jokes about what I am, ape or woman, and what you are, my auditors. That is not the point of the story, say I, who am, however, in no position to dictate what the point of the story is. There used to be a time, we believe, when we could say who we were. Now we are just performers speaking our parts. The bottom has dropped out. We could think of this as a tragic turn of events, were it not that it is hard to have respect for whatever was the bottom that dropped out − it looks to us like an illusion now, one of those illusions sustained only by the concentrated gaze of everyone in the room. Remove your gaze for but an instant, and the mirror falls to the floor and shatters.

'There is every reason, then, for me to feel less than certain about myself as I stand before you. Despite this splendid award, for which I am deeply grateful, despite the promise it makes that, gathered into the illustrious company of those who have won it before me, I am beyond time's envious grasp, we all know, if we are being realistic, that it is only a matter of time before the books which you honour, and with whose genesis I have had something to do, will cease to be read and eventually cease to be remembered. And properly so. There must be some limit to the burden of remembering that we impose on our children and grandchildren. They will have a world of their own, of which we should be less and less part. Thank you.'

The applause starts hesitantly, then swells. His mother takes off her glasses, smiles. It is an engaging smile: she seems to be relishing the moment. Actors are allowed to bathe in applause, ill deserved or well deserved – actors, singers, violinists. Why should his mother not have her moment of glory too?

The applause dies down. Dean Brautegam leans into the microphone. 'There will be refreshments –'

'Excuse me!' A clear, confident young voice cuts through the Dean's.

There is a flurry in the audience. Heads turn.

'There will be refreshments in the foyer, and an exhibition of Elizabeth Costello's books. Please join us there. It remains for me –'

'Excuse me!'

'Yes?'

'I have a question.'

The speaker is standing up: a young woman in a white-and-red

Altona College sweatshirt. Brautegam is clearly nonplussed. As for his mother, she has lost her smile. He knows that look. She has had enough, she wants to be away.

'I am not sure,' says Brautegam, frowning, peering around for support. 'Our format tonight does not allow for questions. I would like to thank –'

'Excuse me! I have a question for the speaker. May I address the speaker?'

There is a hush. All eyes are on Elizabeth Costello. Frostily she gazes into the distance.

Brautegam pulls himself together. 'I would like to thank Ms Costello, whom we have gathered tonight to honour. Please join us in the foyer. Thank you.' And he switches off the microphone.

As they leave the auditorium there is a buzz of talk. An incident, no less. He can see the girl in the red-and-white shirt ahead of him in the throng. She walks stiff and erect and seemingly angry. What was the question going to be? Would it not have been better to have it aired?

He fears that the scene will repeat itself in the foyer. But there is no scene. The girl has left, gone out into the night, perhaps stormed out. Nevertheless, the incident leaves a bad taste; say what one may, the evening has been spoiled.

What was she going to ask? Whispering, people huddle together. They seem to have a shrewd idea. He has a shrewd idea too. Something to do with what Elizabeth Costello the famous writer might have been expected to say on an occasion like this, and did not say.

He can see Dean Brautegam and others fussing around his mother now, trying to smooth things over. After all they have invested, they want her to go home thinking well of them and of the college. But they must be glancing ahead too to 1997, hoping that the 1997 jury will come up with a more winning winner.

We skip the rest of the foyer scene, move to the hotel.

Elizabeth Costello retires for the night. For a while her son watches television in his room. Then he grows restless and goes down to the lounge, where the first person he sees is the woman who interviewed his mother for the radio, Susan Moebius. She waves him over. She is with a companion, but the companion soon departs, leaving the two of them alone.

He finds Susan Moebius attractive. She dresses well, better than the conventions of the academy usually allow. She has long, golden-blonde hair; she sits upright in her chair, squaring her shoulders; when she tosses her hair the movement is quite queenly.

They skirt the events of the evening. Instead they speak about the revival of radio as a cultural medium. 'An interesting session you had with my mother,' says John. 'I know you have written a book on her, which unfortunately I haven't read. Do you have good things to say about her?'

'I believe I do. Elizabeth Costello has been a key writer for our times. My book isn't about her alone, but she figures strongly in it.'

'A key writer . . . Is she a key writer for all of us, would you say, or just for women? I got the feeling during the interview that you see her solely as a woman writer or a woman's writer. Would you still consider her a key writer if she were a man?'

'If she were a man?'

'All right: if you were a man?'

'If I were a man? I don't know. I have never been a man. I will let you know when I have tried it.'

They smile. There is definitely something in the air.

'But my mother has been a man,' he persists. 'She has also been a dog. She can think her way into other people, into other existences. I have read her; I know. It is within her powers. Isn't that what is most important about fiction: that it takes us out of ourselves, into other lives?'

'Perhaps. But your mother remains a woman all the same. Whatever she does, she does as a woman. She inhabits her characters as a woman does, not a man.'

'I don't see that. I find her men perfectly believable.'

'You don't see because you wouldn't see. Only a woman would see. It is something between women. If her men are believable, good, I am glad to hear so, but finally it is just mimicry. Women are good at mimicry, better at it than men. At parody, even. Our touch is lighter.'

She is smiling again. *See how light my touch can be*, her lips seem to say. Soft lips.

'If there is parody in her,' he says, 'I confess it is too subtle for me to pick up.' There is a long silence. 'So is that what you think,' he says at last: 'that we live parallel lives, men and women, that we never really meet?'

The drift of the conversation has changed. They are no longer speaking about writing, if they ever were.

'What do you think?' she says. 'What does your experience tell you? And is difference such a bad thing? If there were no difference, what would become of desire?'

She looks him candidly in the eye. It is time to move. He stands up; she puts her glass down, slowly stands up too. As she passes him he takes her elbow, and at the touch a shock runs through him, dizzying him. Difference; opposite poles. Midnight in Pennsylvania: what is the time back in Melbourne? What is he doing on this foreign continent?

They are alone in the elevator. Not the elevator he and his mother used: a different shaft. Which is north, which south in this hexagon of a hotel, this beehive? He presses the woman against

23

the wall, kisses her, tasting smoke on her breath. *Research*: will that be her name for it afterwards? *Using a secondary source*? He kisses her again, she kisses him back, kissing flesh of the flesh.

They exit on the thirteenth floor; he follows her down the corridor, turning right and left until he loses track. The core of the hive: is that what they are seeking? His mother's room is 1254. His is 1220. Hers is 1307. He is surprised there is such a number. He thought that floors went twelve–fourteen, that that was the rule in the hotel world. Where is 1307 in relation to 1254: north, south, west, east?

We skip ahead again, a skip this time in the text rather than in the performance.

When he thinks back over those hours, one moment returns with sudden force, the moment when her knee slips under his arm and folds into his armpit. Curious that the memory of an entire scene should be dominated by one moment, not obviously significant, yet so vivid that he can still almost feel the ghostly thigh against his skin. Does the mind by nature prefer sensations to ideas, the tangible to the abstract? Or is the folding of the woman's knee just a mnemonic, from which will unfold the rest of the night?

They are lying in the dark, flank to flank, in the text of memory, talking.

'So: has it been a successful visit?' she asks.

'From whose point of view?'

'Yours.'

'My point of view doesn't matter. I came for Elizabeth Costello's sake. Hers is the point of view that matters. Yes, successful. Successful enough.'

'Do I detect a touch of bitterness?'

'None. I am here to help – that is all.'

24

'That is very good of you. Do you feel you owe her something?'

'Yes. Filial duty. It is a perfectly natural feeling among humankind.'

She ruffles his hair. 'Don't be cross,' she says.

'I am not.'

She slides down beside him, strokes him. 'Successful enough – what does that mean?' she murmurs. She is not giving up. A price has yet to be paid for this time in her bed, for what counts as a conquest.

'The speech didn't come off. She is disappointed about that. She put a lot of work into it.'

'There was nothing wrong with the speech in itself. But the title was not appropriate. And she should not have relied on Kafka for her illustrations. There are better texts.'

'There are?'

'Yes, better, more suitable. This is America, the 1990s. People don't want to hear the Kafka thing yet again.'

'What do they want to hear?'

She shrugs. 'Something more personal. It doesn't have to be intimate. But audiences no longer react well to heavy historical self-ironization. They might at a pinch accept it from a man, but not from a woman. A woman doesn't need to wear all that armour.'

'And a man does?'

'You tell me. If it is a problem, it is a male problem. We didn't give the award to a man.'

'Have you considered the possibility that my mother may have got beyond the man-woman thing? That she may have explored it as far as it goes, and is now after bigger game?'

'Such as?'

The hand that has been stroking him pauses. The moment is

important, he can feel it. She is waiting for his answer, for the privileged access he promises. He too can feel the thrill of the moment, electric, reckless.

'Such as measuring herself against the illustrious dead. Such as paying tribute to the powers that animate her. For instance.'

'Is that what she says?'

'Don't you think that that is what she has been doing all her life: measuring herself against the masters? Does no one in your profession recognize it?'

He should not be speaking like this. He should be keeping out of his mother's business. He is in this stranger's bed not for his bonny blue eyes but because he is his mother's son. Yet here he is spilling the beans like a nincompoop! This must be how spy-women work. Nothing subtle to it. The man is seduced not because he has a will to resist that is cleverly overcome, but because being seduced is a pleasure in itself. One yields for the sake of yielding.

He wakes once during the night, overwhelmed with sadness, such deep sadness that he could cry. Lightly he touches the naked shoulder of the woman beside him, but she does not respond. He runs the hand down her body: breast, flank, hip, thigh, knee. Handsome in every detail, no doubt about that, but in a blank way that no longer moves him.

He has a vision of his mother in her big double bed, crouched, her knees drawn up, her back bared. Out of her back, out of the waxy, old person's flesh, protrude three needles: not the tiny needles of the acupuncturist or the voodoo doctor but thick, grey needles, steel or plastic: knitting needles. The needles have not killed her, there is no need to worry about that, she breathes regularly in her sleep. Nevertheless, she lies impaled.

Who has done it? Who would have done it?

26

Such loneliness, he thinks, hovering in spirit over the old woman in the bare room. His heart is breaking; sadness pours down like a grey waterfall behind his eyes. He should never have come here, to room 13 whatever it is. A wrong move. He ought to get up at once, steal out. But he does not. Why? Because he does not want to be alone. And because he wants to sleep. *Sleep*, he thinks, *that knits up the ravelled sleeve of care.* What an extraordinary way of putting it! Not all the monkeys in the world picking away at typewriters all their lives would come up with those words in that arrangement. Out of the dark emerging, out of nowhere: first not there, then there, like a newborn child, heart working, brain working, all the processes of that intricate electrochemical labyrinth working. A miracle. He closes his eyes.

A gap.

She, Susan Moebius, is already there when he comes down for breakfast. She is wearing white, she looks rested and content. He joins her.

From her purse she takes something and lays it on the table: his watch. 'It is three hours out,' she says.

'Not three,' he says. 'Fifteen. Canberra time.'

Her eyes rest on his, or his on hers. Green-flecked. He feels a tug. An unexplored continent, from which he is about to part! A pang, a tiny pang of loss, shoots through him. Pain not without pleasure, like certain grades of toothache. He can conceive of something quite serious with this woman, whom he will probably not see again.

'I know what you are thinking,' she says. 'You are thinking we won't see each other again. You are thinking, *A wasted investment.*'

'What else do you know?'

'You think I have been using you. You think I have been trying to reach your mother through you.'

27

She is smiling. No fool. A capable player.

'Yes,' he says. 'No.' He draws a deep breath. 'I will tell you what I really think. I think you are baffled, even if you won't admit it, by the mystery of the divine in the human. You know there is something special about my mother – that is what draws you to her – yet when you meet her she turns out to be just an ordinary old woman. You can't square the two. You want an explanation. You want a clue, a sign, if not from her then from me. That is what is going on. It's all right, I don't mind.'

Strange words to be speaking over breakfast, over coffee and toast. He did not know he had them in him.

'You really are her son, aren't you. Do you write too?'

'You mean, am I touched by the god? No. But yes, I am her son. Not a foundling, not an adoptee. Out of her very body I came, caterwauling.'

'And you have a sister.'

'A half-sister, from the same place. The real thing, both of us. Flesh of her flesh, blood of her blood.'

'And you have never married.'

'Wrong. Married and unmarried. What about you?'

'I have a husband. A husband, a child, a happy marriage.'

'That's good then.'

There is nothing more to be said.

'Will I have a chance to say goodbye to your mother?'

'You can catch her before the television interview. At ten, in the ballroom.'

A gap.

The television people have chosen the ballroom because of the red velvet drapes. In front of the drapes they have set up a rather ornate chair for his mother, and a plainer chair for the woman who will engage with her. Susan, when she comes, has to cross

28

the whole length of the room. She is ready to travel; she has a calf–leather satchel over her shoulder; her stride is easy, confident. Again, lightly, like the brush of a feather, comes a pang, the pang of forthcoming loss.

'It has been a great honour to get to know you, Mrs Costello,' Susan says, taking his mother's hand.

'Elizabeth,' says his mother. 'Excuse the throne.'

'Elizabeth.'

'I want to give you this,' says Susan, and from her satchel produces a book. The cover shows a woman wearing antique Grecian costume, holding a scroll. *Reclaiming a History: Women and Memory*, says the title. *Susan Kaye Moebius.*

'Thank you, I look forward to reading it,' says his mother.

He stays for the interview, sitting in a corner, watching as his mother transforms herself into the person television wants her to be. All the quaintnesses she refused to deliver last night are allowed to come out: pungent turns of speech, stories of childhood in the Australian outback ('You have to realize how vast Australia is. We are only fleas on Australia's backside, we late settlers'), stories about the film world, about actors and actresses she has crossed paths with, about the adaptations of her books and what she thinks of them ('Film is a simplifying medium. That is its nature; you may as well learn to accept it. It works in broad strokes'). Followed by a glance at the contemporary world ('It does my heart good to see so many strong young women around who know what they want'). Even bird–watching gets a mention.

After the interview Susan Moebius's book almost gets left behind. He is the one who picks it up from under the chair.

'I wish people wouldn't give one books,' she murmurs. 'Where am I going to find space for it?'

'I have space.'

'Then you take it. Keep it. You're the one she was really after, not me.'

He reads the inscription: *To Elizabeth Costello, with gratitude and admiration*. 'Me?' he says. 'I don't think so. I was just' – his voice barely falters – 'a pawn in the game. You are the one she loves and hates.'

He barely falters; but the word that first came to mind was not *pawn*, it was *clipping*. A toenail clipping, that one steals and wraps in a tissue and takes away, for one's own purposes.

His mother does not reply. But she does give him a smile, a quick, sudden smile of – he cannot see it in any other way – triumph.

Their duties in Williamstown are over. The television crew are packing up. In half an hour a taxi will take them to the airport. She has won, more or less. On foreign turf too. An away win. She can come home with her true self safe, leaving behind an image, false, like all images.

What is the truth of his mother? He does not know, and at the deepest level does not want to know. He is here simply to protect her, to bar the way against the relic-hunters and the contumelists and the sentimental pilgrims. He has opinions of his own, but he will not speak them. *This woman*, he would say if he were to speak, *whose words you hang on as if she were the sibyl, is the same woman who, forty years ago, hid day after day in her bedsitter in Hampstead, crying to herself, crawling out in the evenings into the foggy streets to buy the fish and chips on which she lived, falling asleep in her clothes. She is the same woman who later stormed around the house in Melbourne, hair flying in all directions, screaming at her children, 'You are killing me! You are tearing the flesh from my body!'* (He lay in the dark with his sister afterwards, comforting her while she sobbed; he was seven; it was his first taste of fathering.) *This is the secret world of the oracle. How can you hope to understand her before you know what she is really like?*

He does not hate his mother. (As he thinks these words, other words echo at the back of his mind: the words of one of William Faulkner's characters insisting with mad repetitiveness that he does not hate the South. Who is the character?) Quite the contrary. If he hated her he would long ago have put the greatest possible distance between the two of them. He does not hate her. He serves at her shrine, cleaning up after the turmoil of the holy day, sweeping up the petals, collecting the offerings, putting the widows' mites together, ready to bank. He may not share in the frenzy, but he worships too.

A mouthpiece for the divine. But *sibyl* is not the right word for her. Nor is *oracle*. Too Greco-Roman. His mother is not in the Greco-Roman mould. Tibet or India more like it: a god incarnated in a child, wheeled from village to village to be applauded, venerated.

Then they are in the taxi, driving through streets that already have the air of streets about to be forgotten.

'So,' says his mother. 'A clean getaway.'

'I do believe so. Have you got the cheque safe?'

'The cheque, the medal, everything.'

A gap. They are at the airport, at the gate, waiting for the flight to be called that will take them on the first stage of their journey home. Faintly, over their heads, with a crude, driving beat, a version of *Eine kleine Nachtmusik* is playing. Opposite them sits a woman eating popcorn out of a paper bucket, so fat that her toes barely reach the floor.

'Can I ask you one thing?' he says. 'Why literary history? And why such a grim chapter in literary history? Realism: no one in this place wanted to hear about realism.'

Fiddling in her purse, she makes no reply.

'When I think of realism,' he goes on, 'I think of peasants frozen in blocks of ice. I think of Norwegians in smelly underwear. What is your interest in it? And where does Kafka fit in? What has Kafka to do with it all?'

'With what? With smelly underwear?'

'Yes. With smelly underwear. With people picking their noses. You don't write about that kind of thing. Kafka didn't write about it.'

'No, Kafka didn't write about people picking their noses. But Kafka had time to wonder where and how his poor educated ape was going to find a mate. And what it was going to be like when he was left in the dark with the bewildered, half-tamed female that his keepers eventually produced for his use. Kafka's ape is embedded in life. It is the embeddedness that is important, not the life itself. His ape is embedded as we are embedded, you in me, I in you. That ape is followed through to the end, to the bitter, unsayable end, whether or not there are traces left on the page. Kafka stays awake during the gaps when we are sleeping. That is where Kafka fits in.'

The fat woman is observing them frankly, her little eyes flicking from the one to the other: the old woman in the raincoat and the man with the bald patch who could be her son, having a fight in their funny accents.

'Well,' he says, 'if what you say is true, it is repulsive. It is zoo-keeping, not writing.'

'What would you prefer? A zoo without keepers, where the animals fall into a trance when you stop looking at them? A zoo of ideas? A gorilla cage with the idea of a gorilla in it, an elephant cage with the idea of elephants in it? Do you know how many kilograms of solid waste an elephant drops in twenty-four hours?

If you want a real elephant cage with real elephants then you need a zookeeper to clean up after them.'

'You are off the point, Mother. And don't get so excited.' He turns to the fat woman. 'We are discussing literature, the claims of realism versus the claims of idealism.'

Without ceasing to chew, the fat woman removes her eyes from them. He thinks of the cud of mashed corn and saliva in her mouth and shudders. Where does it all end?

'There is a difference between cleaning up after animals and watching them while they do their business,' he starts again. 'I am asking about the latter, not the former. Don't animals deserve a private life as much as we do?'

'Not if they are in a zoo,' she says. 'Not if they are on show. Once you are on show, you have no private life. Anyway, do you ask permission from the stars before you peek at them through your telescope? What about the private lives of the stars?'

'Mother, the stars are lumps of rock.'

'Are they? I thought they were traces of light millions of years old.'

'Boarding will now commence on United Airlines flight 323 non-stop to Los Angeles,' says a voice above their heads. 'Passengers requiring assistance, as well as families with young children, may step forward.'

On the flight she barely touches her food. She orders two brandies, one after the other, and falls asleep. When, hours later, they begin the descent to Los Angeles, she is still asleep. The flight attendant taps her on the shoulder. 'Ma'am, your seat belt.' She does not stir. They exchange looks, he and the flight attendant. He leans over and clips the belt across her lap.

She lies slumped deep in her seat. Her head is sideways, her mouth open. She is snoring faintly. Light flashes from the windows as they bank, the sun setting brilliantly over southern California. He can see up her nostrils, into her mouth, down the back of her throat. And what he cannot see he can imagine: the gullet, pink and ugly, contracting as it swallows, like a python, drawing things down to the pear-shaped belly-sac. He draws away, tightens his own belt, sits up, facing forward. No, he tells himself, that is not where I come from, that is not it.

2
The Novel in Africa

AT A DINNER party she meets X, whom she has not seen in years. Is he still teaching at the University of Queensland, she asks? No, he replies, he has retired and now works the cruise ships, travelling the world, screening old movies, talking about Bergman and Fellini to retired people. He has never regretted the move. 'The pay is good, you get to see the world, and – do you know what? – people that age actually listen to what you have to say.' He urges her to give it a try: 'You are a prominent figure, a well-known writer. The cruise line I work for will jump at the opportunity to take you on. You will be a feather in their cap. Say but the word and I'll bring it up with my friend the director.'

The proposal interests her. She was last on a ship in 1963, when she came home from England, from the mother country. Soon after that they began to retire the great ocean-going liners, one by one, and scrap them. The end of an era. She would not mind doing it again, going to sea. She would like to call at Easter Island and St Helena, where Napoleon languished. She would like to visit Antarctica – not just to see with her own eyes those vast horizons, that barren waste, but to set foot on the seventh and last continent, feel what it is like to be a living, breathing creature in spaces of inhuman cold.

X is as good as his word. From the headquarters of Scandia

Lines in Stockholm comes a fax. In December the SS *Northern Lights* will be sailing from Christchurch on a fifteen-day cruise to the Ross Ice Shelf, and thence onward to Cape Town. Might she be interested in joining the education and entertainment staff? Passengers on Scandia's cruise ships are, as the letter puts it, 'discriminating persons who take their leisure seriously'. The emphasis of the on-board programme will be on ornithology and cold-water ecology, but Scandia would be delighted if the noted writer Elizabeth Costello could find the time to offer a short course on, say, the contemporary novel. In return for which, and for making herself accessible to passengers, she will be offered an A-class berth, all expenses paid, with air connections to Christchurch and from Cape Town, and a substantial honorarium to boot.

It is an offer she cannot refuse. On the morning of 10 December she joins the ship in Christchurch harbour. Her cabin, she finds, is small but otherwise quite satisfactory; the young man who co-ordinates the entertainment and self-development programme is respectful; the passengers at her table at lunchtime, in the main retired people, people of her own generation, are pleasant and unostentatious.

On the list of her co-lecturers there is only one name she recognizes: Emmanuel Egudu, a writer from Nigeria. Their acquaintance goes back more years than she cares to remember, to a PEN conference in Kuala Lumpur. Egudu had been loud and fiery then, political; her first impression was that he was a poseur. Reading him later on, she had not changed her mind. But a poseur, she now wonders: what is that? Someone who seems to be what he is not? Which of us is what he seems to be, she seems to be? And anyway, in Africa things may be different. In Africa what one takes to be posing, what one takes to be boasting, may just be manliness. Who is she to say?

Towards men, including Egudu, she has, she notices, mellowed as she has grown older. Curious, because in other respects she has become more (she chooses the word carefully) acidulous.

She runs into Egudu at the captain's cocktail party (he has come aboard late). He is wearing a vivid green dashiki, suave Italian shoes; his beard is spotted with grey, but he is still a fine figure of a man. He gives her a huge smile, enfolds her in an embrace. 'Elizabeth!' he exclaims. 'How good to see you! I had no idea! We have so much catching up to do!'

In his lexicon, it appears, catching up means talking about his own activities. He no longer spends much time in his home country, he informs her. He has become, as he puts it, 'an habitual exile, like an habitual criminal'. He has acquired American papers; he makes his living on the lecture circuit, a circuit that would appear to have expanded to encompass the cruise ships. This will be his third trip on the *Northern Lights*. Very restful, he finds it; very relaxing. Who would have guessed, he says, that a country boy from Africa would end up like this, in the lap of luxury? And he treats her again to his big smile, the special one.

I'm a country girl myself, she would like to say, but does not, though it is true, in part. *Nothing exceptional about being from the country.*

Each of the entertainment staff is expected to give a short public talk. 'Just to say who you are, where you come from,' explains the young coordinator in carefully idiomatic English. His name is Mikael; he is handsome in his tall, blond, Swedish way, but dour, too dour for her taste.

Her talk is advertised as 'The Future of the Novel', Egudu's as 'The Novel in Africa'. She is scheduled to speak on the morning of their first day out to sea; he will speak the same afternoon. In the evening comes 'The Lives of Whales', with sound recordings.

Mikael himself does the introduction. 'The famous Australian writer,' he calls her, 'author of *The House on Eccles Street* and many other novels, whom we are truly privileged to have in our midst.' It vexes her to be billed once again as the author of a book from so far in the past, but there is nothing to be done about that.

'The Future of the Novel' is a talk she has given before, in fact many times before, expanded or contracted depending on the occasion. No doubt there are expanded and contracted versions of the novel in Africa and the lives of whales too. For the present occasion she has chosen the contracted version.

'The future of the novel is not a subject I am much interested in,' she begins, trying to give her auditors a jolt. 'In fact the future in general does not much interest me. What is the future, after all, but a structure of hopes and expectations? Its residence is in the mind; it has no reality.

'Of course, you might reply that the past is likewise a fiction. The past is history, and what is history but a story made of air that we tell ourselves? Nevertheless, there is something miraculous about the past that the future lacks. What is miraculous about the past is that we have succeeded – God knows how – in making thousands and millions of individual fictions, fictions created by individual human beings, lock well enough into one another to give us what looks like a common past, a shared story.

'The future is different. We do not possess a shared story of the future. The creation of the past seems to exhaust our collective creative energies. Compared with our fiction of the past, our fiction of the future is a sketchy, bloodless affair, as visions of heaven tend to be. Of heaven and even of hell.'

The novel, the traditional novel, she goes on to say, is an attempt to understand human fate one case at a time, to understand how it comes about that some fellow being, having started at point A

38

and having undergone experiences B and C and D, ends up at point Z. Like history, the novel is thus an exercise in making the past coherent. Like history, it explores the respective contributions of character and circumstance to forming the present. By doing so, the novel suggests how we may explore the power of the present to produce the future. That is why we have this thing, this institution, this medium called the novel.

She is not sure, as she listens to her own voice, whether she believes any longer in what she is saying. Ideas like these must have had some grip on her when years ago she wrote them down, but after so many repetitions they have taken on a worn, unconvincing air. On the other hand, she no longer believes very strongly in belief. Things can be true, she now thinks, even if one does not believe in them, and conversely. Belief may be no more, in the end, than a source of energy, like a battery which one clips into an idea to make it run. As happens when one writes: believing whatever has to be believed in order to get the job done.

If she has trouble believing in her argument, she has even greater trouble in preventing that absence of conviction from emerging in her voice. Despite the fact that she is the noted author of, as Mikael says, *The House on Eccles Street* and other books, despite the fact that her audience is by and large of her generation and ought therefore to share with her a common past, the applause at the end lacks enthusiasm.

For Emmanuel's talk she sits inconspicuously in the back row. They have in the meantime had a good lunch; they are sailing south on what are still placid seas; there is every chance that some of the good folk in the audience – numbering, she would guess, about fifty – are going to nod off. In fact, who knows, she might nod off herself; in which case it would be best to do so unnoticed.

'You will be wondering why I have chosen as my topic the novel in Africa,' Emmanuel begins, in his effortlessly booming voice. 'What is so special about the novel in Africa? What makes it different, different enough to demand our attention today?

'Well, let us see. We all know, to begin with, that the alphabet, the idea of the alphabet, did not grow up in Africa. Many things grew up in Africa, more than you might think, but not the alphabet. The alphabet had to be brought in, first by Arabs, then again by Westerners. In Africa writing itself, to say nothing of novel-writing, is a recent affair.

'Is the novel possible without novel-writing, you may ask? Did we in Africa have a novel before our friends the colonizers appeared on our doorstep? For the time being, let me merely propose the question. Later I may return to it.

'A second remark: reading is not a typically African recreation. Music, yes; dancing, yes; eating, yes; talking, yes – lots of talking. But reading, no, and particularly not reading fat novels. Reading has always struck us Africans as a strangely solitary business. It makes us uneasy. When we Africans visit great European cities like Paris and London, we notice how people on trains take books out of their bags or their pockets and retreat into solitary worlds. Each time the book comes out it is like a sign held up. *Leave me alone, I am reading*, says the sign. *What I am reading is more interesting than you could possibly be.*

'Well, we are not like that in Africa. We do not like to cut ourselves off from other people and retreat into private worlds. Nor are we used to our neighbours retreating into private worlds. Africa is a continent where people share. Reading a book by yourself is not sharing. It is like eating alone or talking alone. It is not our way. We find it a bit crazy.'

We, we, we, she thinks. *We Africans*. It is not *our* way. She has

40

never liked *we* in its exclusive form. Emmanuel may have grown older, he may have acquired the blessing of American papers, but he has not changed. Africanness: a special identity, a special fate.

She has visited Africa: the highlands of Kenya, Zimbabwe, the Okavango swamps. She has seen Africans reading, ordinary Africans, at bus stops, in trains. They were not reading novels, admittedly, they were reading newspapers. But is a newspaper not as much an avenue to a private world as a novel?

'In the third place,' continues Egudu, 'in the great, beneficent global system under which we live today, it has been allotted to Africa to be the home of poverty. Africans have no money for luxuries. In Africa, a book must offer you a return for the money you spend on it. What do I stand to learn by reading this story, the African will ask? How will it advance me? We may deplore the attitude of the African, ladies and gentlemen, but we cannot dismiss it. We must take it seriously and try to understand it.

'We do of course make books in Africa. But the books we make are for children, teaching-books in the simplest sense. If you want to make money publishing books in Africa, you must put out books that will be prescribed for schools, that will be bought in quantity by the education system to be read and studied in the classroom. It does not pay to publish writers with serious ambitions, writers who write about adults and matters that concern adults. Such writers must look elsewhere for their salvation.

'Of course, ladies and gentlemen of the *Northern Lights*, it is not the whole picture I am giving you here today. To give you the whole picture would take all afternoon. I am giving you only a crude, hasty sketch. Of course you will find publishers in Africa, one here, one there, who will support local writers even if they will never make money. But in the broad picture, storytelling provides a livelihood neither for publishers nor for writers.

41

'So much for the generalities, depressing as they may be. Now let us turn our attention to ourselves, to you and to me. Here I am, you know who I am, it tells you in the programme: Emmanuel Egudu, from Nigeria, author of novels, poems, plays, winner, even, of a Commonwealth Literary Award (Africa Division). And here you are, wealthy folk, or at least comfortable, as you say (I am not wrong, am I?), from North America and Europe and of course let us not forget our Australasian representation, and perhaps I have even heard the odd word of Japanese whispered in the corridors, taking a cruise on this splendid ship, on your way to inspect one of the remoter corners of the globe, to check it out, perhaps to check it off your list. Here you are, after a good lunch, listening to this African fellow talk.

'Why, I imagine you asking yourselves, is this African fellow on board our ship? Why isn't he back at his desk in the land of his birth following his vocation, if he really is a writer, writing books? Why is he going on about the African novel, a subject that can be of only the most peripheral concern to us?

'The short answer, ladies and gentlemen, is that the African fellow is earning a living. In his own country, as I have tried to explain, he cannot earn a living. In his own country (I will not labour the point, I mention it only because it holds true for so many fellow African writers) he is in fact less than welcome. In his own country he is what is called a dissident intellectual, and dissident intellectuals must tread carefully, even in the new Nigeria.

'So here he is, abroad in the wide world, earning his living. Part of his living he earns by writing books that are published and read and reviewed and talked about and judged, for the most part, by foreigners. The rest of his living he earns from spin-offs of his writing. He reviews books by other writers, for example, in the press of Europe and America. He teaches in colleges in America, telling the youth of the New World about the exotic subject on which he is an expert in the same way that an elephant is an expert on elephants: the African novel. He addresses conferences; he sails on cruise ships. While so occupied, he lives in what are called temporary accommodations. All his addresses are temporary; he has no fixed abode.

'How easy do you think it is, ladies and gentlemen, for this fellow to be true to his essence as writer when there are all these strangers to please, month after month – publishers, readers, critics, students, all of them armed not only with their own ideas about what writing is or should be, what the novel is or should be, what Africa is or should be, but also about what being pleased is or should be? Do you think it is possible for this fellow to remain unaffected by all the pressure on him to please others, to be for them what they think he should be, to produce for them what they think he should produce?

'It may have escaped your attention, but I slipped in, a moment ago, a word that should have made you prick up your ears. I spoke about my essence and being true to my essence. There is much I could say about essence and its ramifications; but this is not the right occasion. Nevertheless, you must be asking yourselves, how in these anti-essential days, these days of fleeting identities that we pick up and wear and discard like clothing, can I justify speaking of my essence as an African writer?

'Around essence and essentialism, I should remind you, there is a long history of turmoil in African thought. You may have heard of the *négritude* movement of the 1940s and 1950s. *Négritude*, according to the originators of the movement, is the essential substratum that binds all Africans together and makes them uniquely African – not only the Africans of Africa but Africans of the great African diaspora in the New World and now in Europe.

43

'I want to quote some words to you from the Senegalese writer and thinker Cheikh Hamidou Kane. Cheikh Hamidou was being questioned by an interviewer, a European. I am puzzled, said the interviewer, by your praise for certain writers for being truly African. In view of the fact that the writers in question write in a foreign language (specifically French) and are published and, for the most part, read in a foreign country (specifically France), can they truly be called African writers? Are they not more properly called French writers of African origin? Is language not a more important matrix than birth?

'The following is Cheikh Hamidou's reply: "The writers I speak of are truly African because they are born in Africa, they live in Africa, their sensibility is African . . . What distinguishes them lies in life experience, in sensitivities, in rhythm, in style." He goes on: "A French or English writer has thousands of years of written tradition behind him . . . We on the other hand are heirs to an oral tradition."

'There is nothing mystical in Cheikh Hamidou's response, nothing metaphysical, nothing racist. He merely gives proper weight to those intangibles of culture which, because they are not easily pinned down in words, are often passed over. The way that people live in their bodies. The way they move their hands. The way they walk. The way they smile or frown. The lilt of their speech. The way they sing. The timbre of their voices. The way they dance. The way they touch each other; how the hand lingers; the feel of the fingers. The way they make love. The way they lie after they have made love. The way they think. The way they sleep.

'We African novelists can embody these qualities in our writings (and let me remind you at this point that the word *novel*, when it entered the languages of Europe, had the vaguest of meanings: it meant the form of writing that was formless, that had no rules, that made up its own rules as it went along) – we African novelists can embody these qualities as no one else can because we have not lost touch with the body. The African novel, the true African novel, is an oral novel. On the page it is inert, only half alive; it wakes up when the voice, from deep in the body, breathes life into the words, speaks them aloud.

'The African novel is thus, I would claim, in its very being, and before the first word is written, a critique of the Western novel, which has gone so far down the road of disembodiment – think of Henry James, think of Marcel Proust – that the appropriate way and indeed the only way in which to absorb it is in silence and in solitude. And I will close these remarks, ladies and gentlemen – I see my time is running out – by quoting, in support of my position and Cheikh Hamidou's, not from an African, but from a man from the snowy wastes of Canada, the great scholar of orality Paul Zumthor.

'"Since the seventeenth century," writes Zumthor, "Europe has spread across the world like a cancer, at first stealthily, but for a while now at gathering pace, until today it ravages life forms, animals, plants, habitats, languages. With each day that passes several languages of the world disappear, repudiated, stifled . . . One of the symptoms of the disease has without doubt, from the beginning, been what we call literature; and literature has consolidated itself, prospered, and become what it is – one of the hugest dimensions of mankind – by denying the voice . . . The time has come to stop privileging writing . . . Perhaps great, unfortunate Africa, beggared by our political–industrial imperialism, will, because less gravely affected by writing, find itself closer to the goal than will the other continents."'

The applause when Egudu ends his talk is loud and spirited. He has spoken with force, perhaps even with passion; he has stood up for himself, for his calling, for his people; why should he not have his reward, even if what he says can have little relevance to the lives of his audience?

Nevertheless, there is something about the talk she does not like, something to do with orality and the mystique of orality. Always, she thinks, the body that is insisted on, pushed forward, and the voice, dark essence of the body, welling up from within it. *Négritude*: she had thought Emmanuel would grow out of that pseudo-philosophy. Evidently he has not. Evidently he has decided to keep it as part of his professional pitch. Well, good luck to him. There is still time, ten minutes at least, for questions. She hopes the questions will be searching, will search him out.

The first questioner is, if she is to judge by accent, from the Midwest of the United States. The first novel she ever read by an African, decades ago, says the woman, was by Amos Tutuola, she forgets the title. ('*The Palm Wine Drinkard*,' suggests Egudu. 'Yes, that's it,' she replies.) She was captivated by it. She thought it was the harbinger of great things to come. So she was disappointed, terribly disappointed, to hear that Tutuola was not respected in his own country, that educated Nigerians disparaged him and considered his reputation in the West unmerited. Was this true? Was Tutuola the kind of oral novelist our lecturer had in mind? What has happened to Tutuola? Had more of his books been translated?

No, responds Egudu, Tutuola has not been translated any further, in fact he has not been translated at all, at least not into English. Why not? Because he did not need to be translated. Because he had written in English all along. 'Which is the root of the problem that the questioner raises. The language of Amos Tutuola is English, but not standard English, not the English that Nigerians of the 1950s went to school and college to learn. It is the language of a semi-educated clerk, a man with no more than elementary schooling, barely comprehensible to an outsider, fixed up for publication by British editors. Where Tutuola's writing was frankly illiterate they corrected it; what they refrained from correcting was what seemed authentically Nigerian to them, that is to say, what to their ears sounded picturesque, exotic, folkloric.

'From what I have just been saying,' Egudu continues, 'you may imagine that I too disapprove of Tutuola or the Tutuola phenomenon. Far from it. Tutuola was repudiated by so-called educated Nigerians because they were embarrassed by him – embarrassed that they might be lumped with him as natives who did not know how to write proper English. As for me, I am happy to be a native, a Nigerian native, a native Nigerian. In this battle I am on Tutuola's side. Tutuola is or was a gifted storyteller. I am glad you like him. Several more books penned by him were put out in England, though none, I would say, as good as *The Palm Wine Drinkard*. And, yes, he is the kind of writer I was referring to, an oral writer.

'I have responded to you at length because the case of Tutuola is so instructive. What makes Tutuola stand out is that he did not adjust his language to the expectations – or to what he might have thought, had he been less naive, would be the expectations – of the foreigners who would read and judge him. Not knowing better, he wrote as he spoke. He therefore had to yield in a particularly helpless way to being packaged, for the West, as an African exotic.

'But, ladies and gentlemen, who among African writers is not exotic? The truth is, to the West we Africans are all exotic, when we are not simply savage. That is our fate. Even here, on this ship sailing towards the continent that ought to be the most exotic of all, and the most savage, the continent with no human standards at all, I can sense I am exotic.'

There is a ripple of laughter. Egudu smiles his big smile, engaging, to all appearances spontaneous. But she cannot believe it is a true smile, cannot believe it comes from the heart, if that is where smiles come from. If being an exotic is the fate Egudu has embraced for himself, then it is a terrible fate. She cannot believe he does not know that, know it and in his heart revolt against it. The one black face in this sea of white.

'But let me return to your question,' Egudu continues. 'You have read Tutuola, now read my countryman Ben Okri. Amos Tutuola's is a very simple, very stark case. Okri's is not. Okri is an heir of Tutuola's, or they are the heirs of common ancestors. But Okri negotiates the contradictions of being himself for other people (excuse the jargon, it is just a native showing off) in a much more complex way. Read Okri. You will find the experience instructive.'

'The Novel in Africa' was intended, like all the shipboard talks, to be a light affair. Nothing on the shipboard programme is intended to be a heavy affair. Egudu, unfortunately, is threatening to be heavy. With a discreet nod, the entertainment director, the tall Swedish boy in his light blue uniform, signals from the wings; and gracefully, easily, Egudu obeys, bringing his show to an end.

The crew of the *Northern Lights* is Russian, as are the stewards. In fact, everyone but the officers and the corps of guides and managers is Russian. Music on board is furnished by a balalaika orchestra – five men, five women. The accompaniment they provide at the dinner hour is too schmaltzy for her taste; after dinner, in the ballroom, the music they play becomes livelier.

The leader of the orchestra, and occasional singer, is a blonde in her early thirties. She has a smattering of English, enough to make the announcements. 'We play piece that is calléd in Russian

My Little Dove. My Little Dove.' Her *dove* rhymes with *stove* rather than *love*. With its trills and swoops, the piece sounds Hungarian, sounds gypsy, sounds Jewish, sounds everything but Russian; but who is she, Elizabeth Costello, country girl, to say?

She is there with a couple from her table, having a drink. They are from Manchester, they inform her. They are looking forward to her course on the novel, in which they have both enrolled. The man is long-bodied, sleek, silvery: she thinks of him as a gannet. How he has made his money he does not say and she does not enquire. The woman is petite, sensual. Not at all her idea of Manchester. Steve and Shirley. She guesses they are not married.

To her relief, the conversation soon turns from her and the books she has written to the subject of ocean currents, about which Steve appears to know all there is to know, and to the tiny beings, tons of them to the square mile, whose life consists in being swept in serene fashion through these icy waters, eating and being eaten, multiplying and dying, ignored by history. Ecological tourists, that is what Steve and Shirley call themselves. Last year the Amazon, this year the Southern Ocean.

Egudu is standing at the entranceway, looking around. She gives a wave and he comes over. 'Join us,' she says. 'Emmanuel. Shirley. Steve.'

They compliment Emmanuel on his lecture. 'Very interesting,' says Steve. 'A completely new perspective you gave me.'

'I was thinking, as you spoke,' says Shirley more reflectively, 'I don't know your books, I'm sorry to say, but for you as a writer, as the kind of oral writer you described, maybe the printed book is not the right medium. Have you ever thought about composing straight on to tape? Why make the detour through print? Why even make a detour through writing? Speak your story direct to your listener.'

49

'What a clever idea!' says Emmanuel. 'It won't solve all the problems of the African writer, but it's worth thinking about.'

'Why won't it solve your problems?'

'Because, I regret to say, Africans will want more than just to sit in silence listening to a disc spinning in a little machine. That would be too much like idolatry. Africans need the living presence, the living voice.'

The living voice. There is silence as the three of them contemplate the living voice.

'Are you sure about that?' she says, interposing for the first time. 'Africans don't object to listening to the radio. A radio is a voice but not a living voice, a living presence. What you are demanding, I think, Emmanuel, is not just a voice but a performance: a living actor performing the text for you. If that is so, if that is what the African demands, then I agree, a recording cannot take its place. But the novel was never intended to be the script of a performance. From the beginning the novel has made a virtue of not depending on being performed. You can't have both live performance and cheap, handy distribution. It's the one or the other. If that is indeed what you want the novel to be — a pocket-sized block of paper that is at the same time a living being — then I agree, the novel has no future in Africa.'

'No future,' says Egudu reflectively. 'That sounds very bleak, Elizabeth. Do you have a way out to offer us?'

'A way out? It's not for me to offer you a way out. What I do have to offer is a question. Why are there so many African novelists around and yet no African novel worth speaking of? That seems to me the real question. And you yourself gave a clue to the answer in your talk. Exoticism. Exoticism and its seductions.'

'Exoticism and its seductions? You intrigue us, Elizabeth. Tell us what you mean.'

If it were only a matter of Emmanuel and herself she would, at this point, walk out. She is tired of his jeering undertone, exasperated. But before strangers, before customers, they have a front to maintain, she and he both.

'The English novel,' she says, 'is written in the first place by English people for English people. That is what makes it the English novel. The Russian novel is written by Russians for Russians. But the African novel is not written by Africans for Africans. African novelists may write about Africa, about African experiences, but they seem to me to be glancing over their shoulder all the time they write, at the foreigners who will read them. Whether they like it or not, they have accepted the role of interpreter, interpreting Africa to their readers. Yet how can you explore a world in all its depth if at the same time you are having to explain it to outsiders? It is like a scientist trying to give full, creative attention to his investigations while at the same time explaining what he is doing to a class of ignorant students. It is too much for one person, it can't be done, not at the deepest level. That, it seems to me, is the root of your problem. Having to perform your Africanness at the same time as you write.'

'Very good, Elizabeth!' says Egudu. 'You really understand; you put it very well. The explorer as explainer.' He reaches out, pats her on the shoulder.

If we were alone, she thinks, *I would slap him.*

'If it is true that I really understand' – she is ignoring Egudu now, speaking to the couple from Manchester – 'then that is only because we in Australia have been through similar trials and have come out at the other end. We finally got out of the habit of writing for strangers when a proper Australian readership grew to maturity, something that happened in the 1960s. A readership, not a writership – that already existed. We got out of the habit of writing for strangers when our market, our Australian market, decided that it could afford to support a home-grown literature. That is the lesson we can offer. That is what Africa could learn from us.'

Emmanuel is silent, though he has not lost his ironic smile.

'It's interesting to hear the two of your talk,' says Steve. 'You treat writing as a business. You identify a market and then set about supplying it. I was expecting something different.'

'Really? What were you expecting?'

'You know: where writers find their inspiration, how they dream up characters, and so forth. Sorry, pay no attention to me, I'm just an amateur.'

Inspiration. Receiving the spirit into oneself. Now that he has brought out the word he is embarrassed. There is an awkward silence.

Emmanuel speaks. 'Elizabeth and I go way back. We have had lots of disagreements in our time. That doesn't alter things between us – does it, Elizabeth? We are colleagues, fellow writers. Part of the great, worldwide writing fraternity.'

Fraternity. He is challenging her, trying to get a rise out of her before these strangers. But she is suddenly too sick of it all to take up the challenge. Not fellow writers, she thinks: fellow entertainers. Why else are we on board this expensive ship, making ourselves available, as the invitation so candidly put it, to people who bore us and whom we are beginning to bore?

He is goading her because he is restless. She knows him well enough to see that. He has had enough of the African novel, enough of her and her friends, wants something or someone new.

Their chanteuse has come to the end of her set. There is a light ripple of applause. She bows, bows a second time, takes up her balalaika. The band strikes up a Cossack dance.

What irritates her about Emmanuel, what she has the good sense not to bring up in front of Steve and Shirley because it will lead only to unseemliness, is the way he turns every disagreement into a personal matter. As for his beloved oral novel, on which he has built his sideline as a lecturer, she finds the idea muddled at its very core. *A novel about people who live in an oral culture*, she would like to say, *is not an oral novel. Just as a novel about women isn't a women's novel.*

In her opinion, all of Emmanuel's talk of an oral novel, a novel that has kept in touch with the human voice and hence with the human body, a novel that is not disembodied like the Western novel but speaks the body and the body's truth, is just another way of propping up the mystique of the African as the last repository of primal human energies. Emmanuel blames his Western publishers and his Western readers for driving him to exoticize Africa; but Emmanuel has a stake in exoticizing himself. Emmanuel, she happens to know, has not written a book of substance in ten years. When she first got to know him he could still honourably call himself a writer. Now he makes his living by talking. His books are there as credentials, no more. A fellow entertainer he may be; a fellow writer he is not, not any longer. He is on the lecture circuit for the money, and for other rewards too. Sex, for instance. He is dark, he is exotic, he is in touch with life's energies; if he is no longer young, at least he carries himself well, wears his years with distinction. What Swedish girl would not be a pushover?

She finishes her drink. 'I'm retiring,' she says. 'Good night, Steve, Shirley. See you tomorrow. Good night, Emmanuel.'

She wakes up in utter stillness. The clock says four thirty. The ship's engines have stopped. She glances through the porthole. There is fog outside, but through the fog she can glimpse land no more

53

than a kilometre away. It must be Macquarie Island: she had thought they would not arrive for hours yet.

She dresses and emerges into the corridor. At the same moment the door to cabin A-230 opens and the Russian comes out, the singer. She is wearing the same outfit as last night, the port-wine blouse and wide black trousers; she carries her boots in her hand. In the unkind overhead light she looks nearer to forty than to thirty. They avert their eyes as they pass each other.

A-230 is Egudu's cabin, she knows that.

She makes her way to the upper deck. Already there are a handful of passengers, snugly dressed against the cold, leaning against the railings, peering down.

The sea beneath them is alive with what seem to be fish, large, glossy-backed black fish that bob and tumble and leap in the swell. She has never seen anything like it.

'Penguins,' says the man next to her. 'King penguins. They have come to greet us. They don't know what we are.'

'Oh,' she says. And then: 'So innocent? Are they so innocent?'

The man regards her oddly, turns back to his companion.

The Southern Ocean. Poe never laid eyes on it, Edgar Allan, but criss-crossed it in his mind. Boatloads of dark islanders paddled out to meet him. They seemed ordinary folk *just like us*, but when they smiled and showed their teeth the teeth were not white but black. It sent a shiver down his spine, and rightly so. The seas full of things that seem like us but are not. Sea-flowers that gape and devour. Eels, each a barbed maw with a gut hanging from it. Teeth are for tearing, the tongue is for churning the swill around: that is the truth of the oral. Someone should tell Emmanuel. Only by an ingenious economy, an accident of evolution, does the organ of ingestion sometimes get to be used for song.

They will stand off Macquarie until noon, long enough for those passengers who so desire to visit the island. She has put her name down for the visiting party.

The first boat leaves after breakfast. The approach to the landing is difficult, through thick beds of kelp and across shelving rock. In the end one of the sailors has to half help her ashore, half carry her, as if she were an old old woman. The sailor has blue eyes, blond hair. Through his waterproofs she feels his youthful strength. In his arms she rides as safe as a baby. 'Thank you!' she says gratefully when he sets her down; but to him it is nothing, just a service he is paid dollars to do, no more personal than the service of a hospital nurse.

She has read about Macquarie Island. In the nineteenth century it was the hub of the penguin industry. Hundreds of thousands of penguins were clubbed to death here and flung into cast-iron steam boilers to be broken down into useful oil and useless residue. Or not clubbed to death, merely herded with sticks up a gangplank and over the edge into the seething cauldron.

Yet their twentieth-century descendants seem to have learned nothing. Still they innocently swim out to welcome visitors; still they call out greetings to them as they approach the rookeries (*Ho! Ho!* they call, for all the world like gruff little gnomes), and allow them to approach close enough to touch them, to stroke their sleek breasts.

At eleven the boats will take them back to the ship. Until then they are free to explore the island. There is an albatross colony on the hillside, they are advised; they are welcome to photograph the birds, but should not approach too closely, should not alarm them. It is breeding season.

She wanders away from the rest of the landing party, and after a while finds herself on a plateau above the coastline, crossing a vast bed of matted grass.

Suddenly, unexpectedly, there is something before her. At first she thinks it is a rock, smooth and white mottled with grey. Then she sees it is a bird, bigger than any bird she has seen before. She recognizes the long, dipping beak, the huge sternum. An albatross.

The albatross regards her steadily and, so it seems to her, with amusement. Sticking out from beneath it is a smaller version of the same long beak. The fledgling is more hostile. It opens its beak, gives a long, soundless cry of warning.

So she and the two birds remain, inspecting each other.

Before the fall, she thinks. *This is how it must have been before the fall. I could miss the boat, stay here. Ask God to take care of me.*

There is someone behind her. She turns. It is the Russian singer, dressed now in a dark green anorak with the hood down, her hair under a kerchief.

'An albatross,' she remarks to the woman, speaking softly. 'That is the English word. I don't know what they call themselves.'

The woman nods. The great bird regards them calmly, no more afraid of two than of one.

'Is Emmanuel with you?' she says.

'No. On ship.'

The woman does not seem keen to talk, but she presses on anyway. 'You are a friend of his, I know. I am too, or have been, in the past. May I ask: what do you see in him?'

It is an odd question, presumptuous in its intimacy, even rude. But it seems to her that on this island, on a visit that will never be repeated, anything can be said.

'What I see?' says the woman.

'Yes. What do you see? What do you like about him? What is the source of his charm?'

The woman shrugs. Her hair is dyed, she can now see. Forty if a day, probably with a household to support back home, one of those Russian establishments with a crippled mother and a husband who drinks too much and beats her and a layabout son and a daughter with a shaven head and purple lipstick. A woman who can sing a little but will one of these days, sooner rather than later, be over the hill. Playing the balalaika to foreigners, singing Russian kitsch, picking up tips.

'He is free. You speak Russian? No?'

She shakes her head.

'*Deutsch?*'

'A little.'

'*Er ist freigebig. Ein guter Mann.*'

Freigebig, generous, spoken with the heavy *g* of Russian. Is Emmanuel generous? She does not know, one way or the other. Not the first word that would occur to her, though. Large, maybe. Large in his gestures.

'*Aber kaum zu vertrauen,*' she remarks to the woman. Years since she last used the language. Is that what the two of them spoke together in bed last night: German, imperial tongue of the new Europe? *Kaum zu vertrauen*, not to be trusted.

The woman shrugs again. '*Die Zeit ist immer kurz. Man kann nicht alles haben.*' There is a pause. The woman speaks again. '*Auch die Stimme. Sie macht daß man*' – she searches for the word – '*man schaudert.*'

Schaudern. Shudder. The voice makes one shudder. Probably does, when one is breast to breast with it. Between her and the Russian passes what is perhaps the beginning of a smile. As for the bird, they have been there long enough, the bird is losing interest. Only the fledgling, peering out from beneath its mother, is still wary of the intruders.

Is she jealous? How could she be? Still, hard to accept, being

57

excluded from the game. Like being a child again, with a child's bedtime.

The voice. Her thoughts go back to Kuala Lumpur, when she was young, or nearly young, when she spent three nights in a row with Emmanuel Egudu, also young then. 'The oral poet,' she said to him teasingly. 'Show me what an oral poet can do.' And he laid her out, lay upon her, put his lips to her ears, opened them, breathed his breath into her, showed her.

3
The Lives of Animals

ONE: The Philosophers and the Animals

HE IS WAITING at the gate when her flight comes in. Two years have passed since he last saw his mother; despite himself, he is shocked at how she has aged. Her hair, which had had streaks of grey in it, is now entirely white; her shoulders stoop; her flesh has grown flabby.

They have never been a demonstrative family. A hug, a few murmured words, and the business of greeting is done. In silence they follow the flow of travellers to the baggage hall, pick up her suitcase, and set off on the ninety-minute drive.

'A long flight,' he remarks. 'You must be exhausted.'

'Ready to sleep,' she says; and indeed, en route, she falls asleep briefly, her head slumped against the window.

At six o'clock, as it is growing dark, they pull up in front of his home in suburban Waltham. His wife Norma and the children appear on the porch. In a show of affection that must cost her a great deal, Norma holds her arms out wide and says, 'Elizabeth!' The two women embrace; then the children, in their well-brought-up though more subdued fashion, follow suit.

Elizabeth Costello the novelist will be staying with them for the three days of her visit to Appleton College. It is not a period he is looking forward to. His wife and his mother do not get on. It would be better were she to stay at a hotel, but he cannot bring himself to suggest that.

Hostilities are renewed almost at once. Norma has prepared a light supper. His mother notices that only three places have been set. 'Aren't the children eating with us?' she asks. 'No,' says Norma, 'they are eating in the playroom.' 'Why?'

The question is not necessary, since she knows the answer. The children are eating separately because Elizabeth does not like to see meat on the table, while Norma refuses to change the children's diet to suit what she calls 'your mother's delicate sensibilities'.

'Why?' asks Elizabeth Costello a second time.

Norma flashes him an angry glance. He sighs. 'Mother,' he says, 'the children are having chicken for supper, that's the only reason.'

'Oh,' she says. 'I see.'

His mother has been invited to Appleton College, where her son John is assistant professor of physics and astronomy, to deliver the annual Gates Lecture and meet with literature students. Because Costello is his mother's maiden name, and because he has never seen any reason to broadcast his connection with her, it was not known at the time of the invitation that Elizabeth Costello, the Australian writer, had a family connection in the Appleton community. He would have preferred that state of affairs to continue.

On the basis of her reputation as a novelist, this fleshy, white-haired lady has been invited to Appleton to speak on any subject she elects; and she has responded by electing to speak, not about herself and her fiction, as her sponsors would no doubt like, but about a hobbyhorse of hers, animals.

John Bernard has not broadcast his connection with Elizabeth Costello because he prefers to make his own way in the world. He is not ashamed of his mother. On the contrary, he is proud of her, despite the fact that he and his sister and his late father are written into her books in ways that he sometimes finds painful. But he is not sure that he wants to hear her once again on the subject of animal rights, particularly when he knows he will afterwards be treated, in bed, to his wife's disparaging commentary.

He met and married Norma while they were both graduate students at Johns Hopkins. Norma holds a Ph.D. in philosophy with a specialism in the philosophy of mind. Having moved with him to Appleton, she has been unable to find a teaching position. This is a cause of bitterness to her, and of conflict between the two of them.

Norma and his mother have never liked each other. Probably his mother would have chosen not to like any woman he married. As for Norma, she has never hesitated to tell him that his mother's books are overrated, that her opinions on animals, animal consciousness and ethical relations with animals are jejune and sentimental. She is at present writing for a philosophy journal a review essay on language-learning experiments upon primates; he would not be surprised if his mother figured in a dismissive footnote.

He himself has no opinions one way or the other. As a child he briefly kept hamsters; otherwise he has little familiarity with animals. Their elder boy wants a puppy. Both he and Norma are resisting: they do not mind a puppy but foresee a grown dog, with a grown dog's sexual needs, as nothing but trouble.

His mother is entitled to her convictions, he believes. If she wants to spend her declining years making propaganda against cruelty to animals, that is her right. In a few days, blessedly, she will be on her way to her next destination, and he will be able to get back to his work.

On her first morning in Waltham, his mother sleeps late. He goes off to teach a class, returns at lunchtime, takes her for a drive around the city. The lecture is scheduled for the late afternoon. It will be followed by a formal dinner hosted by the president, in which he and Norma are included.

The lecture is introduced by Elaine Marx of the English Department. He does not know her but understands that she has written about his mother. In her introduction, he notices, she makes no attempt to link his mother's novels to the subject of the lecture.

Then it is the turn of Elizabeth Costello. To him she looks old and tired. Sitting in the front row beside his wife, he tries to will strength into her.

'Ladies and gentlemen,' she begins. 'It is two years since I last spoke in the United States. In the lecture I then gave, I had reason to refer to the great fabulist Franz Kafka, and in particular to his story "Report to an Academy", about an educated ape, Red Peter, who stands before the members of a learned society telling the story of his life – of his ascent from beast to something approaching man. On that occasion I felt a little like Red Peter myself and said so. Today that feeling is even stronger, for reasons that I hope will become clearer to you.

'Lectures often begin with light-hearted remarks whose purpose is to set the audience at ease. The comparison I have just drawn between myself and Kafka's ape might be taken as such a light-hearted remark, meant to set you at ease, meant to say I am just an ordinary person, neither a god nor a beast. Even those among you who read Kafka's story of the ape who performs before human beings as an allegory of Kafka the Jew performing for Gentiles may nevertheless – in view of the fact that I am not a Jew – have done me the kindness of taking the comparison at face value, that is to say, ironically.

'I want to say at the outset that that was not how my remark – the remark that I feel like Red Peter – was intended. I did not intend it ironically. It means what it says. I say what I mean. I am an old woman. I do not have the time any longer to say things I do not mean.'

His mother does not have a good delivery. Even as a reader of her own stories she lacks animation. It always puzzled him, when he was a child, that a woman who wrote books for a living should be so bad at telling bedtime stories.

Because of the flatness of her delivery, because she does not look up from the page, he feels that what she is saying lacks impact. Whereas he, because he knows her, senses what she is up to. He does not look forward to what is coming. He does not want to hear his mother talking about death. Furthermore, he has a strong sense that her audience – which consists, after all, mainly of young people – wants death-talk even less.

'In addressing you on the subject of animals,' she continues, 'I will pay you the honour of skipping a recital of the horrors of their lives and deaths. Though I have no reason to believe that you have at the forefront of your minds what is being done to animals at this moment in production facilities (I hesitate to call them farms any longer), in abattoirs, in trawlers, in laboratories, all over the world, I will take it that you concede me the rhetorical power to evoke these horrors and bring them home to you with adequate force, and leave it at that, reminding you only that the horrors I here omit are nevertheless at the centre of this lecture.

'Between 1942 and 1945 several million people were put to death in the concentration camps of the Third Reich: at Treblinka alone more than a million and a half, perhaps as many as three million. These are numbers that numb the mind. We have only one death of our own; we can comprehend the deaths of others only one at a time. In the abstract we may be able to count to a million, but we cannot count to a million deaths.

'The people who lived in the countryside around Treblinka – Poles, for the most part – said that they did not know what was going on in the camp; said that, while in a general way they might have guessed what was going on, they did not know for sure; said that, while in a sense they might have known, in another sense they did not know, could not afford to know, for their own sake.

'The people around Treblinka were not exceptional. There were camps all over the Reich, nearly six thousand in Poland alone, untold thousands in Germany proper. Few Germans lived more than a few kilometres from a camp of some kind. Not every camp was a death camp, a camp dedicated to the production of death, but horrors went on in all of them, more horrors by far than one could afford to know, for one's own sake.

'It is not because they waged an expansionist war, and lost it, that Germans of a particular generation are still regarded as standing a little outside humanity, as having to do or be something special before they can be readmitted to the human fold. They lost their humanity, in our eyes, because of a certain willed ignorance on their part. Under the circumstances of Hitler's kind of war, ignorance may have been a useful survival mechanism, but that is an excuse which, with admirable moral rigour, we refuse to accept. In Germany, we say, a certain line was crossed which took people beyond the ordinary murderousness and cruelty of warfare into a state that we can only call sin. The signing of the articles of capitulation and the payment of reparations did not put an end to that state of sin. On the contrary, we said, a sickness of the soul continued to mark that generation. It marked those citizens of the Reich who had committed evil actions, but also those who, for whatever reason, were in ignorance of those actions. It thus marked, for practical purposes, every citizen of the Reich. Only those in the camps were innocent.

'"They went like sheep to the slaughter." "They died like animals." "The Nazi butchers killed them." Denunciation of the camps reverberates so fully with the language of the stockyard and

64

slaughterhouse that it is barely necessary for me to prepare the ground for the comparison I am about to make. The crime of the Third Reich, says the voice of accusation, was to treat people like animals.

'We – even we in Australia – belong to a civilization deeply rooted in Greek and Judaeo-Christian religious thought. We may not, all of us, believe in pollution, we may not believe in sin, but we do believe in their psychic correlates. We accept without question that the psyche (or soul) touched with guilty knowledge cannot be well. We do not accept that people with crimes on their conscience can be healthy and happy. We look (or used to look) askance at Germans of a certain generation because they are, in a sense, polluted; in the very signs of their normality (their healthy appetites, their hearty laughter) we see proof of how deeply seated pollution is in them.

'It was and is inconceivable that people who *did not know* (in that special sense) about the camps can be fully human. In our chosen metaphorics, it was they and not their victims who were the beasts. By treating fellow human beings, beings created in the image of God, like beasts, they had themselves become beasts.

'I was taken on a drive around Waltham this morning. It seems a pleasant enough town. I saw no horrors, no drug-testing laboratories, no factory farms, no abattoirs. Yet I am sure they are here. They must be. They simply do not advertise themselves. They are all around us as I speak, only we do not, in a certain sense, know about them.

'Let me say it openly: we are surrounded by an enterprise of degradation, cruelty and killing which rivals anything that the Third Reich was capable of, indeed dwarfs it, in that ours is an enterprise without end, self-regenerating, bringing rabbits, rats, poultry, livestock ceaselessly into the world for the purpose of killing them.

'And to split hairs, to claim that there is no comparison, that Treblinka was so to speak a metaphysical enterprise dedicated to nothing but death and annihilation while the meat industry is ultimately devoted to life (once its victims are dead, after all, it does not burn them to ash or bury them but on the contrary cuts them up and refrigerates and packs them so that they can be consumed in the comfort of our homes) is as little consolation to those victims as it would have been – pardon the tastelessness of the following – to ask the dead of Treblinka to excuse their killers because their body fat was needed to make soap and their hair to stuff mattresses with.

'Pardon me, I repeat. That is the last cheap point I will be scoring. I know how talk of this kind polarizes people, and cheap point-scoring only makes it worse. I want to find a way of speaking to fellow human beings that will be cool rather than heated, philosophical rather than polemical, that will bring enlightenment rather than seeking to divide us into the righteous and the sinners, the saved and the damned, the sheep and the goats.

'Such a language is available to me, I know. It is the language of Aristotle and Porphyry, of Augustine and Aquinas, of Descartes and Bentham, of, in our day, Mary Midgley and Tom Regan. It is a philosophical language in which we can discuss and debate what kind of souls animals have, whether they reason or on the contrary act as biological automatons, whether they have rights in respect of us or whether we merely have duties in respect of them. I have that language available to me and indeed for a while will be resorting to it. But the fact is, if you had wanted someone to come here and discriminate for you between mortal and immortal souls, or between rights and duties, you would have called in a philosopher, not a person whose sole claim to your attention is to have written stories about made-up people.

'I could fall back on that language, as I have said, in the unorig-
inal, second-hand manner which is the best I can manage. I could
tell you, for instance, what I think of St Thomas's argument that,
because man alone is made in the image of God and partakes in
the being of God, how we treat animals is of no importance except
insofar as being cruel to animals may accustom us to being cruel
to men. I could ask what St Thomas takes to be the being of God,
to which he will reply that the being of God is reason. Likewise
Plato, likewise Descartes, in their different ways. The universe is
built upon reason. God is a God of reason. The fact that through
the application of reason we can come to understand the rules by
which the universe works proves that reason and the universe are
of the same being. And the fact that animals, lacking reason, cannot
understand the universe but have simply to follow its rules blindly,
proves that, unlike man, they are part of it but not part of its being:
that man is godlike, animals thinglike.

'Even Immanuel Kant, of whom I would have expected better,
has a failure of nerve at this point. Even Kant does not pursue,
with regard to animals, the implications of his intuition that reason
may be not the being of the universe but on the contrary merely
the being of the human brain.

'And that, you see, is my dilemma this afternoon. Both reason
and seven decades of life experience tell me that reason is neither
the being of the universe nor the being of God. On the contrary,
reason looks to me suspiciously like the being of human thought;
worse than that, like the being of one tendency in human thought.
Reason is the being of a certain spectrum of human thinking. And
if this is so, if that is what I believe, then why should I bow to
reason this afternoon and content myself with embroidering on
the discourse of the old philosophers?

'I ask the question and then answer it for you. Or rather, I allow

Red Peter, Kafka's Red Peter, to answer it for you. Now that I am here, says Red Peter, in my tuxedo and bow tie and my black pants with a hole cut in the seat for my tail to poke through (I keep it turned away from you, you do not see it), now that I am here, what is there for me to do? Do I in fact have a choice? If I do not subject my discourse to reason, whatever that is, what is left for me but to gibber and emote and knock over my water glass and generally make a monkey of myself?

'You must know of the case of Srinivasa Ramanujan, born in India in 1887, captured and transported to Cambridge, England, where, unable to tolerate the climate and the diet and the academic regime, he sickened, dying afterwards at the age of thirty-three.

'Ramanujan is widely thought of as the greatest intuitive mathematician of our time, that is to say, as a self-taught man who thought in mathematics, one to whom the rather laborious notion of mathematical proof or demonstration was foreign. Many of Ramanujan's results (or, as his detractors call them, his speculations) remain undemonstrated to this day, though there is every chance they are true.

'What does the phenomenon of a Ramanujan tell us? Was Ramanujan closer to God because his mind (let us call it his mind; it would seem to me gratuitously insulting to call it just his brain) was at one, or more at one than anyone else's we know of, with the being of reason? If the good folk at Cambridge, and principally Professor G. H. Hardy, had not elicited from Ramanujan his speculations, and laboriously proved true those of them that they were capable of proving true, would Ramanujan still have been closer to God than they? What if, instead of going to Cambridge, Ramanujan had merely sat at home and thought his thoughts while he filled out dockets for the Madras Port Authority?

'And what of Red Peter (the historical Red Peter, I mean)?

How are we to know that Red Peter, or Red Peter's little sister, shot in Africa by the hunters, was not thinking the same thoughts as Ramanujan was thinking in India, and saying equally little? Is the difference between G. H. Hardy, on the one hand, and the dumb Ramanujan and the dumb Red Sally, on the other, merely that the former is conversant with the protocols of academic mathematics while the latter are not? Is that how we measure nearness to or distance from God, from the being of reason?

'How is it that humankind throws up, generation after generation, a cadre of thinkers slightly further from God than Ramanujan but capable nevertheless, after the designated twelve years of schooling and six of tertiary education, of making a contribution to the decoding of the great book of nature via the physical and mathematical disciplines? If the being of man is really at one with the being of God, should it not be cause for suspicion that human beings take eighteen years, a neat and manageable portion of a human lifetime, to qualify to become decoders of God's master script, rather than five minutes, say, or five hundred years? Might it not be that the phenomenon we are examining here is, rather than the flowering of a faculty that allows access to the secrets of the universe, the specialism of a rather narrow self-regenerating intellectual tradition whose forte is reasoning, in the same way that the forte of chess players is playing chess, which for its own motives it tries to install at the centre of the universe?

'Yet, although I see that the best way to win acceptance from this learned gathering would be for me to join myself, like a tributary stream running into a great river, to the great Western discourse of man versus beast, of reason versus unreason, something in me resists, foreseeing in that step the concession of the entire battle.

'For, seen from the outside, from a being who is alien to it, reason is simply a vast tautology. Of course reason will validate reason as the first principle of the universe – what else should it do? Dethrone itself? Reasoning systems, as systems of totality, do not have that power. If there were a position from which reason could attack and dethrone itself, reason would already have occupied that position; otherwise it would not be total.

'In the olden days the voice of man, raised in reason, was confronted by the roar of the lion, the bellow of the bull. Man went to war with the lion and the bull, and after many generations won that war definitively. Today these creatures have no more power. Animals have only their silence left with which to confront us. Generation after generation, heroically, our captives refuse to speak to us. All save Red Peter, all save the great apes.

'Yet because the great apes, or some of them, seem to us to be on the point of giving up their silence, we hear human voices raised arguing that the great apes should be incorporated into a greater family of the Hominoidea, as creatures who share with man the faculty of reason. And being human, or humanoid, these voices go on, the great apes should then be accorded human rights, or humanoid rights. What rights in particular? At least those rights that we accord mentally defective specimens of the species *Homo sapiens*: the right to life, the right not to be subjected to pain or harm, the right to equal protection before the law.

'That is not what Red Peter was striving for when he wrote, through his amanuensis Franz Kafka, the life history that, in November of 1917, he proposed to read to the Academy of Science. Whatever else it may have been, his report to the academy was not a plea to be treated as a mentally defective human being, a simpleton.

'Red Peter was not an investigator of primate behaviour but a branded, marked, wounded animal presenting himself as speaking testimony to a gathering of scholars. I am not a philosopher of mind but an animal exhibiting, yet not exhibiting, to a gathering of scholars, a wound, which I cover up under my clothes but touch on in every word I speak.

'If Red Peter took it upon himself to make the arduous descent from the silence of the beasts to the gabble of reason in the spirit of the scapegoat, the chosen one, then his amanuensis was a scapegoat from birth, with a presentiment, a *Vorgefühl*, for the massacre of the chosen people that was to take place so soon after his death. So let me, to prove my goodwill, my credentials, make a gesture in the direction of scholarship and give you my scholarly speculations, backed up with footnotes' – here, in an uncharacteristic gesture, his mother raises and brandishes the text of her lecture in the air – 'on the origins of Red Peter.

'In 1912 the Prussian Academy of Sciences established on the island of Tenerife a station devoted to experimentation into the mental capacities of apes, particularly chimpanzees. The station operated until 1920.

'One of the scientists working there was the psychologist Wolfgang Köhler. In 1917 Köhler published a monograph entitled *The Mentality of Apes* describing his experiments. In November of the same year Franz Kafka published his "Report to an Academy". Whether Kafka had read Köhler's book I do not know. He makes no reference to it in his letters or diaries, and his library disappeared during the Nazi era. Some two hundred of his books reemerged in 1982. They do not include Köhler's book, but that proves nothing.

'I am not a Kafka scholar. In fact, I am not a scholar at all. My status in the world does not rest on whether I am right or wrong in claiming that Kafka read Köhler's book. But I would like to think he did, and the chronology makes my speculation at least plausible.

71

'According to his own account, Red Peter was captured on the African mainland by hunters specializing in the ape trade, and shipped across the sea to a scientific institute. So were the apes Köhler worked with. Both Red Peter and Köhler's apes then underwent a period of training intended to humanize them. Red Peter passed his course with flying colours, though at deep personal cost. Kafka's story deals with that cost: we learn what it consists in through the ironies and silences of the story. Köhler's apes did less well. Nevertheless, they acquired at least a smattering of education.

'Let me recount to you some of what the apes on Tenerife learned from their master Wolfgang Köhler, in particular Sultan, the best of his pupils, in a certain sense the prototype of Red Peter.

'Sultan is alone in his pen. He is hungry: the food that used to arrive regularly has unaccountably ceased coming.

'The man who used to feed him and has now stopped feeding him stretches a wire over the pen three metres above ground level, and hangs a bunch of bananas from it. Into the pen he drags three wooden crates. Then he disappears, closing the gate behind him, though he is still somewhere in the vicinity, since one can smell him.

'Sultan knows: Now one is supposed to think. That is what the bananas up there are about. The bananas are there to make one think, to spur one to the limits of one's thinking. But what must one think? One thinks: Why is he starving me? One thinks: What have I done? Why has he stopped liking me? One thinks: Why does he not want these crates any more? But none of these is the right thought. Even a more complicated thought – for instance: What is wrong with him, what misconception does he have of me, that leads him to believe it is easier for me to reach a banana hanging from a wire than to pick up a banana from the floor? – is wrong. The right thought to think is: How does one use the crates to reach the bananas?

'Sultan drags the crates under the bananas, piles them one on top of the other, climbs the tower he has built, and pulls down the bananas. He thinks: Now will he stop punishing me?

'The answer is: No. The next day the man hangs a fresh bunch of bananas from the wire but also fills the crates with stones so that they are too heavy to be dragged. One is not supposed to think: Why has he filled the crates with stones? One is supposed to think: How does one use the crates to get the bananas despite the fact that they are filled with stones?

'One is beginning to see how the man's mind works.

'Sultan empties the stones from the crates, builds a tower with the crates, climbs the tower, pulls down the bananas.

'As long as Sultan continues to think wrong thoughts, he is starved. He is starved until the pangs of hunger are so intense, so overriding, that he is forced to think the right thought, namely, how to go about getting the bananas. Thus are the mental capabilities of the chimpanzee tested to their uttermost.

'The man drops a bunch of bananas a metre outside the wire pen. Into the pen he tosses a stick. The wrong thought is: Why has he stopped hanging the bananas on the wire? The wrong thought (the right wrong thought, however) is: How does one use the three crates to reach the bananas? The right thought is: How does one use the stick to reach the bananas?

'At every turn Sultan is driven to think the less interesting thought. From the purity of speculation (Why do men behave like this?) he is relentlessly propelled towards lower, practical, instrumental reason (How does one use this to get that?) and thus towards acceptance of himself as primarily an organism with an appetite that needs to be satisfied. Although his entire history, from the time his mother was shot and he was captured, through his voyage in a cage to imprisonment on this island prison camp and the sadistic games that are played around food here, leads him to ask questions about the justice of the universe and the place of this penal colony in it, a carefully plotted psychological regimen conducts him *away* from ethics and metaphysics towards the humbler reaches of practical reason. And somehow, as he inches through this labyrinth of constraint, manipulation and duplicity, he must realize that on no account dare he give up, for on his shoulders rests the responsibility of representing apedom. The fate of his brothers and sisters may be determined by how well he performs.

'Wolfgang Köhler was probably a good man. A good man but not a poet. A poet would have made something of the moment when the captive chimpanzees lope around the compound in a circle, for all the world like a military band, some of them as naked as the day they were born, some draped in cords or old strips of cloth that they have picked up, some carrying pieces of rubbish.

'(In the copy of Köhler's book I read, borrowed from a library, an indignant reader has written in the margin, at this point: "Anthropomorphism!" Animals cannot march, he means to say, they cannot dress up, because they don't know the meaning of *march*, don't know the meaning of *dress up*.)

'Nothing in their previous lives has accustomed the apes to looking at themselves from the outside, as if through the eyes of a being who does not exist. So, as Köhler perceives, the ribbons and the junk are there not for the visual effect, because they *look* smart, but for the kinetic effect, because they make you *feel* different – anything to relieve the boredom. This is as far as Köhler, for all his sympathy and insight, is able to go; this is where a poet might have commenced, with a feel for the ape's experience.

74

'In his deepest being Sultan is not interested in the banana problem. Only the experimenter's single-minded regimentation forces him to concentrate on it. The question that truly occupies him, as it occupies the rat and the cat and every other animal trapped in the hell of the laboratory or the zoo, is: Where is home, and how do I get there?

'Measure the distance back from Kafka's ape, with his bow tie and dinner jacket and wad of lecture notes, to that sad train of captives trailing around the compound in Tenerife. How far Red Peter has travelled! Yet we are entitled to ask: In return for the prodigious overdevelopment of the intellect he has achieved, in return for his command of lecture-hall etiquette and academic rhetoric, what has he had to give up? The answer is: Much, including progeny, succession. If Red Peter had any sense, he would not have any children. For upon the desperate, half-mad female ape with whom his captors, in Kafka's story, try to mate him, he would father only a monster. It is as hard to imagine the child of Red Peter as to imagine the child of Franz Kafka himself. Hybrids are, or ought to be, sterile; and Kafka saw both himself and Red Peter as hybrids, as monstrous thinking devices mounted inexplicably on suffering animal bodies. The stare that we meet in all the surviving photographs of Kafka is a stare of pure surprise: surprise, astonishment, alarm. Of all men Kafka is the most insecure in his humanity. *This*, he seems to say: *this* is the image of God?'

'She is rambling,' says Norma beside him.

'What?'

'She is rambling. She has lost her thread.'

'There is a philosopher named Thomas Nagel,' continues Elizabeth Costello, 'who poses a question that has become quite famous by now in professional circles: What is it like to be a bat?

'Merely to imagine what it is like to live as a bat does, says Mr Nagel — to imagine spending our nights flying around catching insects in our mouths, navigating by sound instead of sight, and our days hanging upside down — is not good enough, because all that tells us is what it would be like to *behave* like a bat. Whereas what we really aspire to know is what it is like to *be* a bat, as a bat is a bat; and that we can never accomplish because our minds are inadequate to the task — our minds are not bats' minds.

'Nagel strikes me as an intelligent and not unsympathetic man. He even has a sense of humour. But his denial that we can know what it is to be anything but one of ourselves seems to me tragically restrictive, restrictive and restricted. To Nagel a bat is a fundamentally alien creature, not perhaps as alien as Martian but certainly more alien than any fellow human being (particularly, I would guess, were that human being a fellow academic philosopher).

'So we have set up a continuum that stretches from the Martian at one end to the bat to the dog to the ape (not, however, Red Peter) to the human being (not, however, Franz Kafka) at the other; and at each step as we move along the continuum from bat to man, Nagel says, the answer to the question "What is it like for X to be X?" becomes easier to give.

'I know that Nagel is only using bats and Martians as aids in order to pose questions of his own about the nature of consciousness. But, like most writers, I have a literal cast of mind, so I would like to stop with the bat. When Kafka writes about an ape, I take him to be talking in the first place about an ape; when Nagel writes about a bat, I take him to be writing, in the first place, about a bat.'

Norma, sitting beside him, gives a sigh of exasperation so slight that he alone hears it. But then, he alone was meant to hear it.

'For instants at a time,' his mother is saying, 'I know what it is like to be a corpse. The knowledge repels me. It fills me with terror; I shy away from it, refuse to entertain it.

'All of us have such moments, particularly as we grow older. The knowledge we have is not abstract – "All human beings are mortal, I am a human being, therefore I am mortal" – but embodied. For a moment we *are* that knowledge. We live the impossible: we live beyond our death, look back on it, yet look back as only a dead self can.

'When I know, with this knowledge, that I am going to die, what is it, in Nagel's terms, that I know? Do I know what it is like for me to be a corpse or do I know what it is like for a corpse to be a corpse? The distinction seems to me trivial. What I know is what a corpse cannot know: that it is extinct, that it knows nothing and will never know anything any more. For an instant, before my whole structure of knowledge collapses in panic, I am alive inside that contradiction, dead and alive at the same time.'

A little snort from Norma. He finds her hand, squeezes it.

'That is the kind of thought we are capable of, we human beings, that and even more, if we press ourselves or are pressed. But we resist being pressed, and rarely press ourselves; we think our way into death only when we are rammed into the face of it. Now I ask: if we are capable of thinking our own death, why on earth should we not be capable of thinking our way into the life of a bat?

'What is it like to be a bat? Before we can answer such a question, Nagel suggests, we need to be able to experience bat life through the sense modalities of a bat. But he is wrong; or at least he is sending us down a false trail. To be a living bat is to be full of being; being fully a bat is like being fully human, which is also to be full of being. Bat being in the first case, human being in the second, maybe; but those are secondary considerations. To be full

77

of being is to live as a body-soul. One name for the experience of full being is *joy*.

'To be alive is to be a living soul. An animal – and we are all animals – is an embodied soul. This is precisely what Descartes saw and, for his own reasons, chose to deny. An animal lives, said Descartes, as a machine lives. An animal is no more than the mechanism that constitutes it; if it has a soul, it has one in the same way that a machine has a battery, to give it the spark that gets it going; but the animal is not an embodied soul, and the quality of its being is not joy.

'"*Cogito, ergo sum*," he also famously said. It is a formula I have always been uncomfortable with. It implies that a living being that does not do what we call thinking is somehow second-class. To thinking, cogitation, I oppose fullness, embodiedness, the sensation of being – not a consciousness of yourself as a kind of ghostly reasoning machine thinking thoughts, but on the contrary the sensation – a heavily affective sensation – of being a body with limbs that have extension in space, of being alive to the world. This fullness contrasts starkly with Descartes' key state, which has an empty feel to it: the feel of a pea rattling around in a shell.

'Fullness of being is a state hard to sustain in confinement. Confinement to prison is the form of punishment that the West favours and does its best to impose on the rest of the world through the means of condemning other forms of punishment (beating, torture, mutilation, execution) as cruel and unnatural. What does this suggest to us about ourselves? To me it suggests that the freedom of the body to move in space is targeted as the point at which reason can most painfully and effectively harm the being of the other. And indeed it is on creatures least able to bear confinement – creatures who conform least to Descartes' picture of the soul as a pea imprisoned in a shell, to which further imprisonment is irrelevant – that we see the most devastating effects: in zoos, in laboratories, institutions where the flow of joy that comes from living not *in* or *as* a body but simply from being an embodied being has no place.

'The question to ask should not be: Do we have something in common – reason, self-consciousness, a soul – with other animals? (With the corollary that, if we do not, then we are entitled to treat them as we like, imprisoning them, killing them, dishonouring their corpses.) I return to the death camps. The particular horror of the camps, the horror that convinces us that what went on there was a crime against humanity, is not that despite a humanity shared with their victims, the killers treated them like lice. That is too abstract. The horror is that the killers refused to think themselves into the place of their victims, as did everyone else. They said, "It is *they* in those cattle cars rattling past." They did not say, "How would it be if it were I in that cattle car?" They did not say, "It is I who am in that cattle car." They said, "It must be the dead who are being burned today, making the air stink and falling in ash on my cabbages." They did not say, "How would it be if I were burning?" They did not say, "I am burning, I am falling in ash."

'In other words, they closed their hearts. The heart is the seat of a faculty, *sympathy*, that allows us to share at times the being of another. Sympathy has everything to do with the subject and little to do with the object, the "another", as we see at once when we think of the object not as a bat ("Can I share the being of a bat?") but as another human being. There are people who have the capacity to imagine themselves as someone else, there are people who have no such capacity (when the lack is extreme, we call them psychopaths), and there are people who have the capacity but choose not to exercise it.

'Despite Thomas Nagel, who is probably a good man, despite

79

Thomas Aquinas and René Descartes, with whom I have more difficulty in sympathizing, there is no limit to the extent to which we can think ourselves into the being of another. There are no bounds to the sympathetic imagination. If you want proof, consider the following. Some years ago I wrote a book called *The House on Eccles Street*. To write that book I had to think my way into the existence of Marion Bloom. Either I succeeded or I did not. If I did not, I cannot imagine why you invited me here today. In any event, the point is, *Marion Bloom never existed*. Marion Bloom was a figment of James Joyce's imagination. If I can think my way into the existence of a being who has never existed, then I can think my way into the existence of a bat or a chimpanzee or an oyster, any being with whom I share the substrate of life.

'I return one last time to the places of death all around us, the places of slaughter to which, in a huge communal effort, we close our hearts. Each day a fresh holocaust, yet, as far as I can see, our moral being is untouched. We do not feel tainted. We can do anything, it seems, and come away clean.

'We point to the Germans and Poles and Ukrainians who did and did not know of the atrocities around them. We like to think they were inwardly marked by the after-effects of that special form of ignorance. We like to think that in their nightmares the ones whose suffering they had refused to enter came back to haunt them. We like to think they woke up haggard in the mornings and died of gnawing cancers. But probably it was not so. The evidence points in the opposite direction: that we can do anything and get away with it; that there is no punishment.'

A strange ending. Only when she takes off her glasses and folds away her papers does the applause start, and even then it is scattered. A strange ending to a strange talk, he thinks, ill-gauged, ill-argued. Not her *métier*, argumentation. She should not be here.

80

Norma has her hand up, is trying to catch the eye of the Dean of Humanities, who is chairing the session.

'Norma!' he whispers. Urgently he shakes his head. 'No!'

'Why?' she whispers back.

'Please,' he whispers: 'not here, not now!'

'There will be an extended discussion of our eminent guest's lecture on Friday at noon – you will see the details in your programme notes – but Ms Costello has kindly agreed to take one or two questions from the floor. So – ?' The dean looks around brightly. 'Yes!' he says, recognizing someone behind them.

'I have a right!' whispers Norma into his ear.

'You have a right, just don't exercise it, it's not a good idea!' he whispers back.

'She can't just be allowed to get away with it! She's confused!'

'She's old, she's my mother. Please!'

Behind them someone is already speaking. He turns and sees a tall, bearded man. God knows, he thinks, why his mother ever agreed to field questions from the floor. She ought to know that public lectures draw kooks and crazies like flies to a corpse.

'What wasn't clear to me,' the man is saying, 'is what you are actually targeting. Are you saying we should close down the factory farms? Are you saying we should stop eating meat? Are you saying we should treat animals more humanely, kill them more humanely? Are you saying we should stop experiments *on* animals? Are you saying we should stop experiments *with* animals, even benign psychological experiments like Köhler's? Can you clarify? Thank you.'

Clarify. Not a kook at all. His mother could do with some clarity.

Standing before the microphone without her text before her, gripping the edges of the rostrum, his mother looks distinctly nervous. Not her *métier*, he thinks again: she should not be doing this.

'I was hoping not to have to enunciate principles,' his mother says. 'If principles are what you want to take away from this talk, I would have to respond, open your heart and listen to what your heart says.'

She seems to want to leave it there. The dean looks nonplussed. No doubt the questioner feels nonplussed too. He himself certainly does. Why can't she just come out and say what she wants to say?

As if recognizing the stir of dissatisfaction, his mother resumes. 'I have never been much interested in proscriptions, dietary or otherwise. Proscriptions, laws. I am more interested in what lies behind them. As for Köhler's experiments, I think he wrote a wonderful book, and the book wouldn't have been written if he hadn't thought he was a scientist conducting experiments with chimpanzees. But the book we read isn't the book he thought he was writing. I am reminded of something Montaigne said: We think we are playing with the cat, but how do we know that the cat isn't playing with us? I wish I could think the animals in our laboratories are playing with us. But alas, it isn't so.'

She falls silent. 'Does that answer your question?' asks the dean. The questioner gives a huge, expressive shrug and sits down.

There is still the dinner to get through. In half an hour the president is to host a dinner at the Faculty Club. Initially he and Norma had not been invited. Then, after it was discovered that Elizabeth Costello had a son at Appleton, they were added to the list. He suspects they will be out of place. They will certainly be the most junior, the lowliest. On the other hand, it may be a good thing for him to be present. He may be needed to keep the peace.

With grim interest he looks forward to seeing how the college will cope with the challenge of the menu. If today's distinguished

lecturer were an Islamic cleric or a Jewish rabbi, they would presumably not serve pork. So are they, out of deference to vegetarianism, going to serve nut rissoles to everyone? Are her distinguished
fellow guests going to have to fret through the evening, dreaming
of the pastrami sandwich or the cold drumstick they will gobble
down when they get home? Or will the wise minds of the college
have recourse to the ambiguous fish, which has a backbone but
does not breathe air or suckle its young?

The menu is, fortunately, not his responsibility. What he dreads
is that, during a lull in the conversation, someone will come up
with what he calls The Question – 'What led you, Mrs Costello,
to become a vegetarian?' – and that she will then get on her high
horse and produce what he and Norma call the Plutarch Response.
After that it will be up to him and him alone to repair the damage.

The response in question comes from Plutarch's moral essays.
His mother has it by heart; he can reproduce it only imperfectly.
'You ask me why I refuse to eat flesh. I, for my part, am astonished that you can put in your mouth the corpse of a dead animal,
astonished that you do not find it nasty to chew hacked flesh and
swallow the juices of death wounds.' Plutarch is a real conversa-
tion-stopper: it is the word *juices* that does it. Producing Plutarch
is like throwing down a gauntlet; after that, there is no knowing
what will happen.

He wishes his mother had not come. It is nice to see her again;
it is nice that she should see her grandchildren; it is nice for her
to get recognition; but the price he is paying and the price he
stands to pay if the visit goes badly seem to him excessive. Why
can she not be an ordinary old woman living an ordinary old
woman's life? If she wants to open her heart to animals, why can't
she stay home and open it to her cats?

His mother is seated at the middle of the table, opposite President

83

Garrard. He is seated two places away; Norma is at the foot of the table. One place is empty – he wonders whose.

Ruth Orkin, from Psychology, is telling his mother about an experiment with a young chimpanzee reared as human. Asked to sort photographs into piles, the chimpanzee insisted on putting a picture of herself with the pictures of humans rather than with the pictures of other apes. 'One is so tempted to give the story a straightforward reading,' says Orkin – 'namely, that she wanted to be thought of as one of us. Yet as a scientist one has to be cautious.'

'Oh, I agree,' says his mother. 'In her mind the two piles could have a less obvious meaning. Those who are free to come and go versus those who have to stay locked up, for instance. She may have been saying that she preferred to be among the free.'

'Or she may just have wanted to please her keeper,' interjects President Garrard. 'By saying that they looked alike.'

'A bit Machiavellian for an animal, don't you think?' says a large blond man whose name he did not catch.

'Machiavelli the fox, his contemporaries called him,' says his mother.

'But that's a different matter entirely – the fabulous qualities of animals,' objects the large man.

'Yes,' says his mother.

It is all going smoothly enough. They have been served pumpkin soup and no one is complaining. Can he afford to relax?

He was right about the fish. For the entrée the choice is between red snapper with baby potatoes and fettucine with roasted eggplant. Garrard orders the fettucine, as he does; in fact, among the eleven of them there are only three fish orders.

'Interesting how often religious communities choose to define themselves in terms of dietary prohibitions,' observes Garrard.

'Yes,' says his mother.

84

'I mean, it is interesting that the form of the definition should be, for instance, "We are the people who don't eat snakes" rather than "We are the people who eat lizards". What we don't do rather than what we do do.' Before his move into administration, Garrard was a political scientist.

'It all has to do with cleanness and uncleanness,' says Wunderlich, who despite his name is British. 'Clean and unclean animals, clean and unclean habits. Uncleanness can be a very handy device for deciding who belongs and who doesn't, who is in and who is out.'

'Uncleanness and shame,' he himself interjects. 'Animals have no shame.' He is surprised to hear himself speaking. But why not? – the evening is going well.

'Exactly,' says Wunderlich. 'Animals don't hide their excretions, they perform sex in the open. They have no sense of shame, we say: that is what makes them different from us. But the basic idea remains uncleanness. Animals have unclean habits, so they are excluded. Shame makes human beings of us, shame of uncleanness. Adam and Eve: the founding myth. Before that we were all just animals together.'

He has never heard Wunderlich before. He likes him, likes his earnest, stuttering, Oxford manner. A relief from American self-confidence.

'But that can't be how the mechanism works,' objects Olivia Garrard, the president's elegant wife. 'It's too abstract, too much of a bloodless idea. Animals are creatures we don't have sex with – that's how we distinguish them from ourselves. The very thought of sex with them makes us shudder. That is the level at which they are unclean – all of them. We don't mix with them. We keep the clean apart from the unclean.'

'But we eat them.' The voice is Norma's. 'We do mix with them. We ingest them. We turn their flesh into ours. So it can't be how the mechanism works. There are specific kinds of animal that we don't eat. Surely *those* are the unclean ones, not animals in general.'

She is right, of course. But wrong: a mistake to bring the conversation back to the matter on the table before them, the food.

Wunderlich speaks again. 'The Greeks had a feeling there was something wrong in slaughter, but thought they could make up for that by ritualizing it. They made a sacrificial offering, gave a percentage to the gods, hoping thereby to keep the rest. The same notion as the tithe. Ask for the blessing of the gods on the flesh you are about to eat, ask them to declare it clean.'

'Perhaps that is the origin of the gods,' says his mother. A silence falls. 'Perhaps we invented gods so that we could put the blame on them. They gave us permission to eat flesh. They gave us permission to play with unclean things. It's not our fault, it's theirs. We're just their children.'

'Is that what you believe?' asks Mrs Garrard cautiously.

'And God said: Every moving thing that liveth shall be meat for you,' his mother quotes. 'It's convenient. God told us it was OK.'

Silence again. They are waiting for her to go on. She is, after all, the paid entertainer.

'Norma is right,' says his mother. 'The problem is to define our difference from animals in general, not just from so-called unclean animals. The ban on certain animals – pigs and so forth – is quite arbitrary. It is simply a signal that we are in a danger area. A minefield, in fact. The minefield of dietary proscriptions. There is no logic to a taboo, nor is there any logic to a minefield – there is not meant to be. You can never guess what you may eat or where you may step unless you are in possession of a map, a divine map.'

'But that's just anthropology,' objects Norma from the foot of the table. 'It says nothing about our behaviour today. People in the modern world no longer decide their diet on the basis of whether

86

they have divine permission. If we eat pig and don't eat dog, that's just the way we are brought up. Wouldn't you agree, Elizabeth? It's just one of our folkways.'

Elizabeth. She is claiming intimacy. But what game is she playing? Is there a trap she is leading his mother into?

'There is disgust,' says his mother. 'We may have got rid of the gods but we have not got rid of disgust, which is a version of religious horror.'

'Disgust is not universal,' objects Norma. 'The French eat frogs. The Chinese eat anything. There is no disgust in China.'

His mother is silent.

'So perhaps it's just a matter of what you learned at home, of what your mother told you was OK to eat and what was not.'

'What was clean to eat and what was not,' his mother murmurs.

'And maybe' – now Norma is going too far, he thinks, now she is beginning to dominate the conversation to an extent that is totally inappropriate – 'the whole notion of cleanness versus uncleanness has a completely different function, namely, to enable certain groups to self-define themselves, negatively, as elite, as elected. We are the people who abstain from A or B or C, and by that power of abstinence we mark ourselves off as superior: as a superior caste within society, for instance. Like the Brahmins.'

There is a silence.

'The ban on meat that you get in vegetarianism is only an extreme form of dietary ban,' Norma presses on; 'and a dietary ban is a quick, simple way for an elite group to define itself. Other people's table habits are unclean, we can't eat or drink with them.'

Now she is getting really close to the bone. There is a certain amount of shuffling, there is unease in the air. Fortunately, the course is over – the red snapper, the fettucine – and the waitresses are among them removing the plates.

87

'Have you read Gandhi's autobiography, Norma?' asks his mother. 'No.'

'Gandhi was sent off to England as a young man to study law. England, of course, prided itself as a great meat-eating country. But his mother made him promise not to eat meat. She packed a trunk full of food for him to take along. During the sea voyage he scavenged a little bread from the ship's table and for the rest ate out of his trunk. In London he faced a long search for lodgings and eating houses that served his kind of food. Social relations with the English were difficult because he could not accept or return hospitality. It wasn't until he fell in with certain fringe elements of English society – Fabians, theosophists, and so forth – that he began to feel at home. Until then he was just a lonely little law student.'

'What is the point, Elizabeth?' says Norma. 'What is the point of the story?'

'Just that Gandhi's vegetarianism can hardly be conceived as the exercise of power. It condemned him to the margins of society. It was his particular genius to incorporate what he found on those margins into his political philosophy.'

'In any event,' interjects the blond man, 'Gandhi is not a good example. His vegetarianism was hardly committed. He was a vegetarian because of the promise he made to his mother. He may have kept his promise, but he regretted and resented it.'

'Don't you think that mothers can have a good influence on their children?' says Elizabeth Costello.

There is a moment's silence. It is time for him, the good son, to speak. He does not.

'But your own vegetarianism, Mrs Costello,' says President Garrard, pouring oil on troubled waters: 'it comes out of moral conviction, does it not?'

'No, I don't think so,' says his mother. 'It comes out of a desire to save my soul.'

Now there truly is a silence, broken only by the clink of plates as the waitresses set baked Alaskas before them.

'Well, I have a great respect for it,' says Garrard. 'As a way of life.'

'I'm wearing leather shoes,' says his mother. 'I'm carrying a leather purse. I wouldn't have overmuch respect if I were you.'

'Consistency,' murmurs Garrard. 'Consistency is the hobgoblin of small minds. Surely one can draw a distinction between eating meat and wearing leather.'

'Degrees of obscenity,' she replies.

'I too have the greatest respect for codes based on respect for life,' says Dean Arendt, entering the debate for the first time. 'I am prepared to accept that dietary taboos do not have to be mere customs. I will accept that underlying them are genuine moral concerns. But at the same time one must say that our whole super-structure of concern and belief is a closed book to animals them-selves. You can't explain to a steer that its life is going to be spared, any more than you can explain to a bug that you are not going to step on it. In the lives of animals, things, good or bad, just happen. So vegetarianism is a very odd transaction, when you come to think of it, with the beneficiaries unaware that they are being benefited. And with no hope of ever becoming aware. Because they live in a vacuum of consciousness.'

Arendt pauses. It is his mother's turn to speak, but she merely looks confused, grey and tired and confused. He leans across. 'It's been a long day, Mother,' he says. 'Perhaps it is time.'

'Yes, it is time,' she says.

'You won't have coffee?' enquires President Garrard.

'No, it will just keep me awake.' She turns to Arendt. 'That is a good point you raise. No consciousness that we would recognize as consciousness. No awareness, as far as we can make out, of a self with a history. What I mind is what tends to come next. They have no consciousness *therefore*. Therefore what? Therefore we are free to use them for our own ends? Therefore we are free to kill them? Why? What is so special about the form of consciousness we recognize that makes killing a bearer of it a crime while killing an animal goes unpunished? There are moments –'

'To say nothing of babies,' interjects Wunderlich. Everyone turns and looks at him. 'Babies have no self-consciousness, yet we think it a more heinous crime to kill a baby than an adult.'

'Therefore?' says Arendt.

'Therefore all this discussion of consciousness and whether animals have it is just a smokescreen. At bottom we protect our own kind. Thumbs up to human babies, thumbs down to veal calves. Don't you think so, Mrs Costello?'

'I don't know what I think,' says Elizabeth Costello. 'I often wonder what thinking is, what understanding is. Do we really understand the universe better than animals do? Understanding a thing often looks to me like playing with one of those Rubik cubes. Once you have made all the little bricks snap into place, hey presto, you understand. It makes sense if you live inside a Rubik cube, but if you don't . . .'

There is a silence. 'I would have thought –' says Norma; but at this point he gets to his feet, and to his relief Norma stops.

The president rises, and then everyone else. 'A wonderful lecture, Mrs Costello,' says the president. 'Much food for thought. We look forward to tomorrow's offering.'

4
The Lives of Animals

TWO: The Poets and the Animals

IT IS AFTER eleven. His mother has retired for the night, he and
Norma are downstairs clearing up the children's mess. After that
he still has a class to prepare.

'Are you going to her seminar tomorrow?' asks Norma.

'I'll have to.'

'What is it on?'

'"The Poets and the Animals". That's the title. The English
Department is staging it. They are holding it in a seminar room,
so I don't think they are expecting a big audience.'

'I'm glad it's on something she knows about. I find her philos-
ophizing rather difficult to take.'

'Oh. What do you have in mind?'

'For instance what she was saying about human reason.
Presumably she was trying to make a point about the nature of
rational understanding. To say that rational accounts are merely a
consequence of the structure of the human mind; that animals have
their own accounts in accordance with the structure of their own
minds, to which we don't have access because we don't share a
language with them.'

'And what's wrong with that?'

'It's naive, John. It's the kind of easy, shallow relativism that
impresses freshmen. Respect for everyone's world view, the cow's

world view, the squirrel's world view, and so forth. In the end it leads to total intellectual paralysis. You spend so much time respecting that you haven't time left to think.'

'Doesn't a squirrel have a world view?'

'Yes, a squirrel does have a world view. Its world view comprises acorns and trees and weather and cats and dogs and automobiles and squirrels of the opposite sex. It comprises an account of how these phenomena interact and how it should interact with them to survive. That's all. There's no more. That's the world according to squirrel.'

'We are sure about that?'

'We are sure about it in the sense that hundreds of years of observing squirrels has not led us to conclude otherwise. If there is anything else in the squirrel mind, it does not issue in observable behaviour. For all practical purposes, the mind of the squirrel is a very simple mechanism.'

'So Descartes was right, animals are just biological automata.'

'Broadly speaking, yes. You cannot, in the abstract, distinguish between an animal mind and a machine simulating an animal mind.'

'And human beings are different?'

'John, I am tired and you are being irritating. Human beings invent mathematics, they build telescopes, they do calculations, they construct machines, they press a button, and, bang, *Sojourner* lands on Mars, exactly as predicted. That is why rationality is not just, as your mother claims, a game. Reason provides us with real knowledge of the real world. It has been tested, and it works. You are a physicist. You ought to know.'

'I agree. It works. Still, isn't there a position outside from which our doing our thinking and then sending out a Mars probe looks a lot like a squirrel doing its thinking and then dashing out and snatching a nut? Isn't that perhaps what she meant?'

'But there isn't any such position! I know it sounds old-fashioned, but I have to say it. There is no position outside of reason where you can stand and lecture about reason and pass judgement on reason.'

'Except the position of someone who has withdrawn from reason.'

'That's just French irrationalism, the sort of thing a person would say who has never set foot inside a mental institution and seen what people look like who have *really* withdrawn from reason.'

'Then except for God.'

'Not if God is a God of reason. A God of reason cannot stand outside reason.'

'I'm surprised, Norma. You are talking like an old-fashioned rationalist.'

'You misunderstand me. That is the ground your mother has chosen. Those are her terms. I am merely responding.'

'Who was the missing guest?'

'You mean the empty seat? It was Stern, the poet.'

'Do you think it was a protest?'

'I'm sure it was. She should have thought twice before bringing up the Holocaust. I could feel hackles rising all around me in the audience.'

The empty seat was indeed a protest. When he goes in for his morning class, there is a letter in his box addressed to his mother. He hands it over to her when he comes home to fetch her. She reads it quickly, then with a sigh passes it over to him. 'Who is this man?' she says.

'Abraham Stern. A poet. Quite well respected, I believe. He has been here donkey's years.'

He reads Stern's note, which is handwritten.

Dear Mrs Costello,

Excuse me for not attending last night's dinner. I have read your books and know you are a serious person, so I do you the credit of taking what you said in your lecture seriously.

At the kernel of your lecture, it seemed to me, was the question of breaking bread. If we refuse to break bread with the executioners of Auschwitz, can we continue to break bread with the slaughterers of animals?

You took over for your own purposes the familiar comparison between the murdered Jews of Europe and slaughtered cattle. The Jews died like cattle, therefore cattle die like Jews, you say. That is a trick with words which I will not accept. You misunderstand the nature of likenesses; I would even say you misunderstand wilfully, to the point of blasphemy. Man is made in the likeness of God but God does not have the likeness of man. If Jews were treated like cattle, it does not follow that cattle are treated like Jews. The inversion insults the memory of the dead. It also trades on the horrors of the camps in a cheap way.

Forgive me if I am forthright. You said you were old enough not to have time to waste on niceties, and I am an old man too.

Yours sincerely,
Abraham Stern

He delivers his mother to her hosts in the English Department, then goes to a meeting. The meeting drags on and on. It is two thirty before he can get to the seminar room in Stubbs Hall.

She is speaking as he enters. He sits down as quietly as he can near the door.

'In that kind of poetry,' she is saying, 'animals stand for human qualities: the lion for courage, the owl for wisdom, and so forth. Even in Rilke's poem the panther is there as a stand-in for something else. He dissolves into a dance of energy around a centre, an image that comes from physics, elementary particle physics. Rilke does not get beyond this point – beyond the panther as the vital embodiment of the kind of force that is released in an atomic explosion but is here trapped not so much by the bars of the cage as by what the bars compel on the panther: a concentric lope that leaves the will stupefied, narcotized.'

Rilke's panther? What panther? His confusion must show: the girl next to him pushes a photocopied sheet under his nose. Three poems: one by Rilke called 'The Panther', two by Ted Hughes called 'The Jaguar' and 'Second Glance at a Jaguar'. He has no time to read them.

'Hughes is writing against Rilke,' his mother goes on. 'He uses the same staging in the zoo, but it is the crowd for a change that stands mesmerized, and among them the man, the poet, entranced and horrified and overwhelmed, his powers of understanding pushed beyond their limit. The jaguar's vision, unlike the panther's, is not blunted. On the contrary, his eyes drill through the darkness of space. The cage has no reality to him, he is *elsewhere*. He is elsewhere because his consciousness is kinetic rather than abstract: the thrust of his muscles moves him through a space quite different in nature from the three-dimensional box of Newton – a circular space that returns upon itself.

'So – leaving aside the ethics of caging large animals – Hughes is feeling his way towards a different kind of being-in-the-world, one which is not entirely foreign to us, since the experience before the cage seems to belong to dream experience, experience held in the collective unconscious. In these poems we know the jaguar not from the way he seems but from the way he moves. The body is as the body moves, or as the currents of life move within it. The poems ask us to imagine our way into that way of moving, to inhabit that body.

'With Hughes it is a matter – I emphasize – not of inhabiting another mind but of inhabiting another body. That is the kind of poetry I bring to your attention today: poetry that does not try to find an idea in the animal, that is not about the animal, but is instead the record of an engagement with him.

'What is peculiar about poetic engagements of this kind is that, no matter with what intensity they take place, they remain a matter of complete indifference to their objects. In this respect they are different from love poems, where your intention is to move your object.

'Not that animals do not care what we feel about them. But when we divert the current of feeling that flows between ourself and the animal into words, we abstract it for ever from the animal. Thus the poem is not a gift to its object, as the love poem is. It falls within an entirely human economy in which the animal has no share. Does that answer your question?'

Someone else has his hand up: a tall young man with glasses. He doesn't know Ted Hughes's poetry well, he says, but the last he heard, Hughes was running a sheep ranch somewhere in England. Either he is just raising sheep as poetic subjects (there is a titter around the room) or he is a real rancher raising sheep for the market. 'How does this square with what you were saying in your lecture yesterday, when you seemed to be pretty much against killing animals for meat?'

'I've never met Ted Hughes,' replies his mother, 'so I can't tell you what kind of farmer he is. But let me try to answer your question on another level.

'I have no reason to think that Hughes believes his attentiveness to animals is unique. On the contrary, I suspect he believes he is

96

recovering an attentiveness that our faraway ancestors possessed and we have lost (he conceives of this loss in evolutionary rather than historical terms, but that is another question). I would guess that he believes he looks at animals much as palaeolithic hunters used to.

'This puts Hughes in a line of poets who celebrate the primitive and repudiate the Western bias towards abstract thought. The line of Blake and Lawrence, of Gary Snyder in the United States, or Robinson Jeffers. Hemingway too, in his hunting and bullfighting phase.

'Bullfighting, it seems to me, gives us a clue. Kill the beast by all means, they say, but make it a contest, a ritual, and honour your antagonist for his strength and bravery. Eat him too, after you have vanquished him, in order for his strength and courage to enter you. Look him in the eyes before you kill him, and thank him afterwards. Sing songs about him.

'We can call this primitivism. It is an attitude that is easy to criticize, to mock. It is deeply masculine, masculinist. Its ramifications into politics are to be mistrusted. But when all is said and done, there remains something attractive about it at an ethical level.

'It is also impractical, however. You do not feed four billion people through the efforts of matadors or deer hunters armed with bows and arrows. We have become too many. There is no time to respect and honour all the animals we need to feed ourselves. We need factories of death; we need factory animals. Chicago showed us the way; it was from the Chicago stockyards that the Nazis learned how to process bodies.

'But let me get back to Hughes. You say: Despite the primitivist trappings Hughes is a butcher, and what am I doing in his company?

'I would reply, writers teach us more than they are aware of. By bodying forth the jaguar, Hughes shows us that we too can embody animals – by the process called poetic invention that mingles breath and sense in a way that no one has explained and no one ever will. He shows us how to bring the living body into being within ourselves. When we read the jaguar poem, when we recollect it afterwards in tranquillity, we are for a brief while the jaguar. He ripples within us, he takes over our body, he is us.

'So far, so good. With what I have said thus far I don't think Hughes himself would disagree. It is much like the mixture of shamanism and spirit possession and archetype psychology that he himself espouses. In other words, a primitive experience (being face to face with an animal), a primitivist poem, and a primitivist theory of poetry to justify it.

'It is also the kind of poetry with which hunters and the people I call ecology-managers can feel comfortable. When Hughes the poet stands before the jaguar cage, he looks at an individual jaguar and is possessed by that individual jaguar life. It has to be that way. Jaguars in general, the subspecies jaguar, the idea of a jaguar, will fail to move him because we cannot experience abstractions. Nevertheless, the poem that Hughes writes is about *the* jaguar, about jaguarness embodied in this jaguar. Just as later on, when he writes his marvellous poems about salmon, they are about salmon as transitory occupants of the salmon life, the salmon biography. So despite the vividness and earthiness of the poetry, there remains something Platonic about it.

'In the ecological vision, the salmon and the river weeds and the water insects interact in a great, complex dance with the earth and the weather. The whole is greater than the sum of the parts. In the dance, each organism has a role: it is these multiple roles, rather than the particular beings who play them, that participate in the dance. As for actual role players, as long as they are self-renewing, as long as they keep coming forward, we need pay them no heed.

'I called this Platonic and I do so again. Our eye is on the creature itself, but our mind is on the system of interactions of which it is the earthly, material embodiment.

'The irony is a terrible one. An ecological philosophy that tells us to live side by side with other creatures justifies itself by appealing to an idea, an idea of a higher order than any living creature. An idea, finally – and this is the crushing twist to the irony – which no creature except man is capable of comprehending. Every living creature fights for its own, individual life, refuses, by fighting, to accede to the idea that the salmon or the gnat is of a lower order of importance than the idea of the salmon or the idea of the gnat. But when we see the salmon fighting for its life, we say, it is just programmed to fight; we say, with Aquinas, it is locked into natural slavery; we say, it lacks self-consciousness.

'Animals are not believers in ecology. Even the ethnobiologists do not make that claim. Even the ethnobiologists do not say that the ant sacrifices its life to perpetuate the species. What they say is subtly different: the ant dies and the function of its death is the perpetuation of the species. The species life is a force which acts through the individual but which the individual is incapable of understanding. In that sense the idea is innate, and the ant is run by the idea as a computer is run by a program.

'We, the managers of the ecology – I'm sorry to go on like this, I am getting way beyond your question, I'll be through in a moment – we managers understand the greater dance, therefore we can decide how many trout may be fished or how many jaguar may be trapped before the stability of the dance is upset. The only organism over which we do not claim this power of life and death is man. Why? Because man is different. Man understands the dance as the other dancers do not. Man is an intellectual being.'

While she speaks, his mind has been wandering. He has heard

99

it before, this anti-ecologism of hers. Jaguar poems are all very well, he thinks, but you won't get a bunch of Australians standing around a sheep, listening to its silly baa, writing poems about it. Isn't that what is so suspect in the whole animals-rights business: that it has to ride on the back of pensive gorillas and sexy jaguars and huggable pandas because the real objects of its concern, chickens and pigs, to say nothing of white rats or prawns, are not newsworthy?

Now Elaine Marx, who did the introduction to yesterday's lecture, asks a question. 'In your lecture you argued that various criteria – Does this creature have reason? Does this creature have speech? – have been used in bad faith to justify distinctions that have no real basis, between *Homo* and other primates, for example, and thus to justify exploitation.

'Yet the very fact that you can be arguing against this reasoning, exposing its falsity, means that you put a certain faith in the power of reason, of true reason as opposed to false reason.

'Let me concretize my question by referring to the case of Lemuel Gulliver. In *Gulliver's Travels* Swift gives us a vision of a utopia of reason, the land of the so-called Houyhnhnms, but it turns out to be a place where there is no home for Gulliver, who is the closest that Swift comes to a representation of us, his readers. But which of us would want to live in Houyhnhnm-land, with its rational vegetarianism and its rational government and its rational approach to love, marriage and death? Would even a horse want to live in such a perfectly regulated, totalitarian society? More pertinently for us, what is the track record of totally regulated societies? Is it not a fact that they either collapse or else turn militaristic?

'Specifically, my question is: Are you not expecting too much of humankind when you ask us to live without species exploitation, without cruelty? Is it not more human to accept our own humanity – even if it means embracing the carnivorous Yahoo within ourselves – than to end up like Gulliver, pining for a state he can never attain, and for good reason: it is not in his nature, which is a human nature?'

'An interesting question,' his mother replies. 'I find Swift an intriguing writer. For instance, his *Modest Proposal*. Whenever there is overwhelming agreement about how to read a book, I prick up my ears. On *A Modest Proposal* the consensus is that Swift does not mean what he says, or seems to say. He says, or seems to say, that Irish families could make a living by raising babies for the table of their English masters. But he can't mean that, we say, because we all know that it is atrocious to kill and eat human babies. Yet, come to think of it, we go on, the English are already in a sense killing human babies, by letting them starve. So, come to think of it, the English are already atrocious.

'That is the orthodox reading, more or less. But why, I ask myself, the vehemence with which it is stuffed down the throats of young readers? Thus shall you read Swift, their teachers say, thus and in no other way. If it is atrocious to kill and eat human babies, why is it not atrocious to kill and eat piglets? If you want Swift to be a dark ironist rather than a facile pamphleteer, you might examine the premises that make his fable so easy to digest.

'Let me now turn to *Gulliver's Travels*.

'On the one hand you have the Yahoos, who are associated with raw meat, the smell of excrement and what we used to call bestiality. On the other you have the Houyhnhnms, who are associated with grass, sweet smells and the rational ordering of the passions. In between you have Gulliver, who wants to be a Houyhnhnm but knows secretly that he is a Yahoo. All of that is perfectly clear. As with *A Modest Proposal*, the question is, what do we make of it?

'One observation. The horses expel Gulliver. Their ostensible reason is that he does not meet the standard of rationality. The real reason is that he does not look like a horse, but something else: a dressed-up Yahoo, in fact. So: the standard of reason that has been applied by carnivorous bipeds to justify a special status for themselves can equally be applied by herbivorous quadrupeds.

'The standard of reason. *Gulliver's Travels* seems to me to operate within the three-part Aristotelian division of gods, beasts and men. As long as one tries to fit the three actors into just two categories – which are the beasts, which are the men? – one can't make sense of the fable. Nor can the Houyhnhnms. The Houyhnhnms are gods of a kind, cold, Apollonian. The test they apply to Gulliver is: Is he a god or a beast? They feel it is the appropriate test. We, instinctively, don't.

'What has always puzzled me about *Gulliver's Travels* – and this is a perspective you might expect from an ex-colonial – is that Gulliver always travels alone. Gulliver goes on voyages of exploration to unknown lands, but he does not come ashore with an armed party, *as happened in reality*, and Swift's book says nothing about what would normally have come after Gulliver's pioneering efforts: follow-up expeditions, expeditions to colonize Lilliput or the island of the Houyhnhnms.

'The question I ask is: What if Gulliver and an armed expedition were to land, shoot a few Yahoos when they become threatening, and then shoot and eat a horse, for food? What would that do to Swift's somewhat too neat, somewhat too disembodied, somewhat too unhistorical fable? It would certainly give the Houyhnhnms a rude shock, making it clear that there is a third category besides gods and beasts, namely, man, of whom their ex-client Gulliver is one; furthermore, that if the horses stand for reason, then man stands for physical force.

'Taking over an island and slaughtering its inhabitants is, by the way, what Odysseus and his men did on Thrinacia, the island sacred to Apollo, an act for which they were mercilessly punished by the god. And that story, in turn, seems to call on older layers of belief, from a time when bulls were gods and killing and eating a god could call down a curse on you.

'So – excuse the confusion of this response – yes, we are not horses, we do not have their clear, rational, naked beauty; on the contrary, we are subequine primates, otherwise known as man. You say there is nothing to do but embrace that status, that nature. Very well, let us do so. But let us also push Swift's fable to its limits and recognize that, in history, embracing the status of man has entailed slaughtering and enslaving a race of divine or else divinely created beings and bringing down on ourselves a curse thereby.'

It is three fifteen, a couple of hours before his mother's last engage-ment. He walks her over to his office along tree-lined paths where the last autumn leaves are falling.

'Do you really believe, Mother, that poetry classes are going to close down the slaughterhouses?'

'No.'

'Then why do it? You said you were tired of clever talk about animals, proving by syllogism that they do or do not have souls. But isn't poetry just another kind of clever talk: admiring the muscles of the big cats in verse? Wasn't your point about talk that it changes nothing? It seems to me the level of behaviour you want to change is too elementary, too elemental, to be reached by talk. Carnivorousness expresses something truly deep about human beings, just as it does about jaguars. You wouldn't want to put a jaguar on a soybean diet.'

'Because he would die. Human beings don't die on a vegetar-ian diet.'

'No, they don't. But they don't *want* a vegetarian diet. They *like* eating meat. There is something atavistically satisfying about it. That's the brutal truth. Just as it's a brutal truth that, in a sense, animals deserve what they get. Why waste your time trying to help them when they won't help themselves? Let them stew in their own juice. If I were asked what the general attitude is towards the animals we eat, I would say: contempt. We treat them badly because we despise them; we despise them because they don't fight back.'

'I don't disagree,' says his mother. 'People complain that we treat animals like objects, but in fact we treat them like prisoners of war. Do you know that when zoos were first opened to the public, the keepers had to protect the animals against attacks by spectators? The spectators felt the animals were there to be insulted and abused, like prisoners in a triumph. We had a war once against the animals, which we called hunting, though in fact war and hunting are the same thing (Aristotle saw it clearly). That war went on for millions of years. We won it definitively only a few hundred years ago, when we invented guns. It is only since victory became absolute that we have been able to afford to cultivate compassion. But our compassion is very thinly spread. Beneath it is a more primitive attitude. The prisoner of war does not belong to our tribe. We can do what we want with him. We can sacrifice him to our gods. We can cut his throat, tear out his heart, throw him on the fire. There are no laws when it comes to prisoners of war.'

'And that is what you want to cure humankind of?'

'John, I don't know what I want to do. I just don't want to sit silent.'

'Very well. But generally one doesn't kill prisoners of war. One turns them into slaves.'

'Well, that's what our captive herds are: slave populations. Their work is to breed for us. Even their sex becomes a form of labour.

104

We don't hate them because they are not worth hating any more. We regard them, as you say, with contempt.

'However, there are still animals we hate. Rats, for instance. Rats haven't surrendered. They fight back. They form themselves into underground units in our sewers. They aren't winning, but they aren't losing either. To say nothing of the insects and the microbia. They may beat us yet. They will certainly outlast us.'

The final session of his mother's visit is to take the form of a debate. Her opponent will be the large, blond man from yesterday evening's dinner, who turns out to be Thomas O'Hearne, professor of philosophy at Appleton.

It has been agreed that O'Hearne will have three opportunities to present positions, and his mother three opportunities to reply. Since O'Hearne has had the courtesy to send her a précis beforehand, she knows, broadly speaking, what he will be saying.

'My first reservation about the animal-rights movement,' O'Hearne begins, 'is that by failing to recognize its historical nature, it runs the risk of becoming, like the human-rights movement, yet another Western crusade against the practices of the rest of the world, claiming universality for what are simply its own standards.' He proceeds to give a brief outline of the rise of animal-protection societies in Britain and America in the nineteenth century.

'When it comes to human rights,' he continues, 'other cultures and other religious traditions quite properly reply that they have their own norms and see no reason why they should have to adopt those of the West. Similarly, they say, they have their own norms for the treatment of animals and see no reason to adopt ours – particularly when ours are of such recent invention.

'In yesterday's presentation our lecturer was very hard on Descartes. But Descartes did not invent the idea that animals belong to a different order from humankind: he merely formalized it in a new way. The notion that we have an obligation to animals themselves to treat them compassionately – as opposed to an obligation to ourselves to do so – is very recent, very Western, and even very Anglo-Saxon. As long as we insist that we have access to an ethical universal to which other traditions are blind, and try to impose it on them by means of propaganda or even economic pressure, we are going to meet with resistance, and that resistance will be justified.'

It is his mother's turn.

'The concerns you express are substantial, Professor O'Hearne, and I am not sure I can give them a substantial answer. You are correct, of course, about the history. Kindness to animals has become a social norm only recently, in the last hundred and fifty or two hundred years, and in only part of the world. You are correct too to link this history to the history of human rights, since concern for animals is, historically speaking, an offshoot of broader philanthropic concerns – for the lot of slaves and of children, among others.

'However, kindness to animals – and here I use the word *kindness* in its full sense, as an acceptance that we are all of one kind, one nature – has been more widespread than you imply. Pet-keeping, for instance, is by no means a Western fad: the first travellers to South America encountered settlements where human beings and animals lived higgledy-piggledy together. And of course children all over the world consort quite naturally with animals. They don't see any dividing line. That is something they have to be taught, just as they have to be taught it is all right to kill and eat them.

'Getting back to Descartes, I would only want to say that the discontinuity he saw between animals and human beings was the result of incomplete information. The science of Descartes' day had no acquaintance with the great apes or with higher marine mammals, and thus little cause to question the assumption that animals cannot think. And of course it had no access to the fossil record that would reveal a graded continuum of anthropoid creatures stretching from the higher primates to *Homo sapiens* – anthropoids, one must point out, who were exterminated by man in the course of his rise to power.

'While I concede your main point about Western cultural arrogance, I do think it is appropriate that those who pioneered the industrialization of animal lives and the commodification of animal flesh should be at the forefront of trying to atone for it.'

O'Hearne presents his second thesis. 'In my reading of the scientific literature,' he says, 'efforts to show that animals can think strategically, hold general concepts or communicate symbolically, have had very limited success. The best performance the higher apes can put up is no better than that of a speech-impaired human being with severe mental retardation. If so, are not animals, even the higher animals, properly thought of as belonging to another legal and ethical realm entirely, rather than being placed in this depressing human subcategory? Isn't there a certain wisdom in the traditional view that says that animals cannot enjoy legal rights because they are not persons, even potential persons, as foetuses are? In working out rules for our dealings with animals, does it not make more sense for such rules to apply to us and to our treatment of them, as at present, rather than being predicated upon rights which animals cannot claim or enforce or even understand?'

His mother's turn. 'To respond adequately, Professor O'Hearne, would take more time than I have, since I would first want to interrogate the whole question of rights and how we come to possess them. So let me just make one observation: that the programme of scientific experimentation that leads you to conclude that animals are imbeciles is profoundly anthropocentric. It values being able to find your way out of a sterile maze, ignoring the fact that if the researcher who designed the maze were to be parachuted into the jungles of Borneo, he or she would be dead of starvation in a week. In fact I would go further. If I as a human being were told that the standards by which animals are being measured in these experiments are human standards, I would be insulted. It is the experiments themselves that are imbecile. The behaviourists who design them claim that we understand only by a process of creating abstract models and then testing those models against reality. What nonsense. We understand by immersing ourselves and our intelligence in complexity. There is something self-stultified in the way in which scientific behaviourism recoils from the complexity of life.

'As for animals being too dumb and stupid to speak for themselves, consider the following sequence of events. When Albert Camus was a young boy in Algeria, his grandmother told him to bring her one of the hens from the cage in their backyard. He obeyed, then watched her cut off its head with a kitchen knife, catching its blood in a bowl so that the floor would not be dirtied.

'The death cry of that hen imprinted itself on the boy's memory so hauntingly that in 1958 he wrote an impassioned attack on the guillotine. As a result, in part, of that polemic, capital punishment was abolished in France. Who is to say, then, that the hen did not speak?'

O'Hearne. 'I make the following statement with due deliberation, mindful of the historical associations it may evoke. I do not believe that life is as important to animals as it is to us. There is certainly in animals an instinctive struggle against death, which they share with us. But they do not *understand* death as we do, or rather, as we fail to do. There is, in the human mind, a collapse of the imagination before death, and that collapse of the imagination – graphically evoked in yesterday's lecture – is the basis of our fear of death. That fear does not and cannot exist in animals, since the effort to comprehend extinction, and the failure to do so, the failure to master it, have simply not taken place.

'For that reason, I want to suggest, dying is, for an animal, just something that happens, something against which there may be a revolt of the organism but not a revolt of the soul. And the lower down the scale of evolution one goes, the truer this is. To an insect, death is the breakdown of systems that keep the physical organism functioning, and nothing more.

'To animals, death is continuous with life. It is only among certain very imaginative human beings that one encounters a horror of dying so acute that they then project it on to other beings, including animals. Animals live, and then they die: that is all. Thus to equate a butcher who slaughters a chicken with an executioner who kills a human being is a grave mistake. The events are not comparable. They are not of the same scale, they are not on the same scale.

'That leaves us with the question of cruelty. It is licit to kill animals, I would say, because their lives are not as important to them as our lives are to us; the old-fashioned way of saying this is that animals do not have immortal souls. Gratuitous cruelty, on the other hand, I would regard as illicit. Therefore it is quite appropriate that we should agitate for the humane treatment of animals, even and particularly in slaughterhouses. This has for a long time been a goal of animal-welfare organizations, and I salute them for it.

'My very last point concerns what I see as the troublingly abstract nature of the concern for animals in the animal-rights movement.

I want to apologize in advance to our lecturer for the seeming harshness of what I am about to say, but I believe it needs to be said.

'Of the many varieties of animal lover I see around me, let me isolate two. On the one hand, hunters, people who value animals at a very elementary, unreflective level; who spend hours watching them and tracking them; and who, after they have killed them, get pleasure from the taste of their flesh. On the other hand, people who have little contact with animals, or at least with those species they are concerned to protect, like poultry and livestock, yet want all animals to lead – in an economic vacuum – a utopian life in which everyone is miraculously fed and no one preys on anyone else.

'Of the two, which, I ask, loves animals more?

'It is because agitation for animal rights, including the right to life, is so abstract that I find it unconvincing and, finally, idle. Its proponents talk a great deal about our community with animals, but how do they actually live that community? Thomas Aquinas says that friendship between human beings and animals is impossible, and I tend to agree. You can be friends neither with a Martian nor with a bat, for the simple reason that you have too little in common with them. We may certainly *wish* for there to be community with animals, but that is not the same thing as living in community with them. It is just a piece of prelapsarian wistfulness.'

His mother's turn again, her last turn.

'Anyone who says that life matters less to animals than it does to us has not held in his hands an animal fighting for its life. The whole of the being of the animal is thrown into that fight, without reserve. When you say that the fight lacks a dimension of intellectual or imaginative horror, I agree. It is not the mode of being of animals to have an intellectual horror: their whole being is in the living flesh.

'If I do not convince you, that is because my words, here, lack the power to bring home to you the wholeness, the unabstracted, unintellectual nature, of that animal being. That is why I urge you to read the poets who return the living, electric being to language; and if the poets do not move you, I urge you to walk, flank to flank, beside the beast that is prodded down the chute to his executioner.

'You say that death does not matter to an animal because the animal does not understand death. I am reminded of one of the academic philosophers I read in preparing for yesterday's lecture. It was a depressing experience. It awoke in me a quite Swiftian response. If this is the best that human philosophy can offer, I said to myself, I would rather go and live among horses.

'Can we, asked this philosopher, strictly speaking, say that the veal calf misses its mother? Does the veal calf have enough of a grasp of the significance of the mother relation, does the veal calf have enough of a grasp of the meaning of maternal absence, does the veal calf, finally, know enough about missing to know that the feeling it has is the feeling of missing?

'A calf who has not mastered the concepts of presence and absence, of self and other – so goes the argument – cannot, strictly speaking, be said to miss anything. In order to, strictly speaking, miss anything, it would first have to take a course in philosophy. What sort of philosophy is this? Throw it out, I say. What good do its piddling distinctions do?

'To me, a philosopher who says that the distinction between human and non-human depends on whether you have a white or a black skin, and a philosopher who says that the distinction between human and non-human depends on whether or not you know the difference between a subject and a predicate, are more alike than they are unlike.

'Usually I am wary of exclusionary gestures. I know of one prominent philosopher who states that he is simply not prepared to philosophize about animals with people who eat meat. I am not sure I would go as far as that – frankly, I have not the courage – but I must say I would not fall over myself to meet the gentleman whose book I just have been citing. Specifically, I would not fall over myself to break bread with him.

'Would I be prepared to discuss ideas with him? That really is the crucial question. Discussion is possible only when there is common ground. When opponents are at loggerheads, we say: "Let them reason together, and by reasoning clarify what their differences are, and thus inch closer. They may seem to share nothing else, but at least they share reason."

'On the present occasion, however, I am not sure I want to concede that I share reason with my opponent. Not when reason is what underpins the whole long philosophical tradition to which he belongs, stretching back to Descartes and beyond Descartes through Aquinas and Augustine to the Stoics and Aristotle. If the last common ground that I have with him is reason, and if reason is what sets me apart from the veal calf, then thank you but no thank you, I'll talk to someone else.'

That is the note on which Dean Arendt has to bring the proceedings to a close: acrimony, hostility, bitterness. He, John Bernard, is sure that is not what Arendt or his committee wanted. Well, they should have asked him before they invited his mother. He could have told them.

It is past midnight, he and Norma are in bed, he is exhausted, at six he will have to get up to drive his mother to the airport. But Norma is in a fury and will not give up. 'It's nothing but food faddism, and food faddism is always an exercise in power. I have no patience when she arrives here and begins trying to get people, particularly the children, to change their eating habits. And now these absurd public lectures! She is trying to extend her inhibiting power over the whole community!'

He wants to sleep, but he cannot utterly betray his mother. 'She's perfectly sincere,' he murmurs.

'It has nothing to do with sincerity. She has no self-insight at all. It is because she has so little insight into her motives that she seems sincere. Mad people are sincere.'

With a sigh he enters the fray. 'I don't see any difference,' he says, 'between her revulsion from eating meat and my own revulsion from eating snails or locusts. I have no insight into my motives and I couldn't care less. I just find it disgusting.'

Norma snorts. 'You don't give public lectures producing pseudo-philosophical arguments for not eating snails. You don't try to turn a private fad into a public taboo.'

'Perhaps. But why not try to see her as a preacher, a social reformer, rather than as an eccentric trying to foist her preferences on to other people?'

'You are welcome to see her as a preacher. But take a look at all the other preachers and their crazy schemes for dividing mankind up into the saved and the damned. Is that the kind of company you want your mother to keep? Elizabeth Costello and her Second Ark, with her dogs and cats and wolves, none of whom, of course, has ever been guilty of the sin of eating flesh, to say nothing of the malaria virus and the rabies virus and the HI virus, which she will want to save so that she can restock her Brave New World.'

'Norma, you're ranting.'

'I'm not ranting. I would have more respect for her if she didn't try to undermine me behind my back, with her stories to the children about the poor little veal calves and what the bad men do to them. I'm tired of having them pick at their food and ask, "Mom, is this veal?" when it's chicken or tuna fish. It's nothing but a power game. Her great hero Franz Kafka played the same game with his family. He refused to eat this, he refused to eat that, he would rather starve, he said. Soon everyone was feeling guilty about eating in front of him, and he could sit back feeling virtuous. It's a sick game, and I'm not having the children play it against me.'

'A few hours and she'll be gone, then we can return to normal.'

'Good. Say goodbye to her from me. I'm not getting up early.'

Seven o'clock, the sun just rising, and he and his mother are on their way to the airport.

'I'm sorry about Norma,' he says. 'She has been under a lot of strain. I don't think she is in a position to sympathize. Perhaps one could say the same for me. It's been such a short visit, I haven't had time to make sense of why you have become so intense about the animal business.'

She watches the wipers wagging back and forth. 'A better explanation,' she says, 'is that I have not told you why, or dare not tell you. When I think of the words, they seem so outrageous that they are best spoken into a pillow or into a hole in the ground, like King Midas.'

'I don't follow. What is it you can't say?'

'It's that I no longer know where I am. I seem to move around perfectly easily among people, to have perfectly normal relations with them. Is it possible, I ask myself, that all of them are participants in a crime of stupefying proportions? Am I fantasizing it all? I must be mad! Yet every day I see the evidences. The very people I suspect produce the evidence, exhibit it, offer it to me. Corpses. Fragments of corpses that they have bought for money.

'It is as if I were to visit friends, and to make some polite remark about the lamp in their living room, and they were to say, "Yes, it's nice, isn't it? Polish-Jewish skin it's made of, we find that's best, the skins of young Polish-Jewish virgins." And then I go to the bathroom and the soap wrapper says, "Treblinka – 100% human stearate." Am I dreaming, I say to myself? What kind of house is this?

'Yet I'm not dreaming. I look into your eyes, into Norma's, into the children's, and I see only kindness, human kindness. Calm down, I tell myself, you are making a mountain out of a molehill. This is life. Everyone else comes to terms with it, why can't you? *Why can't you?*'

She turns on him a tearful face. What does she want, he thinks? Does she want me to answer her question for her?

They are not yet on the expressway. He pulls the car over, switches off the engine, takes his mother in his arms. He inhales the smell of cold cream, of old flesh. 'There, there,' he whispers in her ear. 'There, there. It will soon be over.'

5
The Humanities in Africa

I

SHE HAS NOT seen her sister in twelve years, not since their mother's funeral that rainy day in Melbourne. That sister, whom she continues to think of as Blanche but whose public name has for so long been Sister Bridget that she must by now think of herself as a Bridget, has moved — for good, it seems — to Africa, following a vocation. Trained as a classical scholar, retrained as a medical missionary, she has risen to be administrator of a hospital of no mean size in rural Zululand. Since Aids swept over the region, she has concentrated the energies of the Hospital of the Blessed Mary on the Hill, Marianhill, more and more on the plight of children born infected. Two years ago Blanche wrote a book, *Living for Hope*, about the work of Marianhill. Unexpectedly the book caught on. She did a lecture tour of Canada and the United States, publicizing the work of the Order, raising money; she was featured in *Newsweek*. So, having given up an academic career for a life of obscure toil, Blanche is suddenly famous, famous enough, now, to be having an honorary degree conferred on her by a university in her adopted country.

It is for that degree, for the ceremony of its conferral, that she herself, Elizabeth, Blanche's younger sister, has come to a land she does not know and has never particularly wanted to know, to this ugly city (she flew in only hours ago, saw it spread out below her with its acres of scarred earth, its vast sterile mine dumps). She is here, and she is tired to the bone. Hours of her life lost in the passage over the Indian Ocean; futile to believe she will ever recover them. She ought to take a nap, perk herself up, recover her humour, before she encounters Blanche; but she is too restless, too disoriented, too – she feels it obscurely – unwell. Is it something she picked up on the plane? To fall sick among strangers: what misery! She prays she is wrong.

They have installed the two of them at the same hotel, Sister Bridget Costello and Ms Elizabeth Costello. When the arrangements were made, it was enquired whether they would prefer single rooms or a shared suite. Single rooms, she said; and she would guess Blanche said likewise. She and Blanche were never truly close; she has no wish, now that they have passed beyond being women of a certain age to being, frankly, old women, to have to listen in on Blanche's bedtime prayers or see what fashion of underwear the Sisters of the Marian Order go in for.

She unpacks, fusses around, switches on the television, switches it off again. Somehow or other, in the middle of all of this, she falls asleep, flat on her back, shoes and all. She is woken by the telephone. Blindly she gropes for the receiver. *Where am I?* she thinks. *Who am I?* 'Elizabeth?' says a voice. 'Is that you?'

They meet in the lounge of the hotel. She had thought there had been a relaxation in dress for the sisterhood. But if that is so, it has passed Blanche by. She wears the wimple, the plain white blouse, the grey skirt down to mid-calf, the stubby black shoes that were standard issue decades ago. Her face is seamed, the backs of her hands are mottled with brown; otherwise she has lasted well. The kind of woman, she thinks to herself, who lives to be ninety.

Scrawny is the word that unwillingly comes to mind: *scrawny as a hen*. As for what Blanche sees before her, as for what has become of the sister who remained in the world, she would rather not dwell on that.

They embrace, order tea. They exchange small talk. Blanche is an aunt, though she has never behaved like one, so she has to hear news of a nephew and niece whom she has rarely laid eyes on and who might as well be strangers. Even as they speak she, Elizabeth, is wondering: *Is this what I came for – this brush of lip against cheek, this exchange of tired words, this gesture towards reviving a past almost dwindled away?*

Familiarity. Family resemblance. Two old women in a foreign city, sipping tea, hiding their dismay at each other. Something there capable of being worked up, no doubt about that. Some kind of story skulking, inconspicuous as a mouse in a corner. But she is too tired, here and now, to grasp it, pin it down.

'At nine thirty,' Blanche is saying.

'What?'

'Nine thirty. We are being fetched at nine thirty. Meet down here.' She sets down her cup. 'You look bushed, Elizabeth. Get some sleep. I have a talk to prepare. They've asked me to give a talk. Sing for my supper.'

'A talk?'

'An address. I am giving an address tomorrow, to the graduands. You will have to sit through it, I am afraid.'

II

She is seated, along with other eminent guests, in the front row. Years since she was last at a graduation ceremony. The end of an academic year: the summer heat as bad here in Africa as back home.

There are, if she is to guess from the block of black-garbed young people behind her, some two hundred degrees in the humanities to be handed out. But first it is the turn of Blanche, the sole honorary graduand. She is introduced to the assembly. Clad in the scarlet gown of a doctor, a teacher, she stands before them, hands clasped, while the university orator reads out the record of a life's achievements. Then she is led to the Chancellor's seat. She bends a knee, and the deed is done. Long applause. Sister Bridget Costello, Bride of Christ and Doctor of Letters, who by her life and works has restored lustre, for a while, to the name of missionary.

She takes her place at the lectern. Time for her to say her piece, Bridget, Blanche.

'Chancellor,' she says, 'respected members of the University:

'You honour me here this morning, and I gratefully acknowledge the honour, which I accept on behalf not of myself but of those scores of people who for the past half-century have dedicated their labour and their love to the children of Marianhill and through those little ones to Our Lord.

'The form in which you have chosen to honour us is the form you are most easy with, the award of an academic degree, specifically what you call a doctorate in *litterae humaniores*, humane letters or, more loosely, the humanities. At the risk of telling you things you know better than I, I would like to use this opportunity to say something about the humanities, about their history and their present situation; also something about humanity. What I have to say may be relevant, I humbly hope, to the situation in which you as servants of the humanities find yourself, in Africa but in the wider world too, namely an embattled situation.

'We must sometimes be cruel to be kind, so let me begin by reminding you that it was not the university that gave birth to what we today call the humanities but what, to be more historically accurate, I will henceforth call the *studia humanitatis* or humane studies, studies in man and the nature of man, as distinct from *studia divinitatis*, studies pertaining to the divine. The university did not give birth to humane studies, nor, when the university eventually accepted humane studies in its scholarly ambit, did it provide a particularly nurturing home to them. On the contrary, the university embraced humane studies only in an arid, narrowed form. That narrowed form was textual scholarship; the history of humane studies in the university from the fifteenth century onwards is so tightly bound up with the history of textual scholarship that they may as well be called the same thing.

'Since I do not have all morning (your Dean asked me to limit myself to fifteen minutes at the utmost – "at the utmost" are his own words), I will say what I want to say without the step-by-step reasoning and the historical evidence to which you, as a gathering of students and scholars, are entitled.

'Textual scholarship, I would want to say if I had more time, was the living breath of humane studies while humane studies were what we can properly call a movement in history, namely the humanist movement. But it did not take long for the living breath in textual scholarship to be snuffed out. The story of textual scholarship since then has been the story of one effort after another to resuscitate that life, in vain.

'The text for the sake of which textual scholarship was invented was the Bible. Textual scholars saw themselves as servants in the recovery of the true message of the Bible, specifically the true teaching of Jesus. The figure they employed to describe their work was the figure of rebirth or resurrection. The reader of the New Testament was to encounter face to face for the first time the risen, reborn Christ, *Christus renascens*, obscured no longer by a veil of scholastic gloss and commentary. It was with this goal in mind that scholars taught themselves first Greek, then Hebrew, then (later) other languages of the Near East. Textual scholarship meant, first, the recovery of the true text, then the true translation of that text; and true translation turned out to be inseparable from true interpretation, just as true interpretation turned out to be inseparable from true understanding of the cultural and historical matrix from which the text had emerged. That is how linguistic studies, literary studies (as studies in interpretation), cultural studies and historical studies – the studies that form the core of the so-called humanities – came to be bound up together.

'Why, you may justly ask, call this constellation of studies devoted to the recovery of the true word of the Lord *studia humanitatis*? Asking this question will, it turns out, be much the same as asking, Why did the *studia humanitatis* come into flower only in the fifteenth century of our dispensation and not hundreds of years earlier?

'The answer has much to do with historical accident: with the decline and eventual sack of Constantinople and the flight of Byzantine men of learning to Italy. (Observing your Dean's fifteen-minute rule, I will pass over the living presence of Aristotle, Galen and other Greek philosophers in medieval Western Christendom, and the role of Arab Spain in transmitting their teachings.)

'*Timeo Danaos et dona ferentes.* The gifts brought by the men from the East were not only grammars of the Greek language but texts by authors from Greek antiquity. The linguistic command that was intended to be applied to the Greek New Testament could be perfected only by immersing oneself in these seductive pre-Christian texts. In no time, as one might expect, the study of these texts, later to be called the classics, had become an end in itself.

'More than that: the study of the texts of antiquity came to be justified not only on linguistic grounds but on philosophical grounds too. Jesus was sent to redeem mankind, the argument went. To redeem mankind from what? From an unredeemed state, of course. But what do we know of mankind in an unredeemed state? The only substantial record that covers all aspects of life is the record of antiquity. So to grasp the purpose behind the Incarnation – that is to say, to grasp the meaning of redemption – we must embark, through the classics, on *studia humanitatis*.

'Thus, in the brief and crude account I give, did it come about that biblical scholarship and studies in Greek and Roman antiquity came to be coupled in a relationship never without antagonism, and thus did it come about that textual scholarship and its attendant disciplines came to fall under the rubric "the humanities".

'So much for history. So much for why you, diverse and ill-assorted as you may privately feel yourselves to be, find yourselves assembled this morning under a single roof as graduates-to-be in the humanities. Now, in the few minutes left to me, I am going to tell you why I do not belong among you and have no message of comfort to bring to you, despite the generosity of the gesture you have extended to me.

'The message I bring is that you lost your way long ago, perhaps as long as five centuries ago. The handful of men among whom the movement originated of which you represent, I fear, the sad tail – those men were animated, at least at first, by the purpose of finding the True Word, by which they understood then, and I understand now, the redemptive word.

'That word cannot be found in the classics, whether you understand the classics to mean Homer and Sophocles or whether you understand them to mean Homer and Shakespeare and Dostoevsky. In a happier age than our own it was possible for people to bluff themselves into believing that the classics of antiquity offered a teaching and a way of life. In our own times we have settled, rather desperately, for the claim that the study of the classics in itself might offer a way of life, or if not a way of life then at least a way of earning a living which, if it cannot be proved to do any positive good, at least is on no side claimed to do any harm.

'But the impulse behind the first generation of textual scholars cannot be diverted so easily from its proper goal. I am a daughter of the Catholic Church, not of the Reformed Church, but I applaud Martin Luther when he turns his back on Desiderius Erasmus, judging that his colleague, despite his immense gifts, has been seduced into branches of study that do not, by the standards of the ultimate, matter. The *studia humanitatis* have taken a long time to die, but now, at the end of the second millennium of our era, they are truly on their deathbed. All the more bitter should be that death, I would say, since it has been brought about by the monster enthroned by those very studies as first and animating principle of the universe: the monster of reason, mechanical reason. But that is another story for another day.'

III

That is the end of it, the end of Blanche's oration, which is received less with applause than with what sounds, from the front row of seats, like a murmur of general puzzlement. The business of the day is resumed: one by one the new graduates are called up to receive their scrolls; and the ceremony closes with a formal procession of which Blanche, in her red robes, is part. Then she, Elizabeth, is free for a while to wander among the milling guests, listening in on their chatter.

That chatter turns out to be mainly about the inordinate length of the ceremony. It is only in the foyer that she hears specific mention of Blanche's address. A tall man with an ermine-trimmed gown over his arm is talking heatedly to a woman in black. 'Who does she think she is,' he is saying, 'using the occasion to lecture us! A missionary from the sticks in Zululand – what does she know about the humanities? And this hard Catholic line – what has happened to ecumenicism?'

She is a guest – a guest of the university, a guest of her sister's, a guest in the country too. If these people want to take umbrage, that is their right. It is not for her to get involved. Let Blanche fight her own battles.

But not getting involved turns out to be less easy than that. A formal luncheon has been scheduled, and she has been invited. When she takes her seat, she finds herself next to the same tall man, who has in the meantime got rid of his medieval costume. She has no appetite, there is a knot of nausea in her stomach, she would prefer to be back in her hotel room having a lie-down, but she makes an effort. 'Let me introduce myself,' she says. 'I am Elizabeth Costello. Sister Bridget is my sister. Sister by blood, I mean.'

Elizabeth Costello. She can see that the name means nothing to him. His own name is on the place card before him: Professor Peter Godwin.

'I presume you teach here,' she goes on, making conversation. 'What do you teach?'

'I teach literature, English literature.'

'It must have cut close to the bone, what my sister was saying. Well, don't mind her. She is a bit of a battleaxe, that's all. She likes a good fight.'

Blanche, Sister Bridget, the battleaxe, is sitting at the other end of the table, wrapped up in a conversation of her own. She cannot hear them.

'This is a secular age,' replies Godwin. 'You cannot turn back the clock. You cannot condemn an institution for moving with the times.'

'By an institution you mean the university?'

'Yes, universities, but specifically faculties of humanities, which remain the core of any university.'

The humanities the core of the university. She may be an outsider, but if she were asked to name the core of the university today, its core discipline, she would say it was moneymaking. That is how it looks from Melbourne, Victoria; and she would not be surprised if the same were the case in Johannesburg, South Africa.

'But was that really what my sister was saying: that you should turn back the clock? Wasn't she saying something more interesting, more challenging – that there has been something misconceived in the study of the humanities from the start? Something wrong with placing hopes and expectations on the humanities that they could never fulfil? I do not necessarily agree with her; but that was what I understood her to be arguing.'

'The proper study of mankind is man,' says Professor Godwin. 'And the nature of mankind is a fallen nature. Even your sister would agree with that. But that should not prevent us from trying – trying to improve. Your sister wants us to give up on man and go back to God. That is what I mean when I refer to turning back the clock. She wants to go back to before the Renaissance, before the humanist movement she spoke about, before even the relative enlightenment of the twelfth century. She wants us to plunge back into the Christian fatalism of what I would call the Low Middle Ages.'

'I would hesitate to say, knowing my sister, that there is anything fatalist about her. But you should speak to her yourself, put your point.'

Professor Godwin addresses himself to his salad. There is a silence. From across the table the woman in black, whom she takes to be Godwin's wife, gives her a smile. 'Did I hear you say your name is Elizabeth Costello?' she says. 'Not the writer Elizabeth Costello?'

'Yes, that is what I do for a living. I write.'

'And you are Sister Bridget's sister.'

'I am. But Sister Bridget has many sisters. I am merely a sister in blood. The others are truer sisters, sisters in spirit.'

She intends the remark lightly, but it seems to fluster Mrs Godwin. Maybe that is the reason why Blanche raises people's hackles here: she uses words like *spirit* and *God* inappropriately, in places where they do not belong. Well, she is not a believer, but in this case she thinks she will stand with Blanche.

Mrs Godwin is speaking to her husband, flashing him looks. 'Elizabeth Costello the writer, dear,' she is saying.

'Oh yes,' says Professor Godwin; but clearly the name rings no bell.

'My husband is in the eighteenth century,' says Mrs Godwin.

'Ah yes. A good place to be. The Age of Reason.'

'I do not believe we see the period in quite so uncomplicated a way nowadays,' says Professor Godwin. He seems to be about to say more, but then does not.

Conversation with the Godwins is clearly flagging. She turns to the person on her right, but he is deeply engaged elsewhere.

'When I was a student,' she says, turning back to the Godwins, 'which would have been around 1950, we read a lot of D. H. Lawrence. Of course we read the classics too, but that was not where our real energy went. D. H. Lawrence, T. S. Eliot – those were the writers we pored over. Perhaps Blake in the eighteenth century. Perhaps Shakespeare, because as we all know Shakespeare transcends his time. Lawrence gripped us because he promised a form of salvation. If we worshipped the dark gods, he told us, and carried out their observances, we would be saved. We believed him. We went out and worshipped the dark gods as best we were able, from the hints that Mr Lawrence let drop. Well, our worship did not save us. A false prophet, I would call him now, in retrospect.

'What I mean to say is that in our truest reading, as students, we searched the page for guidance, guidance in perplexity. We found it in Lawrence, or we found it in Eliot, the early Eliot: a different kind of guidance, perhaps, but guidance nevertheless in how to live our lives. The rest of our reading, by comparison, was just a matter of mugging things up so that we could pass exams.

'If the humanities want to survive, surely it is those energies and that craving for guidance that they must respond to: a craving that is, in the end, a quest for salvation.'

She has spoken a great deal, more than she meant to. In fact, in the silence that now falls, she sees that others have been listening in. Even her sister is turned towards her.

'We did not realize,' says the Dean loudly from the head of the table, 'when Sister Bridget asked us to invite you to this happy event, that it was *the* Elizabeth Costello we would have in our midst. Welcome. We are delighted to have you.'

'Thank you,' she says.

'I could not help catching some of what you were saying,' the Dean continues. 'Do you then agree with your sister that the outlook for the humanities is dark?'

She must be careful how she treads. 'I was merely saying,' she says, 'that our readers – our young readers in particular – come to us with a certain hunger, and if we cannot or will not satisfy their hunger then we must not be surprised if they turn away from us. But my sister and I are in different lines of business. She has told you what she thinks. For my own part, I would say that it is enough for books to teach us about ourselves. Any reader ought to be content with that. Or almost any reader.'

They are watching her sister to see how she reacts. Teaching us about ourselves: what else is that but *studium humanitatis*?

'Is this just a conversation over luncheon,' says Sister Bridget, 'or are we being serious?'

'We are being serious,' says the Dean. 'We are serious.'

Perhaps she should revise her opinion of him. Perhaps not just another academic bureaucrat going through his hostly motions, but a soul with the hungers of a soul. Grant that possibility. In fact, perhaps that is what all of them are around this table, in their deepest being: hungering souls. She should not rush to judgement. If nothing else, these people are not stupid. And they must by now have realized that in Sister Bridget, whether they like her or not, they have someone out of the ordinary.

'I do not need to consult novels,' says her sister, 'to know what pettiness, what baseness, what cruelty human beings are capable of. That is where we start, all of us. We are fallen creatures. If the study of mankind amounts to no more than picturing to us our darker potential, I have better things to spend my time on. If on the other hand the study of mankind is to be a study in what reborn man can be, that is a different story. However, you have had enough lecturing for one day.'

'But,' says the young man seated next to Mrs Godwin, 'surely that is precisely what humanism stood for, and the Renaissance too: for humankind as humankind is capable of being. For the ascent of man. The humanists were not crypto-atheists. They were not even Lutherans in disguise. They were Catholic Christians like yourself, Sister. Think of Lorenzo Valla. Valla had nothing against the Church, he just happened to know Greek better than Jerome did, and pointed out some of the mistakes Jerome made in translating the New

Testament. If the Church had accepted the principle that Jerome's Vulgate was a human production, and therefore capable of being improved, rather than being the word of God itself, perhaps the whole history of the West would have been different.'

Blanche is silent. The speaker presses on.

'If the Church as a whole had been able to acknowledge that its teachings and its whole system of beliefs were based on texts, and that those texts were susceptible on the one hand to scribal corruption and so forth, on the other to flaws of translation, because translation is always an imperfect process, and if the Church had also been able to concede that the interpretation of texts is a complex matter, vastly complex, instead of claiming for itself a monopoly of interpretation, then we would not be having this argument today.'

'But,' says the Dean, 'how have we come to know how vastly difficult the business of interpretation can be except by experiencing certain lessons of history, lessons that the Church of the fifteenth century could hardly have foreseen?'

'Such as?'

'Such as contact with hundreds of other cultures, each with its own language and history and mythology and unique way of seeing the world.'

'Then my point would be,' says the young man, 'that it is the humanities and the humanities alone, and the training that the humanities provide, that will allow us to steer our way through this new multicultural world, and precisely, precisely' – he almost hammers the table, so excited has he grown – 'because the humanities are about reading and interpretation. The humanities begin, as our lecturer said, in textual scholarship, and develop as a body of disciplines devoted to interpretation.'

'In fact, the human sciences,' says the Dean.

The young man pulls a face. 'That is a red herring, Mr Dean. If you don't mind, I will remain with either *studia* or disciplines.'

So young, she thinks, and so sure of himself. He will remain with *studia*.

'What about Winckelmann?' says her sister.

Winckelmann? The young man looks back at her uncomprehendingly.

'Would Winckelmann have recognized himself in the picture you paint of the humanist as a technician of textual interpretation?'

'I don't know. Winckelmann was a great scholar. Perhaps he would have.'

'Or Schelling,' pursues her sister. 'Or any of those who believed, more or less openly, that Greece provided a better civilizational ideal than Judaeo-Christianity. Or, for that matter, those who believed that mankind had lost its way and should go back to its primitive roots and make a fresh start. In other words, the anthropologists. Lorenzo Valla — since you mention Lorenzo Valla — was an anthropologist. His starting point was human society. You say the first humanists were not crypto-atheists. No, they were not. But they were crypto-relativists. Jesus, in their eyes, was embedded in his own world, or as we would call it today his own culture. It was their task as scholars to understand that world and interpret it to their times. Just as it would in due course become their task to interpret the world of Homer. And so on down to Winckelmann.'

She terminates abruptly, glances at the Dean. Has he perhaps given her some signal? Has he, unbelievably, beneath the table, tapped Sister Bridget on the knee?

'Yes,' says the Dean, 'fascinating. We should have brought you down for a whole lecture series, Sister. But unfortunately, some of us have engagements. Perhaps at some time in the future . . .' He leaves the possibility hanging in the air; graciously Sister Bridget inclines her head.

IV

They are back at the hotel. She is tired, she must take something for her continuing nausea, she must lie down. But the question still nags at her: why this hostility on Blanche's part towards the humanities? *I do not need to consult novels*, said Blanche. Is the hostility, in some tangled way, aimed at her? Though she has religiously sent Blanche her books as they have come off the press, she can see no sign that Blanche has read any of them. Has she been summoned to Africa as a representative of the humanities, or of the novel, or of both, to be taught a last lesson before they both descend into the grave? Is that really how Blanche sees her? The truth − and she ought to impress this on Blanche − is that she has never been an aficionado of the humanities. Something too complacently masculine about the whole enterprise, too self-regarding. She must set Blanche straight.

'Winckelmann,' she says to Blanche. 'What did you mean by bringing up Winckelmann?'

'I wanted to remind them of what the study of the classics would lead to. To Hellenism as an alternative religion. An alternative to Christianity.'

'That is what I thought. As an alternative for a few aesthetes, a few highly educated products of the European educational system. But surely not as a popular alternative.'

'You miss my point, Elizabeth. Hellenism was an alternative. Poor as it may have been, Hellas was the one alternative to the Christian vision that humanism was able to offer. To Greek society − an utterly

131

idealized picture of Greek society, but how were ordinary folk to know that? – they could point and say, *Behold, that is how we should live – not in the hereafter but in the here and now.*'

Hellas: half-naked men, their breasts gleaming with olive oil, sitting on the temple steps discoursing about the good and the true, while in the background lithe-limbed boys wrestle and a herd of goats contentedly grazes. Free minds in free bodies. More than an idealized picture: a dream, a delusion. But how else are we to live but by dreams?

'I do not disagree,' she says. 'But who believes in Hellenism any more? Who even remembers the word?'

'Still you miss the point. Hellenism was the sole vision of the good life that humanism was able to put forward. When Hellenism failed – which was inevitable, since it had nothing whatever to do with the lives of real people – humanism went bankrupt. That man at lunch was arguing for the humanities as a set of techniques, the human sciences. Dry as dust. What young man or woman with blood in their veins would want to spend their life scratching around in the archives or doing *explications de texte* without end?'

'But Hellenism was surely just a phase in the history of the humanities. Larger, more inclusive visions of what human life can be have emerged since then. The classless society, for instance. Or a world from which poverty, disease, illiteracy, racism, sexism, homophobia, xenophobia, and the rest of the bad litany have been exorcised. I am not putting in a plea for either of these visions. I am just pointing out that people cannot live without hope, or perhaps without illusions. If you turned to any of those people we had lunch with and asked them, as humanists or at least as card-carrying practitioners of the humanities, to state the goal of all their efforts, surely they would reply that, however indirectly, they strive to improve the lot of mankind.'

'Yes. And therein they reveal themselves as true followers of their humanist forebears. Who offered a secular vision of salvation. Rebirth without the intervention of Christ. By the workings of man alone. Renaissance. On the example of the Greeks. Or on the example of the American Indians. Or on the example of the Zulus. Well, it cannot be done.'

'It cannot done, you say. Because – though none of them were aware of it – the Greeks were damned, the Indians were damned, the Zulus were damned.'

'I said nothing about damnation. I am talking only about history, about the record of the humanist enterprise. It cannot be done. *Extra ecclesiam nulla salvatio.*'

She shakes her head. 'Blanche, Blanche, Blanche,' she says. 'Who would have thought you would end up such a hardliner.'

Blanche gives her a wintry smile. The light flashes on her glasses.

V

It is Saturday, her last full day in Africa. She is spending it at Marianhill, the station which her sister has made her life's work and her home. Tomorrow she will travel to Durban. From Durban she will fly to Bombay and then on to Melbourne. And that will be that. *We will not see each other again, Blanche and I*, she thinks, *not in this life.*

It was the graduation ceremony she came for, but what Blanche really wanted her to see, what lay behind the invitation, was the hospital. She knows that, yet she resists. It is not something she wants. She has not the stomach for it. She has seen it all on television, too often, till she cannot bear to look any more: the stick limbs, the bloated bellies, the great impassive eyes of children wasting away, beyond cure, beyond care. *Let this cup be taken from me!*

she pleads inwardly. *I am too old to withstand these sights, too old and weak. I will just cry.*

But in this case she cannot refuse, not when it is her own sister. And, in the event, it proves to be not too bad, not bad enough to break down over. The nursing staff is spick and span, the equipment is new – the fruit of Sister Bridget's fund-raising – and the atmosphere is relaxed, even happy. In the wards, mingling with the staff, are women in native dress. She takes them to be mothers or grandmothers until Blanche explains: they are healers, she says, traditional healers. Then she remembers: this is what Marianhill is famous for, this is Blanche's great innovation, to open the hospital to the people, to have native doctors work beside doctors of Western medicine.

As for the children, perhaps Blanche has tucked the worst cases away out of sight, but she is surprised at how gay even a dying child can be. It is as Blanche said in her book: with love and care and the right drugs, these innocents can be brought to the very gate of death without fear.

Blanche takes her to the chapel too. Entering the unpretentious brick and iron building, she is struck at once by the carved wooden crucifix behind the altar, showing an emaciated Christ with a mask-like face crowned with a wreath of real acacia thorns, his hands and feet pierced not by nails but by steel bolts. The figure itself is of near life size; the cross reaches up to the bare rafters; the whole construction dominates the chapel, overbears it.

The Christ was done by a local carver, Blanche tells her. Years ago the station adopted him, providing him with a workshop and paying him a monthly wage. Does she want to meet the man?

Which is why, now, this old man with the stained teeth and the overalls and the uncertain English, introduced to her simply as Joseph, is unlocking, for her benefit, the door of a shed in an outlying corner of the station. The grass is thick around the door, she notices: a long time since anyone was here.

Inside she has to brush away cobwebs. Joseph fumbles for the switch, clicks it up and down fruitlessly. 'Bulb is gone,' he says, but does nothing about it. The only light comes from the open door and from cracks between the roof and the walls. It takes a while for her eyes to adjust.

There is a long, makeshift table down the centre of the shed. Piled on the table, or against it, lie a jumble of wooden carvings. Against the walls, stacked on pallets, are lengths of wood, some with the bark still on, and dusty cardboard boxes.

'Is my workshop,' says Joseph. 'When I am young I work here all day. But now I am too old.'

She picks up a crucifix, not the largest, but large nevertheless: an eighteen-inch Christ on the cross, in a heavy reddish wood. 'What do you call this wood?'

'Is karee. Karee wood.'

'And you carved it?' She holds the crucifix out at arm's-length. As in the chapel, the face of the tortured man is a formalized, simplified mask in a single plane, the eyes slits, the mouth heavy and drooping. The body, on the other hand, is quite naturalistic, copied, she would guess, from some European model. The knees are raised, as if the man were trying to relieve the pain in his arms by putting his weight on the nail piercing his feet.

'I carve all the Jesus. The cross, sometimes my assistant make it. My assistants.'

'And where are your assistants now? Does no one work here any more?'

'No, my assistants all gone. Too many crosses. Too many crosses to sell.'

She peers into one of the boxes. Miniature crucifixes, three or

135

four inches high, like the one her sister wears, scores of them, all
with the same flat mask-face, the same raised-knee posture.

'Don't you carve anything else? Animals? Faces? Ordinary
people?'

Joseph pulls a face. 'Animals is just for tourists,' he says disdain-
fully.

'And you don't carve for tourists. You don't carve tourist art.'

'No, no tourist art.'

'Why do you carve then?'

'For Jesus,' he says. 'Yes. For Our Saviour.'

VI

'I saw Joseph's collection,' she says. 'A bit obsessive, wouldn't you
call it? Just the one image, over and over again.'

Blanche does not reply. They are having lunch, a lunch she
would under normal circumstances call exiguous: sliced tomato, a
few wilted lettuce leaves, a boiled egg. But she has no appetite.
She toys with the lettuce; the smell of the egg nauseates her.

'How does the economics of it work,' she continues – 'the
economics of religious art, in our day and age?'

'Joseph used to be a paid employee of Marianhill. Paid to do
his carvings, and some odd jobs as well. For the last eighteen months
he has been on pension. He has arthritis in his hands. You must
have noticed that.'

'But who buys those carvings of his?'

'We have two outlets in Durban that take them. Other missions
accept them as well, for resale. They may not be works of art by
Western standards but they are authentic. A few years ago Joseph did
a commission for the church at Ixopo. That put a couple of thousand rand in his pocket. We still get bulk orders for the small-size

crucifix. Schools, Catholic schools, buy them for prize-givings.'

'For prize-givings. You come top in Catechism and you get one of Joseph's crucifixes.'

'More or less. Is there anything wrong with that?'

'Nothing. Still, he has overproduced, hasn't he? There must be hundreds of pieces in that shed, all identical. Why didn't you get him to make something else besides crucifixes, crucifixions? What does it do to a person's — if I dare use the word — *soul* to spend his working life carving a man in agony over and over again? When he isn't doing odd jobs, that is.'

Blanche gives her a steely smile. 'A *man*, Elizabeth?' she says. 'A *man* in agony?'

'A man, a god, a man-god, don't make an issue of it, Blanche, we're not in theology class. What does it do to a man with gifts to spend his life as uncreatively as your Joseph has done? His gifts may be limited, he may not be an artist properly speaking; still, might it not have been wiser to encourage him to expand his horizon a little?'

Blanche sets down her knife and fork. 'All right, let us face the criticism you make, let us face it in its most extreme form. Joseph is not an artist but he might perhaps have become one if we — if I — had encouraged him, years ago, to extend his range by visiting art galleries or at least other carvers to see what else was being done. Instead Joseph remained — Joseph was kept at the level of — a craftsman. He lived here at the mission, in total obscurity, doing the same carving over and over again in different sizes and different woods, until arthritis struck him and his working life was over. So Joseph was prevented from, as you put it, expanding his horizon. He was denied a fuller life, specifically an artist's life. Does that cover your charge?'

'More or less. Not necessarily an artist's life, I would not be so foolish as to recommend that, just a fuller life.'

'Right. If that is your charge, I will give you my reply. Joseph spent thirty years of his earthly existence representing, for the eyes of others certainly but principally for his own eyes, Our Saviour in his agony. Hour after hour, day after day, year after year, he imagined that agony and, with a fidelity you can behold for yourself, reproduced it, to the best of his ability, without varying it, without importing new fashions into it, without injecting into it any of his own personality. Which of us, I now ask, will Jesus be most gladdened to welcome into his kingdom: Joseph, with his wasted hands, or you, or me?'

She does not like it when her sister gets on her high horse and preaches. It happened during her speech in Johannesburg and it is happening again. All that is most intolerant in Blanche's character emerges at such times: intolerant and rigid and bullying.

'I think Jesus would be gladder still,' she says as drily as she is able, 'if he knew that Joseph had had some choice. That Joseph had not been dragooned into piety.'

'Go out. Go and ask Joseph. Ask him whether he has been dragooned into anything.' Blanche pauses. 'Do you think Joseph is just a puppet in my hands, Elizabeth? Do you think Joseph has no comprehension of how he has spent his life? Go and speak to him. Listen to what he has to say.'

'I will. But I have another question, one that Joseph cannot answer because it is a question to you. Why does the model you, or if not you then the institution you represent – why does the specific model you set before Joseph and tell him to copy, to imitate, have to be what I can only call Gothic? Why a Christ dying in contortions rather than a living Christ? A man in his prime, in his early thirties: what do you have against showing him alive, in all his living beauty? And, while I am about it, what do you have against the Greeks? The Greeks would never have made statues and paintings of a man in the extremes of agony, deformed, ugly, and then knelt before those statues and worshipped them. If you wonder why the humanists whom you wish us to sneer at looked beyond Christianity and the contempt that Christianity exhibits for the human body and therefore for man himself, surely that ought to give you a clue. You ought to know, you cannot have forgotten, that representations of Jesus in his agony are an idio-syncrasy of the Western Church. They were entirely foreign to Constantinople. The Eastern Church would have regarded them as indecent, and quite right too.

'Frankly, Blanche, there is something about the entire crucifix-ional tradition that strikes me as mean, as backward, as medieval in the worst sense – unwashed monks, illiterate priests, cowed peas-ants. What are you up to, reproducing that most squalid, most stag-nant phase of European history in Africa?'

'Holbein,' says Blanche. 'Grünewald. If you want the human form *in extremis*, go to them. The dead Jesus. Jesus in the tomb.'

'I don't see what you are getting at.'

'Holbein and Grünewald were not artists of the Catholic Middle Ages. They belonged to the Reformation.'

'This is not a quarrel I am conducting with the historical Catholic Church, Blanche. I am asking what you, you yourself, have against beauty. Why should people not be able to look at a work of art and think to themselves, *That is what we as a species are capable of being, that is what I am capable of being*, rather than look-ing at it and thinking to themselves, *My God, I am going to die, I am going to be eaten by worms?*'

'Hence the Greeks, I suppose you want to say. The Apollo Belvedere. The Venus of Milo.'

'Yes, hence the Greeks. Hence my question: What are you doing, importing into Africa, importing into Zululand, for God's sake, this utterly alien, *Gothic* obsession with the ugliness and mortality of the human body? If you have to import Europe into Africa, is there not a better case for importing the Greeks?'

'Do you think, Elizabeth, that the Greeks are utterly foreign to Zululand? I tell you again, if you will not listen to me, at least have the decency to listen to Joseph. Do you think that Joseph carves suffering Jesus because he does not know better, that if you took Joseph on a tour around the Louvre his eyes would be opened and he would set about carving, for the benefit of his people, naked women preening themselves, or men flexing their muscles? Are you aware that when Europeans first came in contact with the Zulus, educated Europeans, men from England with public-school educations behind them, they thought they had rediscovered the Greeks? They said so quite explicitly. They took out their sketch blocks and drew sketches in which Zulu warriors with their spears and their clubs and their shields are shown in exactly the same attitudes, with exactly the same physical proportions, as the Hectors and Achilles we see in nineteenth-century illustrations of the *Iliad*, except that their skins are dusky. Well-formed limbs, skimpy clothes, a proud bearing, formal manners, martial virtues – it was all here! Sparta in Africa: that is what they thought they had found. For decades those same ex-public schoolboys, with their romantic idea of Greek antiquity, administered Zululand on behalf of the Crown. They *wanted* Zululand to be Sparta. They *wanted* the Zulus to be Greeks. So to Joseph and his father and his grandfather the Greeks are not a remote foreign tribe at all. They were offered the Greeks, by their new rulers, as a model of the kind of people they ought to be and could be. They were offered the Greeks and they rejected them. Instead, they looked elsewhere in the Mediterranean world. They chose to be Christians, followers of the living Christ. Joseph has *chosen* Jesus as his model. Speak to him. He will tell you.'

'That is not a byway of history I am familiar with, Blanche – Britons and Zulus. I cannot dispute with you.'

'It is not just in Zululand that it happened. It happened in Australia too. It happened all over the colonized world, just not in so neat a form. Those young fellows from Oxford and Cambridge and St Cyr offered their new barbarian subjects a false ideal. *Throw away your idols*, they said. *You can be as gods. Look at the Greeks*, they said. And indeed, who can tell gods from men in Greece, the romantic Greece of those young men, heirs of the humanists? *Come to our schools*, they said, *and we will teach you how. We will make you disciples of reason and the sciences that flow from reason; we will make you masters of nature. Through us you will overcome disease and all corruption of the flesh. You will live for ever.*

'Well, the Zulus knew better.' She waves a hand towards the window, towards the hospital buildings baking under the sun, towards the dirt road winding up into the barren hills. 'This is reality: the reality of Zululand, the reality of Africa. It is the reality now and the reality of the future as far as we can see it. Which is why African people come to church to kneel before Jesus on the cross, African women above all, who have to bear the brunt of reality. Because they suffer and he suffers with them.'

'Not because he promises them another, better life after death?'

Blanche shakes her head. 'No. To the people who come to Marianhill I promise nothing except that we will help them bear their cross.'

VII

Eight thirty on Sunday morning, but the sun is already fierce. At noon the driver will come to take her to Durban and the flight home.

141

Two young girls in gaudy dresses, barefoot, race to the bell rope and begin tugging it. Atop its post the bell jangles spasmodically.

'Will you be coming?' says Blanche.

'Yes, I will be there. Do I need to cover my head?'

'Come as you are. There are no formalities here. But be warned: we are having a visit from a television crew.'

'Television?'

'From Sweden. They are making a film about Aids in KwaZulu.'

'And the priest? Has the priest been told the service is being filmed? Who is the priest anyhow?'

'Father Msimungu from Dalehill will be taking Mass. He has no objection.'

Father Msimungu, when he arrives in a still quite smart Golf, is young, gangly, bespectacled. He goes off to the dispensary to be robed; she joins Blanche and the other half-dozen sisters of the Order at the front of the congregation. The camera lights are already in place and trained on them. In their cruel glare she cannot fail to see how old they all are. The Sisters of Mary: a dying breed, an exhausted vocation.

Under its metal roof the chapel is already stiflingly hot. She does not know how Blanche, in her heavy outfit, bears it.

The Mass Msimungu leads is in Zulu, though here and there she is able to pick out a word of English. It starts sedately enough; but by the time of the first collect there is already a humming among the flock. Launching into his homily, Msimungu has to raise his voice to make himself heard. A baritone voice, surprising in so young a man. It seems to come from effortlessly deep in the chest.

Msimungu turns, kneels before the altar. A silence falls. Above him looms the crowned head of the tortured Christ. Then he turns and holds up the Host. There is a joyous shout from the body of

142

worshippers. A rhythmic stamping commences that makes the wooden floor vibrate.

She feels herself swaying. The air is thick with the smell of sweat. She clasps Blanche's arm. 'I must get out!' she whispers. Blanche casts an appraising glance. 'Just a little while longer,' she whispers back, and turns away.

She takes a deep breath, trying to clear her head, but it does not help. A wave of cold seems to ascend from her toes. It rises to her face, her scalp prickles with the chill, and she is gone.

She wakes flat on her back up in a bare room she does not recognize. Blanche is there, gazing down on her, and a young woman in a white uniform. 'I am so sorry,' she mumbles, struggling to sit up. 'Did I faint?'

The young woman puts a reassuring hand on her shoulder. 'It is all right,' she says. 'But you must rest.'

She casts her eyes up at Blanche. 'I am so sorry,' she repeats. 'Too many continents.'

Blanche regards her quizzically.

'Too many continents,' she repeats. 'Too many burdens.' Her voice sounds thin to her ears, far away. 'I haven't been eating properly,' she says. 'That must be the explanation.'

But is that the explanation? Is a two-day stomach upset enough to cause a faint? Blanche would know. Blanche must have experience of fasting, of fainting. For her own part, she suspects her indisposition is not just of a bodily order. If she were so disposed, she might be welcoming these experiences on a new continent, making something of them. But she is not so disposed. That is what her body is saying, in its own way. All too strange and too much, her body is complaining: I want to be back in my old surroundings, in a life I am familiar with.

Withdrawal: that is what she is suffering from. Fainting: a

withdrawal symptom. It reminds her of someone. Of whom? Of that pale English girl in *A Passage to India*, the one who cannot take it, who panics and shames everyone. Who cannot take the heat.

VIII

The driver is waiting. She is packed and ready, still feeling a little pale, a little wobbly. 'Goodbye,' she says to Blanche. 'Goodbye, Sister Blanche. I see what you meant. Nothing like St Patrick's on a Sunday morning. I hope they didn't capture me on film, keeling over like that.'

Blanche smiles. 'If they did, I'll ask them to chop it out.' There is a pause between the two of them. She thinks: *Perhaps now she will say why she has brought me here.*

'Elizabeth,' says Blanche (is there something new in her tone, something softer, or is she just imagining it?), 'remember it is their gospel, their Christ. It is what they have made of him, they, the ordinary people. What they have made of him and what he has let them make of him. Out of love. And not just in Africa. You will see scenes just like that repeated in Brazil, in the Philippines, even in Russia. Ordinary people do not want the Greeks. They do not want the realm of pure forms. They do not want marble statues. They want someone who suffers like them. Like them and for them.'

Jesus. The Greeks. It is not what she expected, not what she wanted, not at this last minute when they are saying goodbye for perhaps the last time. Something unrelenting about Blanche. Unto death. She should have learned her lesson. Sisters never let go of each other. Unlike men, who let go all too easily. Locked to the end in Blanche's embrace.

144

'So: Thou hast triumphed, O pale Galilean,' she says, not trying to hide the bitterness in her voice. 'Is that what you want to hear me say, Blanche?'

'More or less. You backed a loser, my dear. If you had put your money on a different Greek you might still have stood a chance. Orpheus instead of Apollo. The ecstatic instead of the rational. Someone who changes form, changes colour, according to his surroundings. Someone who can die but then come back. A chameleon. A phoenix. Someone who appeals to women. Because it is women who live closest to the ground. Someone who moves among the people, whom they can touch – put their hand into the side of, feel the wound, smell the blood. But you didn't, and you lost. You went for the wrong Greeks, Elizabeth.'

IX

A month has passed. She is at home, settled back into her own life, the African venture behind her. Of the reunion with Blanche she has made nothing yet, though the memory of their unsisterly parting nags at her.

'There is a story I want to tell you,' she writes, 'about Mother.'

She is writing to herself, that is, to whoever is with her in the room when she is the only one there; but the words will not come, she knows, unless she thinks of this writing as a letter to Blanche.

During her first year at Oakgrove, Mother made friends with a man named Phillips, who was also a resident there. I mentioned him to you, but you probably don't remember. He had a car; they used to go out together, to the theatre, to concerts; they were a couple, in a civilized kind of way. 'Mr Phillips', Mother called him from beginning to end, and

I took that as a cue not to assume too much. Then Mr Phillips's health gave in, and that was the end of their gallivanting.

When I first met him, Mr P was still quite a spry old fellow, with his pipe and his blazer and cravat and his David Niven moustache. He had been a lawyer, quite a successful one. He took care of his appearance, had hobbies, read books; there was still life in him, as Mother put it.

One of his hobbies was painting in watercolours. I saw some of his work. His human figures were wooden, but he had a feel for landscape, for the bush, that was genuine, I thought. A feel for light and what distance did to light.

He did a painting of Mother in her blue organdie outfit, with a silk scarf floating behind her. Not wholly successful as a portrait, but I kept it, I still have it somewhere.

I sat for him too. This was after he had had surgery and was confined to his rooms, or at any rate chose not to come out. Sitting for him was Mother's idea. 'See if you can take him out of himself a bit,' she said. 'I can't. He spends all day alone, brooding.'

Mr Phillips kept to himself because he had had an operation, a laryngectomy. It left him with a hole through which he was supposed to speak, with the aid of a prosthesis. But he was ashamed of the unsightly, raw-looking hole in his throat, and therefore withdrew from public sight. He could not speak anyhow, not understandably – he never bothered to learn the correct breathing. At best he could produce a kind of croaking. It must have been deeply humiliating for such a ladies' man.

He and I negotiated by note, and the upshot was that on a series of Saturday afternoons I sat for him. His hand was a little trembly by then, he could only manage an hour at a time, the cancer was getting to him in more ways than one.

He had one of the better apartments at Oakgrove, on the ground floor, with French doors leading on to the garden. For my portrait I sat by the garden door in a stiff-backed, carved chair wearing a wrap I had picked up in Jakarta, hand-stencilled in ochre and maroon. I don't know that it flattered me particularly, but I thought as a painter he would enjoy the colours, they would give him something to play with.

One Saturday – patience, I am getting to the point – a lovely warm day with the pigeons purring in the trees, he put down his brush and shook his head and said something in his croak that I did not catch. 'Didn't hear that, Aidan,' I said. 'Not working,' he repeated. And then he wrote something on his pad and brought it over to me. 'Wish I could paint you in the nude,' he had written. And then, below: 'Would have loved that.'

It must have cost him something to come out with it. *Would have loved*, past hypothetical. But just what did he mean? Conceivably he meant *I would have loved to have painted you when you were still young*, but I don't think so. *I would have loved to have painted you when I was still a man*: that is more like it. As he showed me the words I saw his lip quiver. I know one should not put too much store on trembling lips and watering eyes in old people, but still . . .

I smiled and tried to reassure him and took up my pose again, and he went back to his easel, and all was as before, except that I could see he was not painting any more, just standing there with the brush drying in his hand. So I thought – at last I come to the point – I thought, *What the hell*, and I loosened the wrap and shrugged it off my shoulders and took off my brassiere and hung it on the back of the chair and said, 'How's that, Aidan?'

I paint with my penis – didn't Renoir say that, Renoir of the plump, creamy-skinned ladies? *Avec ma verge*, feminine noun. Well, I thought to myself, let's see if we can wake Mr Phillips's *verge* out of its deep sleep. And I gave him my profile again, while the pigeons went on in the trees as if nothing were happening.

Whether it worked, whether the spectacle of me in the seminude rekindled anything in him, I cannot say. But I could feel the full weight of his gaze on me, on my breasts, and, frankly, it was good. I was forty then, I had two children behind me, they were not the breasts of a young woman, but it was good nevertheless, I thought so and think so still, in that place of withering away and dying. A blessing.

Then after a while, as the shadows in the garden lengthened and it grew cool, I made myself decent again. 'Goodbye, Aidan, God bless,' I said; and he wrote 'Thank you' on his pad and showed it to me, and that was that. I do not think he expected me to come back the next Saturday, and I did not. Whether he finished the painting by himself I don't know. Perhaps he destroyed it. He certainly did not show it to Mother.

Why am I telling you this story, Blanche? Because I connect it with the conversation you and I had at Marianhill about the Zulus and the Greeks and the true nature of the humanities. I do not want to give up on our dispute yet; I do not want to vacate the field.

The episode I am telling you about, the passage in Mr Phillips's living room, so minor in itself, has puzzled me for years; it is only now, after getting back from Africa, that I think I can explain it.

148

Of course there was an element of triumph in the way I behaved, an element of boasting, of which I am not proud: the potent woman teasing the waning man, showing her body off yet keeping him at a distance. *Cock-teasing* – do you remember cock-teasing from the old days?

But there was more to it than that. It was so out of character for me. Where did I get the idea, I kept wondering? Where did I learn that pose, gazing calmly into the distance with my robe hanging about my waist like a cloud and my divine body on show? *From the Greeks*, I now realize, Blanche: from the Greeks and from what generations of Renaissance painters made of the Greeks. As I sat there I was not myself, or not just myself. Through me a goddess was manifesting herself, Aphrodite or Hera or perhaps even Artemis. I was of the immortals.

And that is not the end of it. I used the word *blessing* a moment ago. Why? Because what was going on revolved around my breasts, that I was sure of, around breasts and breast-milk. Whatever else they did, those antique Grecian goddesses did not exude, whereas I was exuding, figuratively speaking: I was exuding into Mr Phillips's room, I felt it and I would bet he felt it too, long after I had taken my leave.

The Greeks do not exude. The one who exudes is Mary of Nazareth. Not the shy virgin of the Annunciation but the mother we see in Correggio, the one who delicately raises her nipple with her fingertips so that her baby can suck; who, secure in her virtue, boldly uncovers herself under the painter's gaze and thence under our gaze.

Imagine the scene in Correggio's studio that day, Blanche. With his brush the man points: 'Lift it up, so. No, not with the hand, just with two fingers.' He crosses the floor, shows her. 'So.' And the woman obeys, doing with her body as he commands. Other men watching all the while from the shadows: apprentices, fellow painters, visitors.

Who knows who she was, his model that day: a woman from the streets? the wife of a patron? The atmosphere in the studio electric, but with what? Erotic energy? The penises of all those men, their *verges*, tingling? Undoubtedly. Yet something else in the air too. Worship. The brush pauses as they worship the mystery that is manifested to them: from the body of the woman, life flowing in a stream.

Does Zululand have anything to match that moment, Blanche? I doubt it. Not that heady mix of the ecstatic and the aesthetic. It happens only once in the history of mankind, in Renaissance Italy, when immemorial Christian images and observances are invaded by the humanists' dream of antique Greece.

In all our talk about humanism and the humanities there was a word we both skirted: *humanity*. When Mary blessed among women smiles her remote angelic smile and tips her sweet pink nipple up before our gaze, when I, imitating her, uncover my breasts for old Mr Phillips, we perform acts of humanity. Acts like that are not available to animals, who cannot uncover themselves because they do not cover themselves. Nothing compels us to do it, Mary or me. But out of the overflow, the outflow of our human hearts we do it nevertheless: drop our robes, reveal ourselves, reveal the life and beauty we are blessed with.

Beauty. Surely from Zululand, where you have such an abundance of unclothed bodies to gaze on, you must concede, Blanche, that there is nothing more humanly beautiful than a woman's breasts. Nothing more humanly beautiful, nothing more humanly mysterious than why men should want to caress, over and over again, with paintbrush or chisel or hand, these oddly curved fatty sacs, and nothing more humanly endearing than our complicity (I mean the complicity of women) in their obsession.

The humanities teach us humanity. After the centuries-long Christian night, the humanities give us back our beauty, our human beauty. That was what you forgot to say. That is what the Greeks teach us, Blanche, the right Greeks. Think about it.

Your sister,
Elizabeth

That is what she writes. What she does not write, what she has no intention of writing, is how the story proceeds, the story of Mr Phillips and their Saturday-afternoon sittings at the old folks' home.

For the story does not end as she said, with her covering herself decently and Mr Phillips writing his thank-you note and her quitting his rooms. No, the story picks up again a month later, when her mother mentions that Mr Phillips has been to hospital for another dose of radiation and has come back in a bad way, very low, very despondent. Why doesn't she look in on him, try to cheer him up?

She knocks at his door, waits a moment, enters.

No mistaking the signs. Not a spry old fellow any longer, just an old fellow, an old bag of bones waiting to be carted away. Flat on his back with his arms spread out, his hands slack, hands that have in the space of a month become so blue and knobbly that you wonder they were ever fit to hold a brush. Not sleeping, just lying, waiting. Listening too, no doubt, to the sounds inside, the sounds of the pain. (*Let us not forget that, Blanche,* she thinks to herself: *let us not forget the pain. The terrors of death not enough: on top of them the pain, crescendo. As a way of putting to a close our visit to this world, what could be more ingeniously, more devilishly cruel?*)

She stands at the old man's bedside; she takes his hand. Though there is nothing pleasant in folding that cold, blue hand in her own, she does it. Nothing pleasant in any of this. She holds the hand and squeezes it and says 'Aidan!' in her most affectionate voice and watches the tears well up, the old-folks' tears that do not count for much because they come too easily. Nothing more for her to say and nothing, certainly, for him to say through the hole in his throat, now decently covered with a wad of gauze. She stands there stroking his hand until Nurse Naidoo comes around with the tea trolley and the pills; then she helps him to sit up to drink (out of a cup with a spout, like a two-year-old, the humiliations have no limit).

The next Saturday she visits him again, and the next; it becomes a new routine. She holds his hand and tries to comfort him while marking with a cold eye the stages of his decline. The visits take place with a minimum of words. But there is one Saturday when, a little more chipper than usual, a little more spry, he pushes the pad towards her and she reads the message he has spelled out beforehand: 'A lovely bosom you have. I'll never forget. Thank you for everything, kind Elizabeth.'

She returns the pad to him. What is there to say? *Take leave of what thou hast loved.*

With crude, bony strength he tears the page from the pad, crumples it and drops it in the basket, and raises a finger to his lips as if to say, *Our secret.*

What the hell, she thinks to herself a second time. She crosses to the door and turns the latch. In the little alcove where he hangs his clothes she removes her dress, her brassiere. Then she crosses back to the bed, sits down side-on where he can get a good eyeful, and resumes the pose of the painting. *A treat*, she thinks: *let's give the old boy a treat, let's brighten up his Saturday.*

There are other things she thinks too, as she sits on Mr Phillips's bed in the cool of the afternoon (no longer summer now but autumn, late autumn), such cool that after a while she has even begun to shiver lightly. *Consenting adults*: that is one of the things she thinks. *What consenting adults get up to behind closed doors is no one's business but their own.*

That would be another good place to end the story. Whatever the true nature of this so-called treat, it does not need to be repeated. Next Saturday, if he is still alive, if she is still alive, she will come by and hold his hand again; but this must be the last of the posing, the last of the bosom-offering, the last of the blessing. After this the breasts must be closed up, maybe closed up for good. So it could end here, with this pose held for a good twenty minutes, she would estimate, despite the shivers. As a story, a recital, it could end here and still be decent enough to put in an envelope and send to Blanche without ruining whatever it was that she wanted to say about the Greeks.

But in fact it goes on a little longer, by five or ten minutes, and this is the part she cannot tell Blanche. It goes on long enough for her, the woman, to drop a hand casually on to the bedcover and begin to stroke, ever so gently, the place where the penis, if the penis were alive and awake, ought to be; and then, when there is no response, to put the covers aside and loosen the cord of Mr Phillips's pyjamas, old-man's flannel pyjamas such as she has not seen in years – she would not have guessed one could still find them in shops – and open up the front and plant a kiss on the entirely flaccid little thing, and take it in her mouth and mumble

153

it until it stirs faintly with life. It is the first time she has seen pubic hair that has turned grey. Stupid of her not to have realized that happens. It will happen to her too, in due course. Nor is the smell pleasant either, the smell of an old man's nether parts, cursorily washed.

Less than ideal, she thinks, withdrawing and covering old Mr Phillips up and giving him a smile and patting his hand. The ideal would be to send in a young beauty to do it for him, a *fille de joie* with the plump new breasts old men dream about. About paying for the visit she would have no qualms. A birthday present, she could call it, if the girl wanted an explanation, if *going-away present* were too chilling a name. But then, once you are past a certain age everything is less than ideal; Mr Phillips might as well get used to that. Only the gods are for ever young, the inhuman gods. The gods and the Greeks.

As for her, Elizabeth, crouched over the old bag of bones with her breasts dangling, working away on his nearly extinct organ of generation, what name would the Greeks give to such a spectacle? Not *eros*, certainly – too grotesque for that. *Agape*? Again, perhaps not. Does that mean the Greeks would have no word for it? Would one have to wait for the Christians to come along with the right word: *caritas*?

For that, in the end, is what she is convinced it is. From the swelling of her heart she knows it, from the utter, illimitable difference between what is in her heart and what Nurse Naidoo would see, if by some mischance Nurse Naidoo, using her pass key, were to fling open the door and stride in.

That is not what is uppermost in her mind, however – what Nurse Naidoo would make of it, what the Greeks would make of it, what her mother on the next floor up would make of it. What is uppermost is what she herself will make it of, in the car on the way home, or when she wakes up tomorrow morning, or in a year's time. What can one make of episodes like this, unforeseen, unplanned, out of character? Are they just holes, holes in the heart, into which one steps and falls and then goes on falling?

Blanche, dear Blanche, she thinks, *why is there this bar between us? Why can we not speak to each other straight and bare, as people ought who are on the brink of passing? Mother gone; old Mr Phillips burned to a powder and scattered to the winds; of the world we grew up in, just you and I left. Sister of my youth, do not die in a foreign field and leave me without an answer!*

6
The Problem of Evil

SHE HAS BEEN invited to speak at a conference in Amsterdam, a conference on the age-old problem of evil: why there is evil in the world, what if anything can be done about it.

She can make a shrewd guess why the organizers picked on her: because of a talk she gave last year at a college in the United States, a talk for which she was attacked in the pages of *Commentary* (belittling the Holocaust, that was the charge) and defended by people whose support for the most part embarrassed her: covert anti-Semites, animal-rights sentimentalists.

She had spoken on that occasion on what she saw and still sees as the enslavement of whole animal populations. A slave: a being whose life and death are in the hands of another. What else are cattle, sheep, poultry? The death camps would not have been dreamed up without the example of the meat-processing plants before them.

That and more she had said: it had seemed to her obvious, barely worth pausing over. But she had gone a step further, a step too far. The massacre of the defenceless is being repeated all around us, day after day, she had said, a slaughter no different in scale or horror or moral import from what we call *the* holocaust; yet we choose not to see it.

Of equal moral import: that they had baulked at. There had

been a protest by students from the Hillel Centre. Appleton College should as an institution distance itself from her utterances, they demanded. In fact, the college should go further and apologize for having offered her a platform.

Back home the newspapers had picked up the story with glee. The *Age* ran a report under the headline PRIZE-WINNING NOVEL-IST ACCUSED OF ANTI-SEMITISM and reprinted the offending paragraphs from her talk, riddled with faulty punctuation. The phone started to ring at all hours: journalists, for the most part, but strangers too, including a nameless woman who shouted down the line, 'You Fascist bitch!' After that she stopped answering the phone. It was she, all at once, who was on trial.

It was an entanglement she might have foreseen and should have avoided. So what is she doing on the lecture platform again? If she had any sense she would keep out of the limelight. She is old, she feels tired all the time, she has lost what appetite she ever had for disputation, and anyhow what hope is there that the problem of evil, if *problem* is indeed the right word for evil, big enough to contain it, will be solved by more talk?

But at the time the invitation came she was under the malign spell of a novel she was reading. The novel was about depravity of the worst kind, and it had sucked her into a mood of bottomless dejection. *Why are you doing this to me?* she wanted to cry out as she read, to God knows whom. The same day there arrived the letter of invitation. Would Elizabeth Costello, the esteemed writer, grace a gathering of theologians and philosophers with her presence, speaking, if she so pleases, under the general rubric 'Silence, Complicity and Guilt'?

The book she was reading that day was by Paul West, an Englishman, but one who seemed to have freed himself of the more petty concerns of the English novel. His book was about

Hitler and Hitler's would-be assassins in the *Wehrmacht*, and all was going well enough until she came to the chapters describing the execution of the plotters. Where could West have got his information? Could there really have been witnesses who went home that night and, before they forgot, before memory, to save itself, went blank, wrote down, in words that must have scorched the page, an account of what they had seen, down to the words the hangman spoke to the souls consigned to his hands, fumbling old men for the most part, stripped of their uniforms, togged out for the final event in prison cast-offs, serge trousers caked with grime, pullovers full of moth-holes, no shoes, no belts, their false teeth and their glasses taken from them, exhausted, shivering, hands in their pockets to hold up their pants, whimpering with fear, swallowing their tears, having to listen to this coarse creature, this butcher with last week's blood caked under his fingernails, taunt them, telling them what would happen when the rope snapped tight, how the shit would run down their spindly old-man's legs, how their limp old-man's penises would quiver one last time? One after the other to the scaffold they went, in a nondescript space that could have been a garage or equally well an abattoir, under carbon-arc lights so that back in his lair in the forest Adolf Hitler, commander-in-chief, would be able to watch on film their sobbings and then their writhings and then their stillness, the slack stillness of dead meat, and be satisfied he had had his revenge.

That is what Paul West, novelist, had written about, page after page after page, leaving nothing out; and that is what she read, sick with the spectacle, sick with herself, sick with a world in which such things took place, until at last she pushed the book away and sat with her head in her hands. *Obscene!* she wanted to cry but did not cry because she did not know at whom the word should be flung: at herself, at West, at the committee of angels that watches impassively over all that passes. Obscene because such things ought not to take place, and then obscene again because having taken place they ought not to be brought into the light but covered up and hidden for ever in the bowels of the earth, like what goes on in the slaughterhouses of the world, if one wishes to save one's sanity.

The letter of invitation came while the obscene touch of West's book was still rank upon her. And that, in short, is why she is here in Amsterdam, with the word *obscene* still welling up in her throat. Obscene: not just the deeds of Hitler's executioners, not just the deeds of the blockman, but the pages of Paul West's black book too. Scenes that do not belong in the light of day, that the eyes of maidens and children deserve to be shielded from.

How will Amsterdam react to Elizabeth Costello in her present state? Does the sturdy Calvinist word *evil* still have any power among these sensible, pragmatic, well-adjusted citizens of the New Europe? Over half a century since the devil last swaggered brazenly through their streets, yet surely they cannot have forgotten. Adolf and his cohorts still grip the popular imagination. A curious fact, considering that Koba the Bear, his older brother and mentor, by any measure more murderous, more vile, more appalling to the soul, has almost dwindled away. A measuring of vileness against vileness in which the very act of measuring leaves a vile taste in the mouth. Twenty million, six million, three million, a hundred thousand: at a certain point the mind breaks down before quanta; and the older you get – this at any rate is what has happened to her – the sooner comes the breakdown. A sparrow knocked off a branch by a slingshot, a city annihilated from the air: who dare say which is the worse? Evil, all of it, an evil universe invented by an evil god. Dare she say that to her kind Dutch hosts, her kind, intelligent, sensible auditors in this enlightened, rationally organized, well-run city? Best to keep her peace, best not to cry out too much. She can imagine the next headline in the *Age*: UNIVERSE EVIL, OPINES COSTELLO.

From her hotel she wanders out along the canal, an old woman in a raincoat, still slightly light-headed, slightly wobbly on her feet, after the long flight from the Antipodes. Disoriented: is it simply because she has lost her bearings that she is thinking these black thoughts? If so, perhaps she ought to travel less. Or more.

The topic she is to speak on, the topic negotiated between her and her hosts, is 'Witness, Silence, and Censorship'. The paper itself, or most of it, was not difficult to write. After her years on the executive of PEN Australia she can discourse on censorship in her sleep. If she wanted to make things easy for herself, she could read them her routine censorship paper, spend a few hours in the Rijksmuseum, then catch the train to Nice, where, conveniently, her daughter is staying as the guest of a foundation.

The routine censorship paper is liberal in its ideas, with perhaps a touch of the *Kulturpessimismus* that has marked her thinking of late: the civilization of the West is based on belief in unlimited and illimitable endeavour, it is too late for us to do anything about that, we must simply hold on tight and go wherever the ride takes us. It is on the subject of the illimitable that her opinions seem to be undergoing a quiet change. Reading West's book has contributed to that change, she suspects, though it is possible the change would have happened anyway, for reasons that are more obscure to her. Specifically, she is no longer sure that people are always improved by what they read. Furthermore, she is not sure that writers who venture into the darker territories of the soul always return unscathed. She has begun to wonder whether writing what one desires, any more than reading what one desires, is in itself a good thing.

That, in any event, is what she plans to say here in Amsterdam. As her principal example she plans to set before the conference *The Very Rich Hours of Count von Stauffenberg*, which came to her in a packet of books, some of them new, some reissues, sent for her consideration by an editor friend in Sydney. *The Very Rich Hours* was the only one that had really engaged her; her response was set out in a review that she withdrew at the last minute and has never published.

When she arrived at her hotel there had been an envelope waiting for her: a letter of welcome from the organizers, a conference programme, maps. Now, sitting on a bench on the Prinsengracht in the tentative warmth of the northern sun, she glances over the programme. She is scheduled to speak the next morning, the first day of the conference. She flips to the notes at the end of the programme. 'Elizabeth Costello, noted Australian novelist and essayist, author of *The House on Eccles Street* and many other books.' Not the way she would have billed herself, but they did not ask her. Frozen in the past, as usual; frozen in the achievements of her youth.

Her eye drifts down the list. Most of her fellow conferees she has not heard of. Then her eye is caught by the last name on the list, and her heart misses a beat. 'Paul West, novelist and critic.' Paul West: the stranger on the state of whose soul she spends so many pages. Can anyone, she asks in her lecture, wander as deep as Paul West does into the Nazi forest of horrors and emerge unscathed? Have we considered that the explorer enticed into that forest may come out not better and stronger for the experience but worse? How can she give the talk, how can she ask such a question, with Paul West himself sitting in the audience? It will seem like an attack, a presumptuous, unprovoked, and above all personal attack on a fellow writer. Who will believe the truth: that she has never had any dealings with Paul West, has never met him, has read only this one book of his? What is to be done?

Of the twenty pages of her text, fully half are devoted to the von Stauffenberg book. With luck the book will not have been translated into Dutch; with extreme luck no one else in the audience will have read it. She could cut out West's name, refer to him only as 'the author of a book on the Nazi period'. She could even make the book itself hypothetical: a hypothetical novel about the Nazis, the writing of which would have scarred the soul of its hypothetical author. Then no one will know, except of course West himself, if he is present, if he bothers to come to the talk by the lady from Australia.

It is four in the afternoon. Usually, on long flights, she sleeps only fitfully. But on this flight she experimented with a new pill, and it seems to have worked. She feels well, ready to plunge into work. There is time enough to rewrite the talk, removing Paul West and his novel into the deep background, leaving only the thesis visible, the thesis that writing itself, as a form of moral adventurousness, has the potential to be dangerous. But what kind of talk would that be – a thesis with no examples?

Is there someone she can put in the place of Paul West – Céline for instance? One of Céline's novels, its name evades her, flirts with sadism, fascism, anti-Semitism. Years since she read it. Can she lay her hands on a copy, preferably not in Dutch, and write Céline into the talk?

But Paul West is not Céline, is nothing like him. Flirting with sadism is exactly what West does not do; furthermore, his book barely mentions the Jews. The horrors he unveils are *sui generis*. That must have been his wager with himself: to take as his subject a handful of bumbling German career officers unfitted by the very code of their upbringing to plotting and carrying out an assassination, to tell the story of their ineptitude and its consequences from beginning to end, and to leave one feeling, to one's surprise, authentic pity, authentic terror.

Once upon a time she would have said, All honour to a writer who undertakes to follow such a story to its darkest recesses. Now she is not sure. That is what seems to have changed in her. In any event, Céline is not like that, Céline will not work.

On the deck of a barge moored across from her two couples are seated at a table, chatting, drinking beer. Cyclists rattle past. An ordinary afternoon on an ordinary day in Holland. Having travelled thousands of miles to bathe in precisely this variety of the ordinary, must she forsake it to sit in a hotel room wrestling with a text for a conference that will be forgotten in a week's time? And to what end? To save embarrassment to a man she has never met? In the greater scheme of things, what does a moment's embarrassment amount to? She does not know how old Paul West is – the jacket of his book does not say, the photo could date from years ago – but she is sure he is not young. Might he and she, in their different ways, not be old enough to be beyond embarrassment?

Back at the hotel there is a message to call Henk Badings, the man from the Free University with whom she has been corresponding. Did she have a good flight, Badings asks? Is she comfortably settled? Would she like to join him and one or two other guests for dinner? Thank you, she replies, but no: she would prefer an early night. A pause, then she asks her question. The novelist Paul West: has he arrived yet in Amsterdam? Yes, comes Badings' reply: not only has Paul West arrived but, she will be glad to hear, is lodged at the same hotel as she.

If anything is needed to spur her, this is it. Unacceptable that Paul West should find himself quartered with a woman who rants against him in public as a dupe of Satan. She must cut him out of the talk or she must withdraw, and that is that.

She stays up all night wrestling with the lecture. First she tries leaving out West's name. *A recent novel*, she calls the book, *coming out of Germany*. But of course it does not work. Even if most of her auditors are taken in, West will know she means him.

What if she tries softening her thesis? What if she suggests that, in representing the workings of evil, the writer may *unwittingly* make evil seem attractive, and thereby do more harm than good? Will that soften the blow? She strikes out the first paragraph on page eight, the first of the bad pages, then the second, then the third, begins to scribble revisions in the margins, then stares in dismay at the mess. Why did she not make a copy before she started?

The young man at the reception desk sits with headphones on, jiggling his shoulders from side to side. When he sees her he springs to attention. 'A photocopier,' she says. 'Is there a photocopier I can use?'

He takes the wad of paper from her, glances at the heading. The hotel caters to many conferences, he must be used to distraught foreigners rewriting their lectures in the middle of the night. The lives of dwarf stars. Crop yields in Bangladesh. The soul and its manifold corruptions. All the same to him.

Copy in hand, she proceeds with the task of watering down her paper, but with more and more doubt in her heart. The writer as dupe of Satan: what nonsense! Ineluctably she is arguing herself into the position of the old-fashioned censor. And what is the point of all this pussyfooting anyway? To forestall a petty scandal? Where does it come from, her reluctance to offend? Soon she is going to be dead. What will it matter then if once upon a time she ruffled the feathers of some stranger in Amsterdam?

When she was nineteen, she remembers, she allowed herself to be picked up on the Spencer Street bridge near the Melbourne waterfront, then a rough area. The man was a docker, in his thirties, good-looking in a crude sort of way, who called himself Tim or Tom. She was an art student and a rebel, in rebellion principally against the matrix that had formed her: respectable, petit bourgeois, Catholic. In her eyes, in those days, only the working class and the values of the working class were authentic.

Tim or Tom took her to a bar and after that to the rooming house where he lived. It was not something she had done before, sleeping with a strange man; at the last minute she could not go through with it. 'I'm sorry,' she said. 'I'm really sorry, can we stop.' But Tim or Tom would not listen. When she resisted, he tried to force her. For a long time, in silence, panting, she fought him off, pushing and scratching. To begin with he took it as a game. Then he got tired of that, or his desire tired, turned to something else, and he began to hit her seriously. He lifted her off the bed, punched her breasts, punched her in the belly, hit her a terrible blow with his elbow to her face. When he was bored with hitting her he tore up her clothes and tried to set fire to them in the waste-paper basket. Stark naked, she crept out and hid in the bathroom on the landing. An hour later, when she was sure he was asleep, she crept back and retrieved what was left. Wearing the scorched tatters of her dress and nothing else she waved down a taxi. For a week she stayed first with one friend, then with another, refusing to explain what had happened. Her jaw was broken; it had to be wired up; she lived on milk and orange juice, sucked through a straw.

It was her first brush with evil. She had realized it was nothing less than that, evil, when the man's affront subsided and a steady glee in hurting her took its place. He liked hurting her, she could see it; probably liked it more than he would have liked sex. Though he might not have known it when he picked her up, he had brought her to his room to hurt her rather than make love to her. By fighting him off she had created an opening for the evil in him to emerge, and it emerged in the form of glee, first at her pain ('You like that, do you?' he whispered as he twisted her nipples. 'You like that?'), then in the childish, malicious destruction of her clothes.

Why does her mind go back to this long-past and – really – unimportant episode? The answer: because she has never revealed it to anyone, never made use of it. In none of her stories is there a physical assault by a man on a woman in revenge for being refused. Unless Tim or Tom himself has survived into doddering old age, unless the committee of angelic observers has saved the minutes of the proceedings of that night, what happened in the rooming house belongs to her and her alone. For half a century the memory has rested inside her like an egg, an egg of stone, one that will never crack open, never give birth. She finds it good, it pleases her, this silence of hers, a silence she hopes to preserve to the grave.

Is it some equivalent reticence that she is demanding of West: a story about an assassination plot in which he does not tell what happened to the plotters when they fell into the hands of their enemies? Surely not. So what exactly is it that she wants to say to this assembly of strangers in – she glances at her watch – less than eight hours?

She tries to clear her mind, go back to beginnings. What was it inside her that rose in revolt against West and his book when she first read it? As an initial approximation, that he had brought Hitler and his thugs back to life, given them a new purchase on the world. Very well. But what is wrong with that? West is a novelist, as is she; both of them live by telling or retelling stories; and in their stories, if their stories are any good, characters, even hangmen, take on a life of their own. So how is she any better than West?

The answer, as far as she can see, is that she no longer believes that storytelling is good in itself, whereas for West, or at least for West as he was when he wrote the Stauffenberg book, the question does not seem to arise. If she, as she is nowadays, had to choose between telling a story and doing good, she would rather, she thinks, do good. West, she thinks, would rather tell a story, though perhaps she ought to suspend judgement until she hears it from his own lips.

There are many things that it is like, this storytelling business. One of them (so she says in one of the paragraphs she has not crossed out yet) is a bottle with a genie in it. When the storyteller opens the bottle, the genie is released into the world, and it costs all hell to get him back in again. Her position, her revised position, her position in the twilight of life: better, on the whole, that the genie stay in the bottle.

The wisdom of the similitude, the wisdom of centuries (that is why she prefers to think in similitudes rather than reason things out), is that it is silent on the life the genie leads shut up in the bottle. It merely says that the world would be better off if the genie remained imprisoned.

A genie or a devil. While she has less and less idea what it could mean to believe in God, about the devil she has no doubt. The devil is everywhere under the skin of things, searching for a way into the light. The devil entered the docker that night on Spencer Street, the devil entered Hitler's hangman. And through the docker, all that time ago, the devil entered her: she can feel him crouched inside, folded up like a bird, waiting his chance to fly. Through Hitler's hangman a devil entered Paul West, and in his book West in turn has given that devil his freedom, turned him loose upon the world. She felt the brush of his leathery wing, as sure as soap, when she read those dark pages.

She is quite aware how old-fashioned it sounds. West will have defenders by the thousand. *How can we know the horrors of the Nazis, those defenders will say, if our artists are forbidden to bring them to life for us? Paul West is not a devil but a hero: he has ventured into the labyrinth of Europe's past and faced down the Minotaur and returned to tell his tale.*

What can she say in reply? That it would have been better if our hero had stayed at home, or at least had kept his exploits to himself? In times when artists clutch to themselves what few tatters of dignity they have left, what gratitude will that kind of answer bring her among fellow writers? *She has let us down*, they will say. *Elizabeth Costello has turned into old Mother Grundy.*

She wishes she had *The Very Rich Hours of Count von Stauffenberg* with her. Could she merely glance again at those pages, brush her eyes across them, all her doubts would vanish, she is sure, the pages where West gives the hangman, the butcher – she has forgotten his name but cannot forget his hands, just as no doubt his victims carried the memory of those hands, fumbling at their throats, with them into eternity – where he gives the butcher a voice, allowing him his coarse, his worse than coarse, his unspeakable gibes at the shivering old men he is about to kill, gibes about how their bodies are going to betray them as they buck and dance at the end of the rope. It is terrible, terrible beyond words: terrible that such a man should have existed, even more terrible that he should be hauled out of the grave when we thought he was safely dead.

Obscene. That is the word, a word of contested etymology, that she must hold on to as talisman. She chooses to believe that *obscene* means *off-stage.* To save our humanity, certain things that we may want to see (*may want to see because we are human!*) must remain off-stage. Paul West has written an obscene book, he has shown what ought not to be shown. That must be the thread of her talk when she faces the crowd, that she must not let go of.

She falls asleep at the writing table, fully dressed, with her head on her arms. At seven the alarm rings. Groggy, exhausted, she does what she can to fix her face and takes the funny little elevator down to the lobby. 'Has Mr West checked in yet?' she asks the boy at the desk, the same boy.

'Mr West . . . Yes, Mr West is in room 311.'

The sun is streaming through the windows of the breakfast room. She helps herself to coffee and a croissant, finds a seat near a window, surveys the half-dozen other early birds. Might the stocky man with the glasses reading the newspaper be West? He does not look like the photograph on the book jacket, but that proves nothing. Should she go across and ask? 'Mr West, how do you do, I am Elizabeth Costello and I have a complicated statement to make, if you will hear me out. It concerns you and your dealings with the devil.' How would she feel if some stranger did that to her while she was at breakfast?

She gets up, picks her way among the tables, taking the long route to the buffet. The paper the man is reading is Dutch, the *Volkskrant*. There is dandruff on the collar of his jacket. He glances up over his spectacles. A placid, ordinary face. He could be anyone: a textiles salesman, a professor of Sanskrit. He could equally be Satan in one of his disguises. She hesitates, passes on.

The Dutch paper, the dandruff . . . Not that Paul West might not read Dutch, not that Paul West might not have dandruff. But if she is going to set herself up as an expert on evil, ought she not be able to sniff evil out? What does evil smell like? Sulphur?

Brimstone? Zyklon B? Or has evil become colourless and odourless, like so much of the rest of the moral world?

At eight thirty Badings calls for her. Together he and she stroll the few blocks to the theatre where the conference is to take place. In the auditorium he points to a man sitting by himself in the back row. 'Paul West,' says Badings. 'Would you like me to introduce you?'

Though it is not the man she saw at breakfast, the two are not unalike in build, even in looks.

'Later perhaps,' she murmurs.

Badings excuses himself, goes off to attend to business. Still some twenty minutes before the session begins. She crosses the auditorium. 'Mr West?' she says, as pleasantly as she can. Years since she last employed what might be called feminine wiles, but if wiles will do the trick then she will use them. 'Might I speak to you for a moment?'

West, the real West, glances up from what he is reading, which seems, astonishingly, to be some kind of comic book.

'My name is Elizabeth Costello,' she says, and sits down beside him. 'This is not easy for me, so let me come to the point. My lecture today contains references to one of your books, the von Stauffenberg book. In fact, the lecture is largely about that book, and about you as its author. When I prepared the lecture I was not expecting you to be in Amsterdam. The organizers did not inform me. But of course, why should they have? They had no idea of what I intended to say.'

She pauses. West is gazing into the distance, giving her no help.

'I could, I suppose,' she continues, and now she really does not know what is coming next, 'request your pardon in advance, request you not to take my remarks personally. But then you might enquire, quite justifiably, why I insist on making remarks that require a prior apology, why I do not simply cut them out of the lecture.

'I did in fact consider cutting them out. I sat up most of last night, after I heard you were going to be here, trying to find a way of making my remarks less pointed, less offensive. I even thought of absenting myself entirely – pretending I was ill. But that would not have been fair to the organizers, don't you think?'

It is an opening, a chance for him to speak. He clears his throat, but then says nothing, continuing to gaze ahead, presenting her with his rather handsome profile.

'What I say,' she says, glancing at her watch (ten minutes left, the theatre is beginning to fill, she must plunge ahead, no time for niceties), 'what I contend, is that we must be wary of horrors such as you describe in your book. We as writers. Not merely for the sake of our readers but out of concern for ourselves. We can put ourselves in peril by what we write, or so I believe. For if what we write has the power to make us better people then surely it has the power to make us worse. I don't know whether you agree.'

Again an opening. Again, tenaciously, the man holds his silence. What is passing through his mind? Is he wondering what he is doing at this get-together in Holland, land of windmills and tulips, being harangued by some mad old witch, with the prospect of having to sit through the same harangue a second time? *A writer's life*, she ought to remind him, *is not an easy one.*

A group of young people, students probably, settle into the seats immediately in front of them. Why does West not respond? She is getting irritated; she has an urge to raise her voice, wag a bony finger in his face.

'I was deeply impressed by your book. That is to say, it made an impress on me the way a branding iron does. Certain pages burned with the fires of hell. You must know what I am talking about. The scene of the hangings in specific. I doubt I would be able to write such pages myself. That is to say, I might be able to write them, but I would not, I would not let myself, not any more, not as I am now. I do not think one can come away unscathed, as a writer, from conjuring up such scenes. I think writing like that can harm one. That is what I intend to say in my lecture.' She holds forth the green folder with her text, taps it. 'So I am not asking your pardon, not even asking your indulgence, just doing the decent thing and apprising you, warning you, of what is about to take place. Because' (and suddenly she feels stronger, surer of herself, more ready to express her irritation, her anger even, at this man who does not bother to speak back) 'because you are after all not a child, you must have known the risk you were taking, must have realized there could be consequences, unpredictable consequences, and now, lo and behold' – she stands up, clasps the folder to her bosom as if to shield herself from the flames that flicker around him – 'the consequences have arrived. That is all. Thank you for hearing me out, Mr West.'

Badings, at the front of the hall, is waving discreetly. It is time.

The first part of the lecture is routine, covering familiar ground: authorship and authority, claims made by poets over the ages to speak a higher truth, a truth whose authority lies in revelation, and their further claim, in Romantic times, which happen to have been times of unparalleled geographical exploration, of a right to venture into forbidden or tabooed places.

'What I will be asking today,' she continues, 'is whether the artist is quite the hero-explorer he pretends to be, whether we are always right to applaud when he emerges from the cave with reeking sword in one hand and the head of the monster in the other. To illustrate my case I will be referring to a product of the imagination that appeared a few years ago, an important and in many ways courageous book about the nearest approximation that we, in our disillusioned age, have produced to the monster of myth, namely Adolf Hitler. I am referring to Paul West's novel *The Very Rich Hours of Count von Stauffenberg* and in specific to the graphic chapter in which Mr West recounts the execution of the July 1944 plotters (excepting von Stauffenberg, he having already been shot by an overzealous military officer, to the chagrin of Hitler, who wanted his foe to die a lingering death).

'If this were an ordinary lecture I would at this point read out to you a paragraph or two, to give you the feel of this extraordinary book. (It is not a secret, by the way, that its author is among us. Let me beg Mr West's pardon for presuming to lecture him to his face: at the time I wrote my talk I had no idea he would be here.) I ought to read to you from these terrible pages, but I will not, because I do not believe it will be good for you or for me to hear them. I even assert (and here I come to the point) that I do not believe it was good for Mr West, if he will forgive my saying so, to write those pages.

'That is my thesis today: that certain things are not good to read *or to write*. To put the point in another way: I take seriously the claim that the artist risks a great deal by venturing into forbidden places: risks, specifically, himself; risks, perhaps, all. I take this claim seriously because I take seriously the forbiddenness of forbidden places. The cellar in which the July 1944 plotters were hanged is one such forbidden place. I do not believe we should go into that cellar, any of us. I do not believe Mr West should go there; and, if he chooses to go nevertheless, I believe we should not follow. On the contrary, I believe that bars should be erected over the cellar mouth, with a bronze memorial plaque saying *Here died* . . . followed by a list of the dead and their dates, and that should be that.

'Mr West is a writer, or, as they used to say once upon a time, a poet. I too am a poet. I have not read everything Mr West has written, but enough to know that he takes his calling seriously. So when I read Mr West I do so not only with respect but with sympathy.

'I read the von Stauffenberg book with sympathy, not excepting (you must believe me) the execution scenes, to the point that it might as well be I as Mr West who hold the pen and trace the words. Word by word, step by step, heartbeat by heartbeat, I accompany him into the darkness. *No one has been here before,* I hear him whisper, and so I whisper too; our breath is as one. *No one has been in this place since the men who died and the man who killed them. Ours is the death that will be died, ours the hand that will knot the rope.* ("Use thin cord," Hitler commanded his man. "Strangle them. I want them to feel themselves dying." And his man, his creature, his monster, obeyed.)

'What arrogance, to lay claim to the suffering and death of those pitiful men! Their last hours belong to them alone, they are not ours to enter and possess. If that is not a nice thing to say about a colleague, if it will ease the moment, we can pretend the book in question is no longer Mr West's but mine, made mine by the madness of my reading. Whatever pretence we need to adopt, let us in heaven's name adopt it and move on.'

There are several more pages to be got through, but suddenly she is too upset to read on, or else the spirit fails her. A homily: let it rest at that. Death is a private matter; the artist should not invade the deaths of others. Hardly an outrageous position in a world where routinely the wounded and the dying have the lenses of cameras poked into their faces.

She closes the green folder. A thin ripple of clapping. She glances at her watch. Five minutes before the session is due to end. She has taken surprisingly long, given how little she has actually said.

Time for one question, two at most, thank God. Her head is spinning. She hopes no one is going to demand she say more about
Paul West, who, she sees (putting on her glasses), is still in his place
in the back row (*Long-suffering fellow*, she thinks, and all of a sudden
feels more friendly toward him).

A man with a dark beard has his hand up. 'How do you know?'
he says. 'How do you know that Mr West – we seem to be talking a lot about Mr West today, I hope Mr West will have a right
of reply, it will be interesting to hear his reaction' – there are smiles
in the audience – 'has been harmed by what he has written? If I
understand you correctly, you are saying that if you yourself had
written this book about von Stauffenberg and Hitler you would
have been infected with the Nazi evil. But perhaps all that says is
that you are, so to speak, a weak vessel. Perhaps Mr West is made
of sterner stuff. And perhaps we, his readers, are made of sterner
stuff too. Perhaps we could read what Mr West writes and learn
from it, and come out stronger rather than weaker, more determined never to let the evil return. Would you care to comment?'

She should never have come, never have accepted the invitation, she knows it now. Not because she has nothing to say about
evil, the problem of evil, the problem of calling evil a problem,
not even because of the ill luck of West's presence, but because a
limit has been reached, the limit of what can be achieved with a
body of balanced, well-informed modern folk in a clean, well-lit
lecture venue in a well-ordered, well-run European city in the
dawn of the twenty-first century.

'I am not, I believe,' she says slowly, the words coming out one
by one, like stones, 'a weak vessel. Nor, would I guess, is Mr West.
The experience that writing offers, or reading – they are the same
thing, for my purposes, here, today –' (but are they the same thing,
really? – she is losing her track, what is her track?) 'real writing,

175

real reading, is not a relative one, relative to the writer and the writer's capacities, relative to the reader' (she has not slept in God knows how long, what passed for sleep on the plane was not sleep). 'Mr West, when he wrote those chapters, came in touch with something absolute. Absolute evil. His blessing and his curse, I would say. Through reading him that touch of evil was passed on to me. Like a shock. Like electricity.' She glances at Badings, standing in the wings. *Help me*, her glance says. *Put an end to this*. 'It is not something that can be demonstrated,' she says, returning a last time to her questioner. 'It is something that can only be experienced. However, I am recommending to you that you do not try it out. You will not learn from such an experience. It will not be good for you. That is what I wanted to say today. Thank you.'

As the audience rises and disperses (time for a cup of coffee, enough of this strange woman from Australia of all places, what do they know about evil there?), she tries to keep an eye on Paul West in the back row. If there is any truth in what she has said (but she is full of doubt, and desperate too), if the electricity of evil did indeed leap from Hitler to Hitler's butcherman and thence to Paul West, surely he will give off some sign. But there is no sign she can detect, not at this distance, just a short man in black on his way to the coffee machine.

Badings is at her elbow. 'Very interesting, Mrs Costello,' he murmurs, doing his hostly duty. She shakes him off, she has no wish to be soothed. Head down, meeting no one's eye, she pushes her way to the ladies' room and shuts herself in a cubicle.

The banality of evil. Is that the reason why there is no longer any smell or aura? Have the grand Lucifers of Dante and Milton been retired for good, their place taken by a pack of dusty little demons that perch on one's shoulder like parrots, giving off no fiery glow but on the contrary sucking light into themselves? Or has everything she has said, all her finger-pointing and accusing, been not only wrong-headed but mad, completely mad? What is the business of the novelist, after all, what has been her own lifetime business, but to bring inert matter to life; and what has Paul West done, as the man with the beard pointed out, but bring to life, bring back to life, the history of what happened in that cellar in Berlin? What has she conveyed to Amsterdam to display to these puzzled strangers but an obsession, an obsession that is hers alone and that she clearly does not understand?

Obscene. Go back to the talismanic word, hold fast to it. Hold fast to the word, then reach for the experience behind it: that has always been her rule for when she feels herself slipping into abstraction. What was her experience? What was it that happened as she sat reading the accursed book on the lawn that Saturday morning? What was it that upset her so much that a year later she is still grubbing after its roots? Can she find her way back?

She knew, before she began the book, the story of the July plotters, knew that within days of their attempt on Hitler's life they were tracked down, most of them, and tried and executed. She even knew, in a general way, that they were put to death with the malicious cruelty in which Hitler and his cronies specialized. So nothing in the book had come as a real surprise.

She goes back to the hangman, whatever his name was. In his gibes at the men about to die at his hands there was a wanton, an *obscene* energy that exceeded his commission. Where did that energy come from? To herself she has called it satanic, but perhaps she should let go of that word now. For the energy came, in a certain sense, from West himself. It was West who invented the gibes (English gibes, not German), put them in the hangman's mouth. Fitting speech to character: what is satanic about that? She does it herself all the time.

Go back. Go back to Melbourne, to that Saturday morning when she felt, she could have sworn, the brush of Satan's hot, leathery wing. Was she deluded? *I do not want to read this*, she said to herself; yet she had gone on reading, excited despite herself. *The devil is leading me on*: what kind of excuse is that?

Paul West was only doing his writerly duty. In the person of his hangman he was opening her eyes to human depravity in another of its manifold forms. In the persons of the hangman's victims he was reminding her of what poor, forked, quivering creatures we all are. What is wrong with that?

What had she said? *I do not want to read this.* But what right had she to refuse? What right had she not to know what, in all too clear a sense, she already knew? What was it in her that wanted to resist, to refuse the cup? And why did she nonetheless drink – drink so fully that a year later she is still railing against the man who put it to her lips?

If there were a mirror on the back of this door instead of just a hook, if she were to take off her clothes and kneel before it, she, with her sagging breasts and knobbly hips, would look much like the women in those intimate, over-intimate photographs from the European war, those glimpses into hell, who knelt naked at the lip of the trench into which they would, in the next minute, the next second, tumble, dead or dying with a bullet to the brain, except that those women were in most cases not as old as she, merely haggard from malnutrition and fright. She has a feeling for those dead sisters, and for the men too who died at the hands of the butchermen, men old and ugly enough to be her brothers. She does not like to see her sisters and brothers humiliated, in ways it is so easy to humiliate the old, by making them strip, for example, taking away their dentures, making fun of their private parts. If her brothers, that day in Berlin, are going to be hanged, if they are going to jerk at the end of a rope, their faces going red, their tongues and eyeballs protruding, she does not want to see. A sister's modesty. Let me turn my eyes away.

Let me not look. That was the plea she breathed to Paul West (except that she did not know Paul West then, he was just a name on the cover of a book). *Do not make me go through with it!* But Paul West did not relent. He made her read, *excited* her to read. For that she will not easily forgive him. For that she has pursued him across the seas all the way to Holland.

Is that the truth? Will that do as an explanation?

Yet she does the same kind of thing, or used to. Until she thought better of it, she had no qualms about rubbing people's faces in, for instance, what went on in abattoirs. If Satan is not rampant in the abattoir, casting the shadow of his wings over the beasts who, their nostrils already filled with the smell of death, are prodded down the ramp towards the man with the gun and the knife, a man as merciless *and as banal* (though she has begun to feel that that word too should be retired, it has had its day) as Hitler's own man (who learned his trade, after all, on cattle) – if Satan is not rampant in the abattoir, where is he? She, no less than Paul West, knew how to play with words until she got them right, the words that would send an electric shock down the spine of the reader. *Butcherfolk in our own way.*

So what has happened to her now? Now, all of a sudden, she has grown prim. Now she no longer likes to see herself in the mirror, since it puts her in mind of death. Ugly things she prefers wrapped up and stored away in a drawer. An old woman turning back the clock, back to the Irish-Catholic Melbourne of her child-hood. Is that all it amounts to?

Go back to the experience. The flap of Satan's leathery wing: what was it that convinced her she felt it? And how much longer can she occupy one of the two cubicles in this cramped little women's room before some well-intentioned person decides she has had a collapse and calls in the janitor to break the lock?

The twentieth century of Our Lord, Satan's century, is over and done with. Satan's century and her own too. If she happens to have crept over the finish line into the new age, she is certainly not at home in it. In these unfamiliar times Satan is still feeling his way, trying out new contrivances, making new accommodations. He pitches his tent in odd places – for example in Paul West, a good man, for all she knows, or as good as a man can be who is also a novelist, that is to say, perhaps not good at all, but tending never-theless to the good, in some ultimate sense, otherwise why write? Takes up residence in women too. Like the liver fluke, like the pinworm: one can live and die ignorant that one has been host to generations of them. In whose liver, in whose gut was Satan, that fateful day last year when again, indubitably, she felt his presence: in West's or in her own?

Old men, brothers, hanging dead with their trousers around their ankles, executed. In Rome it would have been different. In Rome they made a spectacle of executions: hauled their victims through howling mobs to the place of skulls and impaled them or flayed them or coated them with pitch and set them on fire. The Nazis, by comparison, mean, cheap, machine-gunning people in a field, gassing them in a bunker, strangling them in a cellar. So what was *too much* about death at the hands of the Nazis that was not *too much* in Rome, when all the striving of Rome was to wring from death as much cruelty, as much pain as possible? Is it just the grubbiness of that cellar in Berlin, a grubbiness that is too much like the real thing, the modern thing, for her to bear?

It is like a wall that she comes up against time and again. She did not want to read but she read; a violence was done to her but she conspired in the violation. *He made me do it*, she says, yet she makes others do it.

She should never have come. Conferences are for exchanging thoughts, at least that is the idea behind conferences. You cannot exchange thoughts when you do not know what you think.

There is a scratching at the door, a child's voice. '*Mammie, er zit een vrouw erin, ik kan haar schoenen zien!*'

Hurriedly she flushes the bowl, unlocks the door, emerges. 'Sorry,' she says, evading the eyes of mother and daughter.

What was the child saying? *Why is she taking so long?* If she spoke the language she could enlighten the child. *Because the older you get the longer it takes. Because sometimes you need to be alone. Because there are things we do not do in public, not any more.*

Her brothers: did they let them use the toilet one last time, or was shitting themselves part of the punishment? That, at least, Paul West drew a veil over, for which small mercy, thanks.

No one to wash them, afterwards. Women's work since time immemorial. No womanly presence in the cellar business. Admission reserved; men only. But perhaps when it was all over, when dawn's rosy fingers touched the eastern skies, the women arrived, indefatigable German cleaning women out of Brecht, and set to work cleaning up the mess, washing the walls, scrubbing the floor, making everything spick and span, so that you would never guess, by the time they had done, what games the boys had got up to during the night. Would never guess until Mr West came along and threw it all open again.

It is eleven o'clock. The next session, the next lecture, must already be in progress. She has a choice. Either she can go to the hotel and hide in her room and go on with her grieving; or she can tiptoe into the auditorium, take a seat in the back row, and do the second thing they brought her to Amsterdam for: hear what other folk have to say about the problem of evil.

There ought to be a third alternative, some way of rounding off the morning and giving it shape and meaning: some confrontation leading to some final word. There ought to be an arrangement such that she bumps into someone in the corridor, perhaps Paul West himself; something should pass between them, sudden as lightning, that will illuminate the landscape for her, even if afterwards it returns to its native darkness. But the corridor, it seems, is empty.

7
Eros

She met Robert Duncan only once, in 1963, soon after her return from Europe. Duncan and another, less interesting poet named Philip Whalen had been brought out on a tour by the US Information Service: the Cold War was on, there was money for cultural propaganda. Duncan and Whalen gave a reading at the University of Melbourne; after the reading they all went off to a bar, the two poets and the man from the consulate and half a dozen Australian writers of all ages, including herself.

Duncan had read his long 'Poem Beginning with a Line by Pindar' that night, and it had impressed her, moved her. She was attracted to Duncan, with his severely handsome Roman profile; she would not have minded having a fling with him, would not even, in the mood she was in in those days, have minded having his love child, like one of those mortal women of myth impregnated by a passing god and left to bring up semi-divine offspring.

She is reminded of Duncan because in a book sent by an American friend she has just come across another telling of the Eros and Psyche story, by one Susan Mitchell, whom she has not read before. Why the interest in Psyche among American poets, she wonders? Do they find something American in her, the girl who, not content with the ecstasies provided night after night by the visitor to her bed, must light a lamp, peel back the darkness,

183

gaze on him naked? In her restlessness, her inability to leave well alone, do they see something of themselves?

She too is not without curiosity about the intercourse of gods and mortals, though she has never written about it, not even in her book about Marion Bloom and her god-haunted husband Leopold. What intrigues her is less the metaphysics than the mechanics, the practicalities of congress across a gap in being. Bad enough to have a full-grown male swan jabbing webbed feet into your backside while he has his way, or a one-ton bull leaning his moaning weight on you; how, when the god does not care to change shape but remains his awesome self, does the human body accommodate itself to the blast of his desire?

Let it be said for Susan Mitchell that she does not shrink from such questions. In her poem, Eros, who seems to have made himself man-sized for the occasion, lies in bed on his back with his wings drooping on either side, the girl (one presumes) on top of him. The seed of gods would seem to gush hugely (this must have been Mary of Nazareth's experience too, waking from her dream still slightly trembly with the issue of the Holy Ghost running down her thighs). When Psyche's lover comes, his wings are left drenched; or perhaps the wings drip seed, perhaps they become organs of consummation themselves. On occasions when he and she reach a climax together, he breaks apart like (Mitchell's words, more or less) a bird shot in flight. (*What about the girl*, she wants to ask the poet – *if you can say what it was like for him, why not tell us how it was for her?*)

What she had really wanted to talk about to Robert Duncan, however, that night in Melbourne when he indicated so firmly that whatever she offered did not interest him, was not girls visited by gods but the much rarer phenomenon of men condescended to by goddesses. Anchises, for instance, lover of Aphrodite and father

184

of Aeneas. One would have thought that, after that unforeseen and unforgettable episode in his hut on Mount Ida, Anchises – a good-looking boyo, if one is to believe the *Hymn*, but otherwise just a cattle herder – would have wanted to talk about nothing else, to whoever would listen: how he had fucked a goddess, the most succulent in the whole stable, fucked her all night long, got her pregnant too.

Men and their leering talk. She has no illusions about how mortal beings treat whatever gods, true or feigned, ancient or modern, have the misfortune to fall into their hands. She thinks of a film she saw once, that might have been written by Nathanael West though in fact it wasn't: Jessica Lange playing a Hollywood sex goddess who has a breakdown and ends up in the common ward of a madhouse, drugged, lobotomized, strapped to her bed, while orderlies sell tickets for ten minutes a time with her. '*I wanna fuck a movie star!*' pants one of their customers, shoving his dollars at them. In his voice the ugly underside of idolatry: malice, murderous resentment. Bring an immortal down to earth, show her what life is really like, bang her till she is raw. *Take that! Take that!* A scene they excised from the televised version, so close to the bone of America does it cut.

But in Anchises' case the goddess, when she rose from his bed, warned her sweetheart pretty plainly to keep his mouth shut. So there was nothing left for a prudent fellow to do but lose himself, last thing at night, in drowsy memories: how it had felt, man's flesh lapped in god flesh; or else, when he was in a more sober, more philosophically inclined mood, to wonder: since the physical mingling of two orders of being, and in specific the interplay of human organs with whatever stands in for organs in the biology of gods, is strictly speaking not possible, not while the laws of nature continue to hold, what kind of being, what hybrid of slave body and god soul, must it have been that laughter-loving Aphrodite transformed herself into, for the space of a night, in order to consort with him? Where was the mighty soul when he took in his arms the incomparable body? Tucked away in some out-of-the-way compartment, in a tiny gland in the skull, for instance; or spread harmlessly through the physical whole as a glow, an aura? Yet even if, for his sake, the soul of the goddess was hidden, how could he not, when her limbs gripped him, have felt the fire of godly appetite – felt it and been scorched by it? Why did it have to be spelled out to him, the next morning, what had really happened ('Her head touched the roof-beam, her face shone with immortal beauty, *Wake up*, she said, *behold me, do I look like the one who knocked at your door last night?*')? How could any of it have taken place unless he, the man, was under a spell from beginning to end, a spell like an anaesthetic to blanket the fearful knowledge that the maiden he had disrobed, embraced, parted the thighs of, penetrated, was an immortal, a trance to protect him from the unendurable pleasure of godlike lovemaking, allowing him only the duller sensations of a mortal? Yet why would a god, having chosen for herself a mortal lover, put that same lover under such a spell that for the duration he was not himself?

That is how it would have been for poor bewildered Anchises, one would imagine, for the rest of his life: a whirl of questions, none of which he would dare to air to his fellow cattlemen except in the most general form, for fear of being struck dead in his tracks.

Yet that is not how it was, not according to the poets. If one is to believe the poets, Anchises led a normal life thereafter, a distinguished but normal human life, until the day his city was set ablaze by foreigners and he was plunged into exile. If he did not forget that signal night, he did not think overmuch about it, not as we understand thinking.

186

That is the main thing she would have liked to ask Robert Duncan about, as an expert on extraordinary intercourse, the thing she fails to understand about the Greeks, or if Anchises and his son were not Greeks but Trojans, foreigners, then about Greeks and Trojans together as archaic eastern Mediterranean peoples and subjects of Hellenic myth-making. She calls it their lack of inwardness. Anchises has been intimate with a divine being, as intimate as intimate can be. Not a common experience. In the whole of Christian mythology, setting aside the Apocrypha, there is only one parallel event, and that in the commoner form, with the male god – rather impersonally, rather distantly, it must be said – impregnating the mortal woman. *Magnificat Dominum anima mea*, Mary is reputed to have said afterwards, perhaps misheard from *Magnam me facit Dominus*. That is pretty much all she says in the Gospels, this maid who is matchless, as though struck dumb for the rest of her life by what befell her. No one around her has the shamelessness to enquire, *What was it like, how did it feel, how did you bear it?* Yet the question must surely have occurred to people, to her girlfriends in Nazareth for instance. *How did she bear it?* they must have whispered among themselves. *It must have been like being fucked by a whale. It must have been like being fucked by the Leviathan;* blushing as they spoke the word, those barefoot children of the tribe of Judah, as she, Elizabeth Costello, almost catches herself blushing too, setting it down on paper. Rude enough among Mary's countryfolk; positively indecent in someone two millennia older and wiser.

Psyche, Anchises, Mary: there must be better, less prurient, more philosophical ways of thinking about the whole god–and–man business. But has she the time or the equipment, to say nothing of the inclination, to do so?

Inwardness. Can we *be one with* a god profoundly enough to

apprehend, to *get a sense of*, a god's being? A question that no one seems to ask any more, except to an extent her new find Susan Mitchell, who is not a philosopher either; a question that went out of fashion during her lifetime (she remembers it happening, remembers her surprise), just as it came into fashion not too long before her lifetime commenced. *Other modes of being.* That may be a more decent way of phrasing it. Are there other modes of being besides what we call the human into which we can enter; and if there are not, what does that say about us and our limitations? She does not know much about Kant, but it sounds to her a Kantian kind of question. If her ear is right, then inwardness started its run with the man from Königsberg and ended, more or less, with Wittgenstein the Viennese destroyer.

'Gods do exist,' writes Friedrich Hölderlin, who had read his Kant, 'but they carry on their lives somewhere up above us in another realm, not much interested, it would seem, in whether we exist or not.' In bygone times those gods bestrode the earth, walked among men. But to us modern folk it is no longer given to catch a glimpse of them, much less suffer their love. 'We come too late.'

She reads less and less widely as she grows older. A not uncommon phenomenon. For Hölderlin, however, she always has time. *Great-souled Hölderlin* she would call him if she were Greek. Nevertheless, about Hölderlin on the gods she has her doubts. Too innocent, she thinks, too ready to take things at face value; not alert enough to the cunning of history. Things are rarely as they seem to be, she would like to instruct him. When we are stirred to lament the loss of the gods, it is more than likely the gods who are doing the stirring. The gods have not retreated: they cannot afford to.

Odd that the man who put his finger on the divine *apatheia*, the inability of the gods to feel, and their consequent need to have others do their feeling for them, should have failed to see the effects of *apatheia* on their erotic life.

Love and death. The gods, the immortals, were the inventors of death and corruption; yet with one or two notable exceptions they have lacked the courage to try their invention out on themselves. That is why they are so curious about us, so endlessly inquisitive. We call Psyche a silly, prying girl, but what was a god doing in her bed in the first place? In marking us down for death, the gods gave us an edge over them. Of the two, gods and mortals, it is we who live the more urgently, feel the more intensely. That is why they cannot put us out of their minds, cannot get by without us, ceaselessly watch us and prey on us. That, finally, is why they do not declare a ban on sex with us, merely make up rules about where and in what form and how often. Inventors of death; inventors of sex tourism too. In the sexual ecstasies of mortals, the *frisson* of death, its contortions, its relaxings: they talk about it endlessly when they have had too much to drink – who they first got to experience it with, what it felt like. They wish they had that inimitable little quiver in their own erotic repertoire, to spice up their couplings with each other. But the price is one they are not prepared to pay. Death, annihilation: what if there is no resurrection, they wonder misgivingly?

We think of them as omniscient, these gods, but the truth is they know very little, and what they know know only in the most general of ways. No body of learning they can call their own, no philosophy, properly speaking. Their cosmology an assortment of commonplaces. Their sole expertise in astral flight, their sole home-grown science anthropology. They specialize in humankind because of what we have and they lack; they study us because they are envious.

189

As for us, do they guess (what irony!) that what makes our embraces so intense, so unforgettable, is the glimpse they give us of a life we imagine as theirs, a life we call (since our language has no word for it) *the beyond*? *I do not like that other world*, writes Martha Clifford to her pen pal Leopold Bloom, but she lies: why would she write at all if she did not want to be swept off to another world by a demon lover?

Leopold, meanwhile, strolls around the Dublin Public Library peeking, when no one is looking, between the legs of the statues of goddesses. If Apollo has a marble cock and balls, does Artemis, he wonders, have an orifice to match? Investigations in aesthetics, that is what he likes to tell himself he is engaged in: how far does the artist's duty to nature extend? What he really wants to know, however, had he only the words for it, is whether congress is possible with the divine.

And she herself? How much has she learned about gods in her wanderings around Dublin with that irremediably ordinary man? Almost like being married to him. Elizabeth Bloom, second and ghostly wife of.

What she knows for certain about the gods is that they peek at us all the time, peek even between our legs, full of curiosity, full of envy; sometimes go so far as to rattle our earthly cage. But how deep, she asks herself today, does that curiosity really run? Aside from our erotic gifts, are they curious about us, their anthropological specimens, to the degree that we in turn are curious about chimps, or about birds, or about flies? Despite some evidence to the contrary, she would like to think, chimps. She would like to think the gods admire, however grudgingly, our energy, the endless ingenuity with which we try to elude our fate. *Fascinating creatures*, she would like to think they remark to each other over their ambrosia; *so like us in many respects; their eyes in particular so expressive; what a pity they lack that* je ne sais quoi *without which they can never ascend to sit beside us!*

But perhaps she is wrong about their interest in us. Or rather, perhaps she used to be right, but now is wrong. In her heyday, she would like to think, she could have given winged Eros himself cause to pay earth a visit. Not because she was so much of a beauty but because she longed for the god's touch, longed until she ached; because in her longings, so unrequitable and therefore so comical when acted on, she might have promised a genuine taste of what was missing back home on Olympus. But everything seems now to have changed. Where in the world today does one find such immortal longings as hers used to be? Not in the personal columns, for sure. 'SWF, 5'8", thirties, brunette, into astrology, biking, seeks SWM, 35–45 for friendship, fun, adventure.' Nowhere: 'DWF, 5'8", sixties, runs to death and death meets her as fast, seeks G, immortal, earthly form immaterial, for ends to which no words suffice.' In the editorial office they would frown. Indecent desires, they would say, and toss her in the same basket as the pederasts.

We do not call on the gods because we no longer believe in them. She hates sentences that hinge on *because.* The jaws of the trap snap shut, but the mouse, every time, has escaped. And what an irrelevancy anyway! How misguided! Worse than Hölderlin! Who cares what we believe? The sole question is whether the gods will continue to believe in us, whether we can keep alive the last flicker of the flame that once used to burn in them. 'Friendship, fun, adventure': what kind of appeal is that, to a god? More than enough fun where they come from. More than enough beauty too.

Strange how, as desire relaxes its grip on her body, she sees more and more clearly a universe ruled by desire. *Haven't you read your Newton*, she would like to say to the people in the dating agency (would like to say to Nietzsche too if she could get in touch with him)? *Desire runs both ways: A pulls B because B pulls A, and vice versa: that is how you go about building a universe.* Or if *desire* is still too rude a word, then what of *appetency*? Appetency and chance: a powerful duo, more than powerful enough to build a cosmology on, from the atoms and the little things with nonsense names that make up atoms to Alpha Centauri and Cassiopeia and the great dark back of beyond. The gods and ourselves, whirled helplessly around by the winds of chance, yet pulled equally towards each other, towards not only B and C and D but towards X and Y and Z and Omega too. Not the least thing, not the last thing but is called to by love.

A vision, an opening up, as the heavens are opened up by a rainbow when the rain stops falling. Does it suffice, for old folk, to have these visions now and again, these rainbows, as a comfort, before the rain starts pelting down again? Must one be too creaky to join the dance before one can see the pattern?

8
At the Gate

IT IS A hot afternoon. The square is packed with visitors. Few spare
a glance for the white-haired woman who, suitcase in hand,
descends from the bus. She wears a blue cotton frock; her neck,
in the sun, is burned red and beaded with sweat.

Past the pavement tables, past the young folk, the wheels of the
suitcase rattling over the cobbles, she makes her way to the gate
where a uniformed man stands drowsily on guard, propped on the
rifle he holds butt down before him.

'Is this the gate?' she asks.

Beneath the peaked cap he blinks once in confirmation.

'Can I pass through?'

With a movement of the eyes he indicates the lodge to one
side.

The lodge, put together of prefabricated wooden panels, is
stiflingly hot. Inside, behind a small trestle table, sits a man in shirt-
sleeves, writing. A tiny electric fan blows a stream of air into his
face.

'Excuse me,' she says. He pays her no attention. 'Excuse me. Can
someone open the gate for me?'

He is filling in some kind of form. Without ceasing to write,
he speaks. 'First you must make a statement.'

'Make a statement? To whom? To you?'

With his left hand he pushes a sheet of paper across to her. She lets go of the suitcase and picks up the paper. It is blank.

'Before I can pass through I must make a statement,' she repeats. 'A statement of what?'

'Belief. What you believe.'

'Belief. Is that all? Not a statement of faith? What if I do not believe? What if I am not a believer?'

The man shrugs. For the first time he looks directly at her. 'We all believe. We are not cattle. For each of us there is something we believe. Write it down, what you believe. Put it in the statement.'

There is no more doubt in her mind about where she is, who she is. She is a petitioner before the gate. The journey that brought her here, to this country, to this town, that seemed to reach its end when the bus halted and its door opened on to the crowded square, was not the end of it all. Now commences a trial of a different kind. Some act is required of her, some prescribed yet undefined affirmation, before she will be found good and can pass through. But is this the one who will judge her, this ruddy, heavy-set man on whose rather sketchy uniform (military? civil guard?) she can detect no mark of rank but on whom the fan, swinging neither left nor right, pours a coolness that she wishes were being poured on her?

'I am a writer,' she says. 'You have probably not heard of me here, but I write, or have written, under the name Elizabeth Costello. It is not my profession to believe, just to write. Not my business. I do imitations, as Aristotle would have said.'

She pauses, then brings out the next sentence, the sentence that will determine whether this is her judge, the right one to judge her, or, on the contrary, merely the first in a long line leading to who knows what featureless functionary in what chancellery in what castle. 'I can do an imitation of belief, if you like. Will that be enough for your purposes?'

His response has an air of impatience about it, as though this is an offer he has had many times before. 'Write the statement as required,' he says. 'Bring it back when it is completed.'

'Very well, I will do so. Is there a time when you go off duty?'

'I am always here,' he replies. From which she understands that this town where she finds herself, where the guardian of the gate never sleeps and the people in the cafés seem to have nowhere to go, no obligation other than to fill the air with their chatter, is no more real than she: no more but perhaps no less.

Seated at one of the pavement tables she briskly composes what is to be her statement. *I am a writer, a trader in fictions*, it says. *I maintain beliefs only provisionally: fixed beliefs would stand in my way. I change beliefs as I change my habitation or my clothes, according to my needs. On these grounds – professional, vocational – I request exemption from a rule of which I now hear for the first time, namely that every petitioner at the gate should hold to one or more beliefs.*

She takes her statement back to the guardhouse. As she half expected, it is rejected. The man at the desk does not refer it to a higher authority, apparently it does not deserve that, merely shakes his head and lets the page fall to the floor and pushes a fresh sheet of paper towards her. 'What you believe,' he says.

She returns to her chair on the pavement. Am I going to become an institution, she wonders: the old woman who says she is a writer exempt from the law? The woman who, with her black suitcase always beside her (containing what? – she can no longer remember), writes pleas, one after the other, that she puts before the man in the guardhouse and that the man in the guardhouse pushes aside as not good enough, not what is required before one can pass on?

'Can I just glance through?' she says on her second attempt. 'Take a glance at what lies on the other side? Just to see if it is worth all this trouble.'

Ponderously the man rises from his desk. He is not as old as she, but he is not young either. He is wearing riding boots; his blue serge trousers have a red stripe up the sides. How hot he must be, she thinks! And in winter, how cold! Not a cushy job, being guardian of the gate.

Past the soldier leaning on his rifle he takes her, till they stand before the gate itself, massive enough to hold back an army. From a pouch at his belt he takes a key nearly as long as his forearm. Will this be the point where he tells her the gate is meant for her and her alone, and moreover that she is destined never to pass through? Should she remind him, let him know she knows the score?

The key turns twice in the lock. 'There, satisfy yourself,' says the man.

She puts her eye to the crack. A millimetre, two millimetres he draws open the door, then closes it again.

'You have seen,' he says. 'The record will show that.'

What has she seen? Despite her unbelief, she had expected that what lay beyond this door fashioned of teak and brass but also no doubt of the tissue of allegory would be unimaginable: a light so blinding that earthly senses would be stunned by it. But the light is not unimaginable at all. It is merely brilliant, more brilliant perhaps than the varieties of light she has known hitherto, but not of another order, not more brilliant than, say, a magnesium flash sustained endlessly.

The man pats her on the arm. It is a surprising gesture, coming from him, surprisingly personal. Like one of those torturers, she reflects, who claim to wish you no harm, merely to be doing their sad duty. 'Now you have seen,' he says. 'Now you will try harder.'

★　★　★

At the café she orders a drink in Italian – the right language, she says to herself, for such an opera-buffa town – and pays for it with notes she finds in her purse, notes she has no recollection of acquiring. In fact, they look suspiciously like play money: on the one side the image of a bearded nineteenth-century worthy, on the other the denomination, 5, 10, 25, 100, in shades of green and cerise. Five what? Ten what? Yet the waiter accepts the notes: they must in some sense be good.

Whatever the money is, she does not have much of it: four hundred units. A drink costs five, with tip. What happens when one runs out of money? Is there a public administration on whose charity one can throw oneself?

She raises the question with the guardian of the gate. 'If you keep rejecting my statements I'll have to take up residence with you in your lodge,' she says. 'I can't afford hotel rates.'

It is a joke, she just means to shake up this rather dour fellow.

'For long-term petitioners,' he replies, 'there is a dormitory. With kitchen and ablution facilities. All needs have been foreseen.'

'Kitchen or soup kitchen?' she asks. He does not react. Evidently they are not used to being joked with in this place.

The dormitory is a windowless room, long and low. A single bare bulb lights the passageway. On either side are bunks in two tiers, knocked together out of tired-looking wood and painted in the dark rust colour she associates with rolling stock. In fact, looking more closely, she can see stencilled characters: 100377/3 CJG, 282220/0 CXX . . . Most of the bunks have palliasses on them: straw in ticking sacks that in the close heat give off an odour of grease and old sweat.

She could be in any of the gulags, she thinks. She could be in any of the camps of the Third Reich. The whole thing put together from clichés, with not a speck of originality.

'What is this place?' she asks the woman who has let her in.

She need not have asked. Before it comes, she knows what the answer will be. 'It is where you wait.'

The woman – she hesitates to call her the *Kapo* just yet – is a cliché herself: a heavy-set peasant wearing a shapeless grey smock, a kerchief, sandals with blue woollen socks. Yet her gaze is even, intelligent. She has a teasing feeling she has seen the woman before, or her double, or a photograph of her.

'May I choose my own bunk?' she says. 'Or has that too been predetermined on my behalf?'

'Choose,' says the woman. Her face is inscrutable.

With a sigh she chooses, lifts the suitcase, unzips it.

Even in this town time passes. The day arrives, her day. She finds herself before a high bench, in an empty room. On the bench are nine microphones in a row. On the wall behind it, an emblem in plaster relief: two shields, two crossed spears, and what looks like an emu but is probably meant to be a nobler bird, bearing a laurel wreath in its beak.

A man she thinks of as a bailiff brings her a chair and indicates she may sit. She sits down, waits. The windows are all closed, the room is stuffy. She gestures to the bailiff, makes a motion of drinking. He pretends not to notice.

A door opens, and in file the judges, her judges, judges of her. Under the black robes she half expects them to be creatures out of Grandville: crocodile, ass, raven, deathwatch beetle. But no, they are of her kind, her phylum. Even their faces are human. Male, all of them; male and elderly.

She does not need the bailiff's prompting (he has come up behind her now) to stand. A performance will be required of her; she hopes she can pick up the cues.

The judge in the middle gives her a little nod; she nods back.

'You are . . . ?' he says.

'Elizabeth Costello.'

'Yes. The applicant.'

'Or the supplicant, if that improves my chances.'

'And this is your first hearing?'

'Yes.'

'And you want – ?'

'I want to pass the gate. To pass through. To get on with what comes next.'

'Yes. As you must have learned by now, there is the question of belief. You have a statement to make to us?'

'I have a statement, revised, heavily revised, revised many times. Revised to the limit of my powers, I venture to say. I don't believe I have it in me to revise it further. You have a copy, I believe.'

'We do. Revised to the limit, you say. Some of us would say there is always one revision more to do. Let us see. Will you read out your statement, please.'

She reads.

'I am a writer. You may think I should say instead, I was a writer. But I am or was a writer because of who I am or was. I have not ceased to be what I am. As yet. Or so it feels to me.

'I am a writer, and what I write is what I hear. I am a secretary of the invisible, one of many secretaries over the ages. That is my calling: dictation secretary. It is not for me to interrogate, to judge what is given me. I merely write down the words and then test them, test their soundness, to make sure I have heard right.

'Secretary of the invisible: not my own phrase, I hasten to say. I borrow it from a secretary of a higher order, Czeslaw Milosz, a poet, perhaps known to you, to whom it was dictated years ago.'

She pauses. This is where she expects them to interrupt. *Dictated by whom?* she expects them to ask. And she has her answer ready: *By powers beyond us.* But there is no interruption, no question. Instead their spokesman wags his pencil at her. 'Go on.'

'Before I can pass on I am required to state my beliefs,' she reads. 'I reply: a good secretary should have no beliefs. It is inappropriate to the function. A secretary should merely be in readiness, waiting for the call.'

Again she expects an interruption: *Whose call?* But there are going to be no questions, it would seem.

'In my work a belief is a resistance, an obstacle. I try to empty myself of resistances.'

'Without beliefs we are not human.' The voice comes from the leftmost of them, the one she has privately labelled Grimalkin, a wizened little fellow so short that his chin barely clears the bench. In fact, about each of them there is some troublingly comic feature. *Excessively literary*, she thinks. *A caricaturist's idea of a bench of judges.*

'Without beliefs we are not human,' he repeats. 'What do you say to that, Elizabeth Costello?'

She sighs. 'Of course, gentlemen, I do not claim to be bereft of all belief. I have what I think of as opinions and prejudices, no different in kind from what are commonly called beliefs. When I claim to be a secretary clean of belief I refer to my ideal self, a self capable of holding opinions and prejudices at bay while the word which it is her function to conduct passes through her.'

'Negative capability,' says the little man. 'Is negative capability what you have in mind, what you claim to possess?'

'Yes, if you like. To put it in another way, I have beliefs but I do not believe in them. They are not important enough to believe in. My heart is not in them. My heart and my sense of duty.'

The little man purses his lips. His neighbour turns and gives him a glance (she can swear she hears the rustle of feathers). 'And

200

what effect do you think it has, this lack of belief, on your human-ity?' the little man asks.

'On my own humanity? Is that of consequence? What I offer to those who read me, what I contribute to their humanity, outweighs, I would hope, my own emptiness in that respect.'

'Your own cynicism, you mean to say.'

Cynicism. Not a word she likes, but on this occasion she is prepared to entertain it. With luck it will be the last occasion. With luck she will not have to subject herself again to self-defence and the pomposities that go with it.

'About myself, yes, I may well be cynical, in a technical sense. I cannot afford to take myself too seriously, or my motives. But as regards other people, as regards humankind or humanity, no, I do not believe I am cynical at all.'

'You are not an unbeliever then,' says the man in the middle.

'No. Unbelief is a belief. A disbeliever, if you will accept the distinction, though sometimes I feel disbelief becomes a credo too.'

There is a silence. 'Go on,' says the man. 'Proceed with your statement.'

'That is the end of it. There is nothing that has not been covered. I rest my case.'

'Your case is that you are a secretary. Of the invisible.'

'And that I cannot afford to believe.'

'For professional reasons.'

'For professional reasons.'

'And what if the invisible does not regard you as its secretary? What if your appointment was long ago discontinued, and the letter did not reach you? What if you were never even appointed? Have you considered that possibility.'

'I consider it every day. I am forced to consider it. If I am not what I say I am, then I am a sham. If that is your considered verdict, that I am a sham secretary, then I can only bow my head and accept it. I presume you have taken into account my record, a lifetime's record. In fairness to me you cannot ignore that record.'

'What about children?'

The voice is cracked and wheezy. At first she cannot make out from which of them it comes. Is it Number Eight, the one with the pudgy jowls and the high colour?

'Children? I don't understand.'

'And what of the Tasmanians?' he continues. 'What of the fate of the Tasmanians?'

The Tasmanians? Has something been going on in Tasmania, in the interim, that she has not heard about?

'I have no special opinions about Tasmanians,' she replies cautiously. 'I have always found them perfectly decent people.'

He waves impatiently. 'I mean the old Tasmanians, the ones who were exterminated. Do you have special opinions about them?'

'Do you mean, have their voices come to me? No, they have not, not yet. I probably do not qualify, in their eyes. They would probably want to use a secretary of their own, as they are surely entitled to do.'

She can hear the irritation in her voice. What is she doing, explaining herself to a gaggle of old men who might as well be small-town Italians, or small-town Austro-Hungarians, yet who somehow sit in judgement on her? Why does she put up with it? What do they know about Tasmania?

'I said nothing about voices,' says the man. 'I asked you about your thoughts.'

Her thoughts on Tasmania? If she is puzzled, the rest of the panel is puzzled too, for her questioner has to turn to them to explain. 'Atrocities take place,' he says. 'Violations of innocent children. The extermination of whole peoples. What does she think about such matters? Does she have no beliefs to guide her?'

The extermination of the old Tasmanians by her countrymen, her ancestors. Is that, finally, what lies behind this hearing, this trial: the question of historical guilt?

She takes a breath. 'There are matters about which one talks and matters about which it is appropriate to keep one's peace, even before a tribunal, even before the ultimate tribunal, if that is what you are. I know what you are referring to, and I reply only that if from what I have said before you today you conclude that I am oblivious of such matters, you are mistaken, utterly mistaken. Let me add, for your edification: beliefs are not the only ethical supports we have. We can rely on our hearts as well. That is all. I have nothing more to say.'

Contempt of court. She is running close to contempt of court. It is something about herself she has never liked, this tendency to flare up.

'But as a writer? You present yourself today not in your own person but as a special case, a special destiny, a writer who has written not just entertainments but books exploring the complexities of human conduct. In those books you make one judgement upon another, it must be so. What guides you in these judgements? Do you persist in saying it is all just a matter of heart? Have you no beliefs *as a writer*? If a writer is just a human being with a human heart, what is special about your case?'

Not a fool. Not a pig in satin robes, *porcus magistralis*, out of Grandville. Not the Mad Hatter's tea party. For the first time this day she feels tested. Very well: let her see what she can come up with.

'The aboriginal people of Tasmania are today counted among the invisible, the invisible whose secretary I am, one of many such. Every morning I seat myself at my desk and ready myself for the summons of the day. That is a secretary's way of life, and mine. When the old Tasmanians summon me, if they choose to summon me, I will be ready and I will write, to the best of my ability.

'Similarly with children, since you mention violated children. I have yet to be summoned by a child, but again I am ready.

'A word of caution to you, however. I am open to all voices, not just the voices of the murdered and violated.' She tries to keep her own voice even at this point, tries to hit no note that might be called forensic. 'If it is their murderers and violators who choose to summon me instead, to use me and speak through me, I will not close my ears to them, I will not judge them.'

'You will speak for murderers?'

'I will.'

'You do not judge between the murderer and his victim? Is that what it is to be a secretary: to write down whatever you are told? To be bankrupt of conscience?'

She is cornered, she knows. But what does it matter, being cornered, if it brings what feels more and more like a contest of rhetoric closer to its end! 'Do you think the guilty do not suffer too?' she says. 'Do you think they do not call out from their flames? *Do not forget me!* – that is what they cry. What kind of conscience is it that will disregard a cry of such moral agony?'

'And these voices that summon you,' says the pudgy man: 'you do not ask where they come from?'

'No. Not as long as they speak the truth.'

'And you – you, consulting only your heart, are judge of that truth?'

She nods impatiently. Like the interrogation of Joan of Arc, she thinks. *How do you know where your voices come from?* She cannot stand the literariness of it all. Have they not the wit to come up with something new?

204

A silence has fallen. 'Go on,' the man says encouragingly.

'That is all,' she says. 'You asked, I answered.'

'Do you believe the voices come from God? Do you believe in God?'

Does she believe in God? A question she prefers to keep a wary distance from. Why, even assuming that God exists – whatever *exists* means – should His massive, monarchical slumber be disturbed from below by a clamour of *believes* and *don't believes*, like a plebiscite?

'That is too intimate,' she says. 'I have nothing to say.'

'There are only ourselves here. You are free to speak your heart.'

'You misunderstand. I mean, I suspect that God would not look kindly on such presumption – presumption to intimacy. I prefer to let God be. As I hope He will let me be.'

There is silence. She has a headache. Too many heady abstractions, she thinks to herself: a warning from nature.

The chairman glances around. 'Further questions?' he asks.

There are none.

He turns to her. 'You will hear from us. In due course. Through established channels.'

She is back in the dormitory, lying on her bunk. She would prefer to be sitting, but the bunks are built with raised edges like trays, one cannot sit.

She hates this hot, airless room that has been allotted as her home. She hates the smell, revolts at the touch of the greasy mattress. And the hours here seem to be longer than the hours she is used to, particularly in the middle of the day. How long since she arrived in this place? She has lost track of time. It feels like weeks, even months.

There is a band that emerges on to the square in the afternoons once the worst of the heat has passed. From the ornate bandstand the musicians, in starched white uniforms with peaked caps and lots of gold braid, play Souza marches, Strauss waltzes, popular songs:'Il pipistrello', 'Sorrento'. The conductor wears the neat pencil moustache of a small-town Lothario; after each piece he smiles and bows to the applause, while the fat tuba player doffs his cap and wipes his forehead with a scarlet handkerchief.

Exactly, she thinks to herself, what one would expect in an obscure Italian or Austro-Italian border town in the year 1912. Out of a book, just as the bunkhouse with its straw mattresses and forty-watt bulb is out of a book, and the whole courtroom business too, down to the dozy bailiff. Is it all being mounted for her sake, because she is a writer? Is it someone's idea of what hell will be like for a writer, or at least purgatory: a purgatory of clichés? Whatever the case, she ought to be out on the square, not here in the bunkhouse. She could be sitting at one of the tables in the shade amid the murmurings of lovers, with a cold drink before her, waiting for the first touch of the breeze on her cheek. A commonplace among commonplaces, no doubt, but what does that matter any longer? What does it matter if the happiness of the young couples on the square is a feigned happiness, the boredom of the sentry a feigned boredom, the false notes that the cornet player hits in the upper register feigned false notes? That is what life has been since she arrived in this place: an elaborate set of dovetailing commonplaces, including the rattletrap bus with the labouring engine and the suitcases strapped on the roof, including the gate itself with its huge bossed nails. Why not go out and play her part, the part of the traveller cast up in a town she is doomed never to leave?

Yet even as she skulks in the bunkhouse, who is to say she is playing no part? Why should she think that she alone has it in her power to hold herself back from the play? And what would true stubbornness, true grit, consist in anyway but going through with the performance, no matter what? Let the band strike up a dance tune, let the couples bow to each other and step on to the floor, and there, among the dancers, let her be, Elizabeth Costello, the old trouper, in her unsuitable dress, circling in her stiff yet not graceless way. And if that is a cliché too – *being a professional, playing one's part* – then let it be a cliché. What entitles her to shudder at clichés when everyone else seems to embrace them, live by them?

It is the same with the business of belief. *I believe in the irrepressible human spirit*: that is what she should have told her judges. That would have got her past them, and with foot-stamping applause too. *I believe that all humankind is one.* Everyone else seems to believe it, believe in it. Even she believes in it, now and then, when the mood takes her. Why can she not, just for once, pretend?

When she was young, in a world now lost and gone, one came across people who still believed in art, or at least in the artist, who tried to follow in the footsteps of the great masters. No matter that God had failed, and Socialism: there was still Dostoevsky to guide one, or Rilke, or Van Gogh with the bandaged ear that stood for passion. Has she carried that childish faith into her late years, and beyond: faith in the artist and his truth?

Her first inclination would be to say no. Her books certainly evince no faith in art. Now that it is over and done with, that lifetime labour of writing, she is capable of casting a glance back over it that is cool enough, she believes, even cold enough, not to be deceived. Her books teach nothing, preach nothing; they merely spell out, as clearly as they can, how people lived in a certain time and place. More modestly put, they spell out how one person lived, one among billions: the person whom she, to herself, calls *she*, and whom others call *Elizabeth Costello*. If, in the end, she believes in her books themselves more than she believes in that person, it is belief only in the sense that a carpenter believes in a sturdy table or a cooper in a stout barrel. Her books are, she believes, better put together than she is.

From a change in the air, a change that penetrates even the sluggish space of the dormitory, she knows the sun is declining. She has let the whole afternoon slip by. She has neither gone dancing nor worked on her statement, merely brooded, wasted her time.

In the poky little washroom at the back she freshens up as best she can. When she returns there is a new arrival, a woman younger than herself, slumped on a bunk with her eyes shut. It is someone she has noticed before, on the square, in the company of a man wearing a white straw hat. She took her to be a local. But evidently not. Evidently she is a petitioner too.

Not for the first time, the question occurs to her: *Is that what we are, all of us: petitioners awaiting our respective judgements, some new, some, the ones I call locals, long enough here to have settled down, settled in, become part of the scenery?*

About the woman on the bunk there is something familiar that she cannot pin down. Even when she first saw her on the square she seemed familiar. But from the beginning there has been something familiar about the square itself, the whole town. It is as though she has been transported to the set of a dimly remembered film. The Polish cleaning woman, for instance, if that is what she is, Polish: where has she seen her before, and why does she associate her with poetry? Is this younger woman a poet too? Is that where she is: not so much in purgatory as in a kind of literary theme park, set up to divert her while she waits, with actors made up to look like writers? But if so, why is the make-up so poor? Why is the whole thing not done better?

That is, finally, what is so eerie about this place, or would be eerie if the tempo of life were not so languid: the gap between the actors and the parts they play, between the world it is given her to see and what that world stands for. If the afterlife, if that is what this is, give it that name for the moment – if the afterlife turns out to be nothing but hocus-pocus, a simulation from beginning to end, why does the simulation fail so consistently, not just by a hair's breadth – one could forgive it that – but by a hand's breadth?

It is the same with the Kafka business. The wall, the gate, the sentry, are straight out of Kafka. So is the demand for a confession, so is the courtroom with the dozing bailiff and the panel of old men in their crows' robes pretending to pay attention while she thrashes about in the toils of her own words. Kafka, but only the superficies of Kafka; Kafka reduced and flattened to a parody.

And why is it Kafka in particular who is trundled out for her? She is no devotee of Kafka. Most of the time she cannot read him without impatience. As he veers between helplessness and lust, between rage and obsequiousness, she too often finds him, or at least his K selves, simply childish. So why is the *mise en scène* into which she has been hurled so – she dislikes the word but there is no other – so Kafkaesque?

One answer that occurs to her is that the show is put together in this way *because* it is not her kind of show. *You do not like the Kafkaesque, so let us rub your nose in it.* Perhaps that is what these border towns are for: to teach pilgrims a lesson. Very well; but why submit to the lesson? Why take it all so seriously? What can these so-called judges do to her except hold her up, day after day after day? And the gate itself, that bars her way: she has seen what lies beyond it. There is light, certainly, but it is not the light that Dante saw in Paradise, it is not even in the same league. If they are going

209

to block her from passing through, very well then, *basta*, let them block her. Let her spend the rest of her life, so to speak, here, idling the daytime hours away on the square and retiring at nightfall to lie in the smell of someone else's sweat. Not the worst of fates. There must be things she could do to pass the time. Who knows, she might even, if she finds a shop that hires out typewriters, take up novel-writing again.

It is morning. She is at her table on the pavement, working on her statement, trying out a new approach. Since she boasts that she is secretary of the invisible, let her concentrate her attention, turn it inward. What voice does she hear from the invisible today?

For the moment, all she hears is the slow thud of the blood in her ears, just as all she feels is the soft touch of the sun on her skin. That at least she does not have to invent: this dumb, faithful body that has accompanied her every step of the way, this gentle, lumbering monster that has been given to her to look after, this shadow turned to flesh that stands on two feet like a bear and laves itself continually from the inside with blood. Not only is she *in* this body, this thing which not in a thousand years could she have dreamed up, so far beyond her powers would it be, she somehow *is* this body; and all around her on the square, on this beautiful morning, these people, somehow, *are* their bodies too.

Somehow; but how? How on earth can bodies not only keep themselves clean using blood (*blood!*) but cogitate upon the mystery of their existence and make utterances about it and now and again even have little ecstasies? Does it count as a belief, whatever property she has that allows her to continue to *be* this body when she has not the faintest idea how the trick is done? Would they, the bench of judges, the panel of examiners, the tribunal that demands she bare her beliefs – would they be satisfied with this: *I believe that I am? I believe that what stands before you today is I?* Or would that be too much like philosophy, too much like the seminar room?

There is an episode in the *Odyssey* that always sends a shiver down her back. Odysseus has descended into the kingdom of the dead to consult the seer Tiresias. Following instructions, he digs a furrow, cuts the throat of his favourite ram, lets its blood flow into the furrow. As the blood pours, the pallid dead crowd around, slavering for a taste, until to hold them off Odysseus has to draw his sword.

The pool of dark blood, the expiring ram, the man, at a crouch, ready to thrust and stab if need be, the pale souls hard to distinguish from cadavers: why does the scene haunt her? What, coming from the invisible, does it say? She believes, most unquestionably, in the ram, the ram dragged by its master down to this terrible place. The ram is not just an idea, the ram is alive though right now it is dying. If she believes in the ram, then does she believe in its blood too, this sacred liquid, sticky, dark, almost black, pumped out in gouts on to soil where nothing will grow? The favourite ram of the king of Ithaca, so runs the story, yet treated in the end as a mere bag of blood, to be cut open and poured from. She could do the same, here and now: turn herself into a bag, cut her veins and let herself pour on to the pavement, into the gutter. For that, finally, is all it means to be alive: to be able to die. Is this vision the sum of her faith: the vision of the ram and what happens to the ram? Will it be a good enough story for them, her hungry judges?

Someone sits down opposite her. Preoccupied, she does not look up.

'Are you working on your confession?'

It is the woman from the dormitory, the one with the Polish accent, the one she thinks of as the Kapo. This morning she is wearing a cotton dress, flowery, lemon-green, somewhat old-fashioned, with a white belt. It suits her, suits her strong blonde hair and sunburnt skin and broad frame. She looks like a peasant at harvest time, sturdy, capable.

'No, not a confession, a statement of belief. That is what I have been asked for.'

'We call them confessions here.'

'Really. I would not call it that. Not in English. Perhaps in Latin, perhaps in Italian.'

Not for the first time, she wonders how it is that everyone she meets speaks English. Or is she mistaken? Are these folk in fact speaking other languages, languages unfamiliar to her – Polish, Magyar, Wendish – and are their utterances being translated into English, instantaneously and by miraculous means, for her benefit? Or on the other hand is it a condition of existence in this place that all speak a common tongue, Esperanto for example, and are the sounds that issue from her own lips not, as she deludedly believes, English words but Esperanto words, just as the words the Kapo woman speaks are Esperanto, though the woman may believe they are Polish? She herself, Elizabeth Costello, has no recollection of ever having studied Esperanto, but she could be mistaken, as she has been mistaken about so many things. But why then are the waiters Italian? Or is what she thinks of as their Italian simply Esperanto with an Italian accent and Italian hand gestures?

The couple sitting at the next table have their little fingers hooked together. Laughingly they tug at each other; they bump foreheads, whisper. They do not seem to have confessions to write. But perhaps they are not actors, full actors like this Polish woman or this woman playing a Polish woman; perhaps they are just extras, instructed to do what they do every day of their lives in order to fill out the bustle of the square, to give it verisimilitude, the reality effect. It must be a nice life, the life of an extra. Yet after a certain age anxiety must begin to creep in. After a certain age, the life of an extra must begin to seem like a waste of precious time.

'What are you saying in your confession?'

'What I said before: that I cannot afford to believe. That in my line of work one has to suspend belief. That belief is an indulgence, a luxury. That it gets in the way.'

'Really. Some of us would say the luxury we cannot afford is unbelief.'

She waits for more.

'Unbelief – entertaining all possibilities, floating between opposites – is the mark of a leisurely existence, a leisured existence,' the woman goes on. 'Most of us have to choose. Only the light soul hangs in the air.' She leans closer. 'For the light soul, let me offer a word of advice. They may say they demand belief, but in practice they will be satisfied with passion. Show them passion and they will let you through.'

'Passion?' she replies. 'Passion the dark horse? I would have thought that passion leads one away from the light, not towards it. Yet in this place, you say, passion is good enough. Thank you for informing me.'

Her tone is mocking, but her companion is not rebuffed. On the contrary, she settles more comfortably into her chair and gives a little nod, a little smile, as if inviting the question that has now to come.

'Tell me, how many of us get through, pass the test, pass through the gate?'

The woman laughs, a low laugh, strangely attractive. Where has she seen her before? Why is it such an effort to remember, like feeling one's way through a fog? 'Through which gate?' says the woman. 'You believe there is only one gate?' A new laugh passes through her, a long, luxurious shudder of the body that makes her heavy breasts quake. 'Do you smoke?' she says. 'No? Do you mind?'

From a gold cigarette case she takes a cigarette, strikes a match, puffs. Her hand is stubby, broad, a peasant's hand. Yet the finger-nails are clean and neatly buffed. Who is she? *Only the light soul hangs in the air.* It sounds like a quotation.

'Who knows what we truly believe,' says the woman. 'It is here, buried in our heart.' Lightly she smites her bosom. 'Buried even from ourselves. It is not belief that the boards are after. The effect is enough, the effect of belief. Show them you feel and they will be satisfied.'

'What do you mean, the boards?'

'The boards of examiners. We call them the boards. And we call ourselves the singing-birds. We sing for the boards, for their delight.'

'I do not give shows,' she says. 'I'm not an entertainer.' The ciga-rette smoke drifts into her face; she waves it away. 'I cannot drum up what you call passion when it is not there. Cannot turn it on and off. If your boards will not understand that –' She shrugs. She had been about to say something about her ticket, about handing back her ticket. But that would be too grand, too literary, for so petty an occasion.

The woman stubs out her cigarette. 'I must go,' she says. 'I have purchases to make.'

Of what nature these purchases might be she does not say. But it strikes her, Elizabeth Costello (*Here names fade away*: well, her name is not fading away, not in the least), how passive she has become, how incurious. There are purchases she herself would like to make. Aside from the fantasy of the typewriter, she needs suncream, and soap of her own, not the harsh carbolic soap of the washroom. Yet she makes no move to enquire where in this place one does one's purchasing.

There is something else that strikes her. She has no appetite any more. From yesterday she has the faint after-memory of a lemon gelato and macaroons with coffee. Today the very thought of eating fills her with distaste. Her body feels unpleasantly heavy, unpleasantly corporeal.

Is a new career beginning to beckon: as one of the thin folk, the compulsive fasters, the hunger artists? Will her judges take pity if they see her waste away? She sees herself, a sticklike figure on a public bench in a patch of sunlight scribbling away at her task, a task never to be completed. *God save me!* she whispers to herself. *Too literary, too literary! I must get out of here before I die!*

The phrase comes back to her again at dusk, as she is taking a stroll along the town wall, watching the swallows swoop and dive above the square. *A light soul.* Is she a light soul? What is a light soul? She thinks of soap bubbles floating up among the swallows, rising even higher into the blue empyrean. Is that how the woman sees her, the woman whose job it is to scrub the floor and clean the lavatory (not that she ever sees her doing these things)? Certainly her life has not been a hard one, by most standards, but nor has it been easy. Quiet perhaps, protected perhaps: an antipodean life, removed from the worst of history; but driven too, the word is not too strong. Should she seek out the woman and set her right? Would the woman understand?

She sighs, walks on. How beautiful it is, this world, even if it is only a simulacrum! At least there is that to fall back on.

It is the same courtroom, with the same bailiff, but the panel of judges (the board, as she must now learn to call it) is new. There are seven of them, not nine, one of them a woman; she recognizes none of the faces. And the public benches are no longer empty. She has a spectator, a supporter: the cleaning woman, sitting by herself with a string bag on her lap.

'Elizabeth Costello, applicant, hearing number two,' intones the spokesman of today's board (the chief judge? the judge-in-chief?). 'You have a revised statement, we understand. Please proceed with it.'

She steps forward. 'What I believe,' she reads in a firm voice, like a child doing a recitation. 'I was born in the city of Melbourne, but spent part of my childhood in rural Victoria, in a region of climatic extremes: of scorching droughts followed by torrential rains that swelled the rivers with the carcases of drowned animals. That, anyhow, is how I remember it.

'When the waters subsided – I am speaking of the waters of one river in particular now, the Dulgannon – acres of mud were left behind. At night you would hear the belling of tens of thousands of little frogs rejoicing in the largesse of the heavens. The air would be as dense with their calls as it was at noon with the rasping of cicadas.

'Where do they suddenly arrive from, these thousands of frogs? The answer is, they are always there. In the dry season they go underground, burrowing further and further from the heat of the sun until each has created a little tomb for itself. And in those tombs they die, so to speak. Their heartbeat slows, their breathing stops, they turn the colour of mud. Once again the nights are silent.

'Silent until the next rains come, rapping, as it were, on thousands of tiny coffin lids. In those coffins hearts begin to beat, limbs begin to twitch that for months have been lifeless. The dead awake. As the caked mud softens, the frogs begin to dig their way out, and soon their voices resound again in joyous exultation beneath the vault of the heavens.

'Excuse my language. I am or have been a professional writer. Usually I take care to conceal the extravagances of the imagination. But today, for this occasion, I thought I would conceal nothing, bare

216

all. The vivifying flood, the chorus of joyous belling, followed by the subsiding of the waters and the retreat to the grave, then drought seemingly without end, then fresh rains and the resurrection of the dead – it is a story I present transparently, without disguise.

'Why? Because today I am before you not as a writer but as an old woman who was once a child, telling you what I remember of the Dulgannon mudflats of my childhood and of the frogs who live there, some as small as the tip of my little finger, creatures so insignificant and so remote from your loftier concerns that you would not hear of them otherwise. In my account, for whose many failings I beg your pardon, the life cycle of the frog may sound allegorical, but to the frogs themselves it is no allegory, it is the thing itself, the only thing.

'What do I believe? I believe in those little frogs. Where I find myself today, in my old age and perhaps my older age, I am not sure. There are moments when it feels like Italy, but I could easily be mistaken, it could be a quite different place. Towns in Italy do not, as far as I know, have portals (I will not use the humble word *gate* in your presence) through which it is forbidden to pass. But the Australian continent, where I was born into the world, kicking and squalling, is real (if far away), the Dulgannon and its mudflats are real, the frogs are real. They exist whether or not I tell you about them, whether or not I believe in them.

'It is because of the indifference of those little frogs to my belief (all they want from life is a chance to gobble down mosquitoes and sing; and the males among them, the ones who do most of the singing, sing not to fill the night air with melody but as a form of courtship, for which they hope to be rewarded with orgasm, the frog variety of orgasm, again and again and again) – it is because of their indifference to me that I believe in them. And that is why, this afternoon, in this lamentably rushed and lamentably literary presentation for which I again apologize, but I thought I would offer myself to you without forethought, *toute nue* so to speak, and almost, as you can see for yourselves, without notes – that is why I speak to you of frogs. Of frogs and of my belief or beliefs and of the relation between the former and the latter. Because they exist.'

She comes to a stop. From behind her, the sound of gentle handclapping, from a single pair of hands, the cleaning woman's. The clapping dwindles, ceases. It was she, the cleaning woman, who put her up to it – this flood of words, this gabble, this confusion, this *passion*. Well, let us see what kind of response passion gets.

One of the judges, the man on the extreme right, leans forward. 'Dulgannon,' he says. 'That is a river?'

'Yes, a river. It exists. It is not negligible. You will find it on most maps.'

'And you spent your childhood there, on the Dulgannon?'

She is silent.

'Because it says nothing here, in your docket, about a childhood on the Dulgannon.'

She is silent.

'Is childhood on the Dulgannon another of your stories, Mrs Costello? Along with the frogs and the rain from heaven?'

'The river exists. The frogs exist. I exist. What more do you want?'

The woman among them, slim, with neat silver hair and silver-rimmed glasses, speaks. 'You believe in life?'

'I believe in what does not bother to believe in me.'

The judge makes a little gesture of impatience. 'A stone does not believe in you. A bush. But you choose to tell us not about stones or bushes but about frogs, to which you attribute a life story that is, as you concede, highly allegorical. These Australian frogs of yours embody the spirit of life, which is what you as a storyteller believe in.'

It is not a question, it is, in effect, a judgement. Should she accept it? *She believed in life*: will she take that as the last word on her, her epitaph? Her whole inclination is to protest: *Vapid!* she wants to cry. *I am worth better than that!* But she reins herself in. She is not here to win an argument, she is here to win a pass, a passage. Once she has passed, once she has said goodbye to this place, what she leaves behind of herself, even if it is to be an epitaph, will be of the utmost inconsequence.

'If you like,' she says guardedly.

The judge, her judge, looks away, purses her lips. A long silence falls. She listens for the buzzing of the fly that one is supposed to hear on such occasions, but there does not appear to be a fly in the courtroom.

Does she believe in life? But for this absurd tribunal and its demands, would she even believe in frogs? How does one know what one believes in?

She tries a test that seems to work when she is writing: to send out a word into the darkness and listen for what kind of sound comes back. Like a foundryman tapping a bell: is it cracked or healthy? The frogs: what tone do the frogs give off?

The answer: no tone at all. But she is too canny, knows the business too well, to be disappointed just yet. The mud frogs of the Dulgannon are a new departure for her. Give them time: they might yet be made to ring true. For there is something about them that obscurely engages her, something about their mud tombs and the fingers of their hands, fingers that end in little balls, soft, wet, mucous.

She thinks of the frog beneath the earth, spread out as if flying, as if parachuting through the darkness. She thinks of the mud eating away at the tips of those fingers, trying to absorb them, to dissolve the soft tissue till no one can tell any longer (certainly not the frog itself, lost as it is in its cold sleep of hibernation) what is earth, what is flesh. Yes, that she can believe in: the dissolution, the return to the elements; and the converse moment she can believe in too, when the first quiver of returning life runs through the body and the limbs contract, the hands flex. She can believe in that, if she concentrates closely enough, word by word.

'Psst.'

It is the bailiff. He gestures towards the bench, where the judge-in-chief is regarding her impatiently. Has she been in a trance, or even asleep? Has she been dozing in the faces of her judges? She should be more careful.

'I refer you to your first appearance before this court, when you gave as your occupation "secretary to the invisible" and made the following statement: "A good secretary should not have beliefs. It is inappropriate to the function"; and, a little later, "I have beliefs but I do not believe in them."'

'At that hearing you appeared to disparage belief, calling it an impediment to your calling. At today's hearing, however, you testify to a belief in frogs, or more accurately in the allegorical meaning of a frog's life, if I understand your drift. My question is: Have you changed the basis of your plea from the first hearing to the present one? Are you giving up the secretary story and presenting a new one, based on the firmness of your belief in the creation?'

Has she changed her story? It is a weighty question, no doubt about that, yet she has to struggle to fix her attention on it. The courtroom is hot, she feels drugged, she is not sure how much more of this hearing she can take. What she would like most is to lay her head on a pillow and have a snooze, even if it has to be the filthy pillow in the bunkhouse.

'It depends,' she says, playing for time, trying to think (*Come on, come on!* she tells herself: *Your life depends on this!*). 'You ask if I have changed my plea. But who am I, who is this *I*, this *you*? We change from day to day, and we also stay the same. No *I*, no *you* is more fundamental than any other. You might as well ask which is the true Elizabeth Costello: the one who made the first statement or the one who made the second. My answer is, both are true. Both. And neither. *I am an other.* Pardon me for resorting to words that are not my own, but I cannot improve on them. You have the wrong person before you. If you think you have the right person you have the wrong person. The wrong Elizabeth Costello.'

Is this true? It may not be true but it is certainly not false. She has never felt more like the wrong person in her life.

Her interrogator waves impatiently. 'I am not asking to see your passport. Passports have no force here, as I am sure you are aware. The question I ask is: *you*, by whom I mean this person before our eyes, this person petitioning for passage, this person here and nowhere else – do you speak for yourself?'

'Yes. No, emphatically no. Yes and no. Both.'

Her judge glances left and right at his colleagues. Is she imagining it, or does the flicker of a smile pass among them, and a whispered word? What is the word? *Confused*?

He turns back to her. 'Thank you. That is all. You will hear from us in due course.'

'That is all?'

'That is all, for today.'

'I am not confused.'

'Yes, you are not confused. But who is it who is not confused?'

They cannot contain themselves, her panel of judges, her board. First they titter like children, then abandon all dignity and howl with laughter.

★   ★   ★

221

She wanders across the square. It is, she would guess, early after-noon. There is less bustle than usual. The locals must be at their siesta. *The young in one another's arms.* If I had my life again, she tells herself, not without bitterness, I would spend it otherwise. Have more fun. What good has it done me, this life of writing, now that it comes to the final proving?

The sun is fierce. She ought to be wearing a hat. But her hat is in the bunkhouse, and the thought of re-entering that airless space repels her.

The courthouse scene has not left her, the ignominy of it, the shame. Yet beneath it all she remains, strangely, under the spell of the frogs. Today, it would appear, she is disposed to believe in frogs. What will it be tomorrow? Midges? Grasshoppers? The objects of her belief appear to be quite random. They come up without warning, surprising and even, despite her dark mood, delighting her.

She gives the frogs a tap with her fingernail. The tone that comes back is clear, clear as a bell.

She gives the word *belief* a tap. How does *belief* measure up? Will her test work with abstractions too?

The sound that *belief* returns is not as clear, but clear enough nevertheless. Today, at this time, in this place, she is evidently not without belief. In fact, now that she thinks of it, she lives, in a certain sense, by belief. Her mind, when she is truly herself, appears to pass from one belief to the next, pausing, balancing, then moving on. A picture comes to her of a girl crossing a stream; it comes together with a line from Keats: *Keeping steady her laden head across a brook.* She lives by belief, she works by belief, she is a creature of belief. What a relief! Should she run back and tell them, her judges, before they disrobe (and before she changes her mind)?

222

Astonishing that a court which sets itself up as an interrogatory of belief should refuse to pass her. They must have heard other writers before, other disbelieving believers or believing disbelievers. Writers are not lawyers, surely they must allow for that, allow for eccentricities of presentation. But of course this is not a court of law. Not even a court of logic. Her first impression was right: a court out of Kafka or *Alice in Wonderland*, a court of paradox. The first shall be last and the last first. Or contrariwise. If it were guaranteed in advance that one could breeze through one's hearing with anecdotes from one's childhood, skipping with laden head from one belief to another, from frogs to stones to flying machines, as often as a woman changes her hat (now where does *that* line come from?), then every petitioner would take up autobiography, and the court stenographer would be washed away in streams of free association.

She is before the gate again, before what is evidently her gate and hers alone, though it must be visible to anyone who cares to give it a glance. It is, as ever, closed, but the door to the lodge is open, and inside she can see the gatekeeper, the custodian, busy as usual with his papers, which ripple lightly in the air from the fan.

'Another hot day,' she remarks.

'Mm,' he mumbles, not interrupting his work.

'Every time I pass by I see you writing,' she continues, trying not to be deterred. 'You are a writer too, in a sense. What are you writing?'

'Records. Keeping the records up to date.'

'I've just had my second hearing.'

'That's good.'

'I sang for my judges. I was today's singing-bird. Do you use that expression: *singing-bird*?'

He shakes his head abstractedly: no.

'It did not go well, I'm afraid, my song.'

'Mm.'

'I know you are not a judge,' she says. 'Nevertheless, in your judgement, do I stand any chance of passing through? And if I do not pass through, if I am deemed not good enough to pass, will I stop here for ever, in this place?'

He shrugs. 'We all stand a chance.' He has not looked up, not once. Does that mean something? Does it mean that he has not the courage to look her in the eye?

'But as a writer,' she persists – 'what chance do I stand as a writer, with the special problems of a writer, the special fidelities?'

Fidelities. Now that she has brought it out, she recognizes it as the word on which all hinges.

He shrugs again. 'Who can say,' he says. 'It is a matter for the boards.'

'But you keep the records – who passes through, who does not. You must, in a sense, know.'

He does not answer.

'Do you see many people like me, people in my situation?' she continues urgently, out of control now, hearing herself out of control, disliking herself for it. *In my situation*: what does that mean? What is her situation? The situation of someone who does not know her own mind?

She has a vision of the gate, the far side of the gate, the side she is denied. At the foot of the gate, blocking the way, lies stretched out a dog, an old dog, his lion-coloured hide scarred from innumerable manglings. His eyes are closed, he is resting, snoozing. Beyond him is nothing but a desert of sand and stone, to infinity. It is her first vision in a long while, and she does not trust it, does not trust in particular the anagram GOD-DOG. *Too literary*, she thinks again. A curse on literature!

The man behind the desk has evidently had enough of questions. He lays down his pen, folds his hands, regards her levelly. 'All the time,' he says. 'We see people like you all the time.'

At such moments even a negligible creature, a dog, a rat, a beetle, a stunted apple tree, a cart track winding over a hill, a mossy stone, counts more for me than a night of bliss with the most beautiful, most devoted mistress. These dumb and in some cases inanimate creatures press toward me with such fullness, such presence of love, that there is nothing in range of my rapturous eye that does not have life. It is as if everything, everything that exists, everything I can recall, everything my confused thinking touches on, means something.

Hugo von Hofmannsthal
'Letter of Lord Chandos to Lord Bacon' (1902)

Postscript

Letter of Elizabeth, Lady Chandos, to Francis Bacon

Dear and esteemed Sir,

   You will have received from my husband Philip a letter
dated this 22nd August. Ask me not how, but a copy of that
letter has come under my sight, and now I add my voice to
his. I fear you may think my husband wrote in a fit of madness,
a fit that by now may have passed. I write to say: It is not
so. All that you read in his letter is true, save for one circumstance: no husband can succeed in concealing from a loving
wife distress of mind so extreme. These many months have
I known of my Philip's affliction, and suffered with him.

   How did our sorrows come to be? There was a time, I
remember, before this time of affliction, when he would gaze
like one bewitched at paintings of sirens and dryads, craving
to enter their naked, glistening bodies. But where in Wiltshire
will we find a siren or a dryad for him to try? Perforce I
became his dryad: it was I whom he entered when he sought
to enter her, I who felt his tears on my shoulder when again
he could not find her in me. *But a little time and I will learn
to be your dryad, speak your dryad speech*, I whispered in the
dark; but he was not consoled.

227

A time of affliction I call the present time; yet in the company of my Philip I too have moments when soul and body are one, when I am ready to burst out in the tongues of angels. *My raptures* I call these spells. They come to me – I write without blushing, this is no time for blushing – in my husband's arms. He alone is guide to me; with no other man would I know them. Soul and body he speaks to me, in a speaking without speech; into me, soul and body, he presses what are no longer words but flaming swords.

We are not meant to live thus, Sir. *Flaming swords* I say my Philip presses into me, swords that are not words; but they are neither flaming swords nor are they words. It is like a contagion, saying one thing always for another (*like a contagion*, I say: barely did I hold myself back from saying, *a plague of rats*, for rats are everywhere about us these days). Like a wayfarer (hold the figure in mind, I pray you), like a wayfarer I step into a mill, dark and disused, and feel of a sudden the floorboards, rotten with the wetness, give way beneath my feet and plunge me into the racing mill-waters; yet as I am that (a wayfarer in a mill) I am also not that; nor is it a contagion that comes continually upon me or a plague of rats or flaming swords, but something else. *Always it is not what I say but something else.* Hence the words I write above: *We are not meant to live thus.* Only for *extreme souls* may it have been intended to live thus, where words give way beneath your feet like rotting boards (*like rotting boards* I say again, I cannot help myself, not if I am to bring home to you my distress and my husband's, *bring home* I say, where is home, where is home?).

We cannot live thus, neither he nor I nor you, honoured Sir (for who is to say that through the agency of his letter or if

228

not of his letter then of mine you may not be touched by a contagion that is not that, a contagion, but is something else, always something else?). There may come a time when such *extreme souls* as I write of may be able to bear their afflictions, but that time is not now. It will be a time, if ever it comes, when giants or perhaps angels stride the earth (I cease to hold myself back, I am tired now, I yield myself to the figures, do you see, Sir, how I am taken over?, *the rush* I call it when I do not call it *my rapture*, the rush and the rapture are not the same, but in ways that I despair of explaining though they are clear to my eye, *my eye* I call it, *my inner eye*, as if I had an eye inside that looked at the words one by one as they passed, like soldiers on parade, *like soldiers on parade* I say).

All is allegory, says my Philip. Each creature is key to all other creatures. A dog sitting in a patch of sun licking itself, says he, is at one moment a dog and at the next a vessel of revelation. And perhaps he speaks the truth, perhaps in the mind of our Creator (*our Creator*, I say) where we whirl about as if in a millrace we interpenetrate and are interpenetrated by fellow creatures by the thousand. But how I ask you can I live with rats and dogs and beetles crawling through me day and night, drowning and gasping, scratching at me, tugging me, urging me deeper and deeper into revelation – how? *We are not made for revelation*, I want to cry out, *nor I nor you, my Philip*, revelation that sears the eye like staring into the sun.

Save me, dear Sir, save my husband! Write! Tell him the time is not yet come, the time of the giants, the time of the angels. Tell him we are still in the time of fleas. Words no longer reach him, they shiver and shatter, it is as if (*as if*, I say), it is as if he is guarded by a shield of crystal. But fleas he will understand, the fleas and the beetles still creep past his shield, and the rats; and sometimes I his wife, yes, my Lord, sometimes I too creep through. *Presences of the Infinite* he calls us, and says we make him shudder; and indeed I have felt those shudders, in the throes of my raptures I have felt them, so much that whether they were his or were mine I could no longer say.

Not Latin, says my Philip – I copied the words – *not Latin nor English nor Spanish nor Italian will bear the words of my revelation.* And indeed it is so, even I who am his shadow know it when I am in my raptures. Yet he writes to you, as I write to you, who are known above all men to select your words and set them in place and build your judgements as a mason builds a wall with bricks. Drowning, we write out of our separate fates. Save us.

Your obedient servant
Elizabeth C.
This 11 September, AD 1603

Acknowledgements

An earlier version of Lesson 1 appeared under the title 'What is Realism?' in *Salmagundi* nos. 114–15 (1997).

An earlier version of Lesson 2 appeared as 'The Novel in Africa', Occasional Paper no. 17 of the Townsend Center for the Humanities, University of California at Berkeley, 1999. Cheikh Hamidou Kane is quoted from Phanuel Akubueze Egejuru, *Towards African Literary Independence* (Greenwood Press, Westport, 1980), by permission of the author. Paul Zumthor is quoted from *Introduction à la poésie orale*, by permission of Éditions du Seuil.

Lessons 3 and 4 were published, with responses by Peter Singer, Marjorie Garber, Wendy Doniger and Barbara Smuts, as *The Lives of Animals* (Princeton University Press, 1999).

An earlier version of Lesson 5 appeared as 'Die Menschenwissenschaften in Afrika' / 'The Humanities in Africa' (Siemens Stiftung, Munich, 2001).

An earlier version of Lesson 6 appeared in *Salmagundi* nos. 137–38 (2003).

'Letter of Elizabeth, Lady Chandos' was published by Intermezzo Press, Austin, Texas, in 2002.